ONE MAN'S WAR

a novel

P. M. KIPPERT

ACADEMY

CHICA

Copyright © 2016 by P. M. Kippert

First edition
Published by Academy Chicago Publishers
An imprint of Chicago Review Press Incorporated
814 North Franklin Street
Chicago, Illinois 60610

ISBN 978-1-61373-356-1

Library of Congress Cataloging-in-Publication Data

Names: Kippert, P. M.
Title: One man's war / P. M. Kippert.
Description: First edition. | Chicago : Academy Chicago Publishers, 2016.
Identifiers: LCCN 2015033743 | ISBN 9781613733561 (trade paper)
Subjects: LCSH: Soldiers—United States—Fiction. | World War,
    1939–1945—Personal narratives, American—Fiction. | GSAFD:
War stories
Classification: LCC PS3611.I675 O54 2016 | DDC 813/.6—dc23
LC record available at http://lccn.loc.gov/2015033743

Cover design: Andrew Brozyna, AJB Design, Inc.
Cover images: photo of GI, Picture Collection, The New York Public
Library, Astor, Lenox and Tilden Foundations; ruined city photo from
Andrew Brozyna's collection.
Interior design: Sarah Olson
Interior layout: Nord Compo

Printed in the United States of America
5 4 3 2 1

PREFACE

One Man's War is, as the title is meant to suggest, the story of one soldier's journey through World War II. As a member of a line rifle company, a soldier rarely knew the larger canvas of the action in which he took part. To the man on the line, it was "Take that hill" or "Hold that bridge" or "Get up and march." The grander picture was not usually known and, in essence, not that important in a day-to-day view of survival and keeping your head down.

As such, often in this novel the broader context of the action is lost, left untold, because it would have been beyond the ken of the protagonists of the book. For that reason, I have supplied an author's note at the end of the text as an aid to the reader who might want a broader understanding of the grand canvas of this particular theater of the war.

1

Bob Kafak landed at Anzio on January 22, 1944, D-day for Operation Shingle, the invasion of Anzio. He walked ashore from the gate of an LCI without getting his feet wet, a good landing.

"Where the fuck is everybody?" Kafak asked Willie Marshak, a friend he'd made in North Africa during his time there.

"I guess we fooled the fucking Krauts, huh?" Marshak said.

It was eerily silent, Kafak thought. He'd arrived in Africa in November 1943, in time to spend his nineteenth birthday there. He'd missed all the fighting and felt glad of it, though he didn't admit that to anyone.

He'd expected to be met by German guns the minute he stepped out of the landing craft, and when nothing happened he felt great relief. Great disappointment, as well. He wanted to get it over with, his first time under fire. He wanted to make sure he could take it, that he wouldn't be a coward. He figured a guy never knew if he could take it until he was in it. That was another thing he didn't mention to anyone.

In the event, there had been just too much coastline for the Germans to protect. They knew the Allies would be coming, they just didn't know where. They had had to pick and choose their spots. They hadn't chosen Anzio-Nettuno.

A sergeant met them just off the beach.

"Who you sonsa bitches with?" the sergeant said, his voice the growl Kafak had become used to from noncommissioned officers.

"We ain't been assigned yet, Sarge," Marshak said.

"You're here as replacements, then," the sergeant said. "Report to the rear. Ask for Lieutenant Dunphy."

Kafak and Marshak wandered around the beach and what was left of the town. It had been wracked by shells, both Allied and German. After asking about a dozen people, they finally found the lieutenant.

"You've been sent as replacements for the Third?" Dunphy asked.

"Seems like, sir," Kafak said.

"Well, the landing didn't cost us much, so we've got nobody for you to replace just yet. We'll put you in the rear until we can assign you."

"Sounds good to me, sir," Marshak said, and grinned.

Dunphy asked, "You fellas ain't seen any combat yet, have you?"

"No, sir, that's right," Kafak said.

Dunphy grunted at them and directed them where to go. There was sporadic shelling. It would get worse. Everyone told them so. They listened to the shells dropping, listened to the men who had seen combat, listened and waited, and tried not to show the fear they felt.

"Hell of a spot they stuck us in, ain't it?" Marshak said.

"What?" Kafak said. "That fucking ammo dump?"

"Yeah, fucking ammo dump. Right fucking next door. Hell, the Krauts don't get us, the fucking US Army will."

"Ain't it always the way."

They laughed over it, being encamped next to an ammo dump with German shells dropping closer and closer and more and more regularly as the days passed.

Other than listening, they spent their time training. The Third Division was always training. If you weren't in combat, you were training. It was, everyone told them, what made the Third such a great fighting unit.

One day during this training, a sergeant told Kafak, "You want to get yourself a helmet with netting, soldier."

"Why's that, Sarge?"

"Cuz when it rains, that helmet you're wearing will shine like a fucking beacon. Get one with netting, it kills the rain, kills the shine. Your head won't be such a nice target for some German sniper."

"Sure thing, Sarge," Kafak said. He got some netting and put it onto his helmet. He promised himself never to be without it.

On one of their days at the rear they heard the loud wail of planes overhead. Then the roll of machine gun fire. They looked up and saw a dogfight going on. It didn't last long before one of the planes started smoking. A pilot ejected, and they traced his chute against the sky. They saw the plane go down into the water off the coast. It didn't hit any of the ships constantly unloading men and supplies onto the beach.

"Let's chase that fucker down!" Marshak said. "We could get us our first POW!"

Kafak didn't expect so, but he followed along with half a dozen other guys. They found the pilot who had bailed out. He was a Brit, pilot of a Spitfire. He'd lost the dogfight. They brought him back to camp to be returned to his base.

Another time a German shell dropped in the water just yards from the beach. The explosion rattled Kafak's teeth. They were false teeth he'd been given by the army after enlisting. His own had rotted from lack of care. He'd been too poor for any dentist back in Detroit, where he'd grown up.

"Son of a bitch," Marshak said. "That sounded like God hisself smacking the water!"

"Fuckin-A," Kafak said.

Marshak let loose a low whistle.

A nearby NCO laughed.

"Say hello to Anzio Annie, boys," he told them. "That's the Germans' big gun. It fires from way the fuck over the other side of their lines and lands way the fuck over here. They can reach out to the ocean with that fucking gun."

"Well, that don't seem fair at all," Marshak said.

"Welcome to war, boys," he said.

After a week of training, they were told they were ready for the front lines.

"Fuckin-A right we are," Marshak said.

"Sure," Kafak said.

Both men were assigned to L Company, Fifteenth Regiment of the Third Infantry Division. The Rock of the Marne. As Dunphy passed out the squad assignments, a few German mortar shells started to whistle overhead. Kafak dove for the nearest foxhole. Dunphy landed right on top of him.

"Sorry, soldier," Dunphy said.

"Nice landing, Lieutenant," Kafak said.

"That's good reaction time, Private. You keep that up and you might survive this war."

"Sure thing, Lieutenant," Kafak said.

They climbed out of the foxhole. Kafak and Marshak headed for the front line and their assigned squads. Arriving there, the two men dug themselves a foxhole. German guns were lobbing shells at a fairly consistent rate onto the beach.

"Things sure have picked up some since we first got here, ain't they?" Marshak said.

"Seems like."

"Only a week, but them goddamned Krauts don't wait around for nobody, ya know?"

"Don't want us walking into Rome, I guess."

"We could've, though, is what I heard."

"Sure."

"Why it was so quiet when we got here. Hardly any German troops around. Thirty miles from Rome and we could've marched right in. I heard a patrol actually made it there, but when they come back and told General Lucas there wasn't a Kraut between us and Rome, he wouldn't believe them."

"I guess I wouldn't't've believed it."

"Well, it might not have sounded true, but it was true. Leastwise, from all I heard about it."

"Rumors are rumors, Willie."

"Sitting on the fucking beach while the Germans fill up them mountains surrounding us ain't no rumor."

"No," Kafak said, "I guess it ain't."

It was January 29.

Kafak lay in his foxhole, wondering when he would face his first battle. There was occasional sniper fire. If the Germans saw anything move, they took a shot at it. A guy learned quick to keep his ass and head down during the daylight hours. Shells fell constantly now as well, exploded nearby. Sometimes very nearby.

"You've got to listen for them being fired," a vet of combat had told Kafak while he trained on the beach. "If you wait until you hear them landing, you're dead. You're too late."

The lesson had served him well when that mortar shell had been lobbed over.

Late that night, Kafak heard the sounds of troops moving up through the Allied lines. He peeked over the lip of his foxhole and saw a guy he knew from Africa, a member of the Third's reconnaissance group.

"Jennings," Kafak said, his voice kept low. Sounds carried farther at night. He knew that much. "What the fuck's going on?"

"We're moving up on Cisterna. We're supporting the Rangers."

"A fucking night attack," Marshak said. He shook his head. "You wonder what these fucking generals are thinking half the time."

"Better than attacking in the daylight."

"Yeah," Marshak said. "The fucking Germans can see every goddamned thing we do during the daytime." Marshak shook his head again. "Still, they're asking to get themselves fucked."

Kafak shrugged. He heard a jeep, maybe more than one, heading along with the advancing troops. He wondered about that. Why would they have a jeep when they were trying to surprise the Germans in the middle of the night? It didn't make sense to him. He thought maybe Marshak was right after all.

The next morning, Kafak was just finishing a can of stew for his breakfast when he heard the loud, tearing whine of a jeep in gear racing down the road from the direction of Cisterna. The jeep barreled past his foxhole drawing a few random shells from German gunners. None of them hit. The jeep swerved behind a building, and Kafak could hear the driver standing hard on the brakes. The jeep slid to a halt behind the half-blown structure, and the men leaped out, racing toward the command post.

"I guess I was right," Marshak said. "I guess they got fucked pretty good after all."

"Seems like," Kafak said.

Not long after, smoke machines started up, providing some cover. They could hear movement all round them. Their sergeant, Boyle, slid into their foxhole.

"Get your shit ready," he told them. "We're moving out."

"Where we going, Sarge?" Marshak asked.

"Up the road. We're going to hook up with the Rangers. They're pinned down near Cisterna. Make sure you take plenty of ammo and get yourself ready to move. Soon and fast. Got it?"

"Sure thing, Sarge," Kafak said.

Kafak used his routine of readying his gear to try not to think about the upcoming fight. This would be it, he knew. His first time under direct enemy fire.

Being shelled was one thing and it was a horrible thing and a guy had to learn how to get used to that. Some men never did. The sometimes constant explosions broke them. The rest of them just kept their heads down and prayed for it to end.

Being shot at, small arms fire, was another thing entirely. People shooting at you, trying to kill you, was another thing you had to face, had to be able to face. It took a whole other kind of getting used to.

At least, that's what the veterans had spoken about.

Kafak hoped he could take it.

"All right, let's go," a voice shouted.

Kafak didn't know whose voice it was. It was a voice of command, a shout from an officer or NCO. It sounded like it might have been Lieutenant Dunphy. Kafak had one of the new M1 Garand gas-powered rifles. He had plenty of extra ammunition in his pouch and pockets. He scrambled out of the foxhole and moved up with the rest of the men, Marshak right beside him.

They formed up with their sergeant. He led the squad forward. They could hear shells exploding up ahead of them, from the direction in which they were heading. They moved along in skirmish formation. A tank and a tank destroyer accompanied them. Before long, both machines ground to a halt. Dunphy put his hand up, and everyone dropped to the ground, waiting. Dunphy went back to talk to the tank driver, see what was wrong. When he came back up front, he told them both the tank and the tank destroyer had developed mechanical problems. They'd be on their own from here on out.

They moved forward. An occasional rifle or machine gun bullet whizzed by like some steel bee. Nothing necessarily aimed at them, though, just random fire from the front toward which they moved.

Kafak saw they were approaching a bridge. They were in no-man's-land now. The Germans couldn't be far away. Everyone moved in a crouch, eyes swiveling in every direction at once. A machine gun opened up on Kafak's squad. Two men went down, wounded; the rest of them dove to the ground. Kafak ducked his head as machine gun and rifle fire whizzed over him. He flattened himself, wanting to crawl into the ground.

"Where is it? Where the fuck is it?" Marshak said.

Kafak assumed he meant the machine gun nest. He raised his eyes to look for it but a roll of fire ducked him quick back down again. He started to hear another sort of gun firing. M1s. The sound of his own squad members returning fire.

Right, Kafak thought to himself, we're supposed to fire back. He put himself into position to fire his rifle from flat on his belly. He pulled the trigger. It made him feel a little better that he could fight back. He saw where the machine gun nest was then. The Germans there were concentrating their fire on the more forward members of the squad. Those guys had ducked down behind some rocks. The ground here was very flat, though, not much natural cover offered at all. Kafak couldn't see the German gunners, only the ugly barrel of the MG42. He fired toward it. Along with everyone else. He didn't figure he hit anything, but it seemed to suppress some of the machine gun's barrage of the forward men, and they were able to move up close enough to toss a few grenades at the machine gunners. Everyone rose up and ran forward under the bursts of the explosions. Kafak followed along with the other guys. He had just reloaded his rifle, so now he fired from his hip as he ran forward, emptying another clip.

"Fuck! Fuck! Fuck!" he said.

The other guys were shouting as well, cursing, as they ran forward.

Kafak's rifle ejected the stripper clip automatically once he fired all eight shots it held. He grabbed a grenade from his belt and pulled the pin with his one hand still holding his rifle. It wasn't easy. He wasn't sure how he managed it. He was just moving now, reacting. He didn't feel afraid. He didn't feel anything. The training had taken over. He threw the grenade toward the machine gun nest. It exploded alongside half a dozen others from the rest of the guys in his squad.

They had reached the nest by then. The gunners were both dead, lying draped over their weapon. A few other German riflemen lay dead or wounded nearby. Four more Germans were retreating, only one of them half turning back as he ran to fire his machine pistol at the Americans. Kafak dropped to one knee, reloaded a new clip, and fired at the running Germans. All four of them fell, dead or wounded. He didn't know if he'd hit any one of them. Everybody in his squad was doing exactly what he was doing.

They saw to their two wounded. One guy was bleeding from a hit across his biceps. He'd already wrapped it tight with a bandage that had turned completely red. The other guy had been hit in the hip. He couldn't move. A medic came up and called for assistance to remove the man back to the field hospital. The guy with the wounded arm stayed with them.

Kafak moved forward with the rest of his squad, behind his sergeant. He still wasn't thinking, just moving and acting. Looking everywhere for another ambush. They moved forward and hooked up with a couple other squads. Mortar shells started falling in among them. Every few steps they would all drop to the ground and wait for the shells to land and blow. It was slow moving, but they were advancing.

Their numbers continued to increase as they met other advancing squads. Kafak heard growling behind him and looked back. The tank and the tank destroyer had fixed their problems and rejoined the group. Kafak felt better about that. They had a good-sized force now, Kafak thought. They could really do some damage.

The Germans must have thought so too, he figured, because then everything the Germans had started hitting them. Small arms fire as well as mortars and self-propelled vehicle cannons and artillery. German 88s flew overhead. They made a sound but only after they exploded. You never heard it before. You could hear the guns popping, though, and every time he did, Kafak hugged the ground. He didn't wait for the shells to blow.

The noise was deafening. Most shells hit the ground when they burst, so the shrapnel flew up and outward, fountaining in every direction. If you got low and flat, it would usually fly over you. Air and tree bursts were the worst, though. When a shell prematurely detonated while still in the air, or when it hit the top of a tree, then the shrapnel rained down everywhere and being flat was no protection at all. Then you had only luck to keep you from being hit. No skill the army could teach you could help you survive that. Only luck.

A lot of the guys were firing their weapons, so Kafak did his as well. He fired in the direction he saw the other men firing. He had no idea what they were all shooting at. He figured someone had seen a German in that direction. He couldn't see a thing, though. Only dirt cascading up into the air, smoke from burning vehicles nearby, and the sweat in his eyes. He continued to fire. It might do some good, he thought.

He wondered what the tank and tank destroyer were doing. He didn't hear them any longer so he figured their mechanical problems had returned and they were out of it. Well, good for them, but not the rest of the troop.

An 88 shell landed fairly close to him, nearly on top of a guy he'd met once but didn't really know. He saw the guy's body fly up into the air and then plop down in about twenty different pieces.

The force of the explosion rattled him, slammed him harder against the earth. He felt like the air had been ripped out of his lungs and like his entire chest had been shoved backward, slamming into his spine. He felt compressed. That was the word, he thought, but thought it only later, when he had time to think. Just then he didn't think anything at all. He just felt.

"Fuck! Shit! Fuck!" he said.

All of that was more in his head than in his mouth, though. He didn't have the breath to really shout out loud just then.

He tried to shove himself deeper into the ground. He felt something tug at his jacket. He thought it might be a bullet hitting him. He looked up and saw his sergeant yelling at him. He couldn't hear anything the guy was saying. It seemed obvious, though, that the sergeant was telling him to get up and advance. Kafak got up to his knees, wobbled a bit. The sergeant pulled him to his feet by his jacket. He started running in a crouch. Advancing. Right next to the sergeant. Suddenly, the sergeant was no longer beside him. Kafak looked back and didn't see the guy. He glanced down. The sergeant lay in a twisted heap on the ground, his chest seeping blood, his eyes wide open. Kafak knew he was dead.

He kept moving.

Later he would think about that. Think about how the bullet had taken a guy out right next to him. *Right next to him.* But not him. Why that man not four feet away, yet he, Kafak, went unscathed? How did that work?

He knew there was no answer. God. Fate. Your time. Whatever you wanted to say to give yourself comfort. It was luck. Pure and simple dumb luck. Bad for one guy, good for another.

He didn't deserve it. He knew that much. When the shit was coming down like that, he understood that no one deserved it, no one deserved to live through that. If you did, you had only luck or God or fate or whatever else you wanted to thank for it, but it was nothing you'd done to deserve it. The good died just as readily as the bad. Everyone died, he thought. Or everyone should have.

Kafak moved along with the rest of the men in his troop. When they hit the ground, he hit the ground. When they advanced, he advanced. They fired, he emptied his rifle right alongside them.

They kept going, bullets whistling with that eerie, mechanical whizzing all round them. All morning long. It just never stopped. Shells kept exploding. The concussions slammed him, oftentimes knocking him to the ground. Each time he thought he was dead. Or something close to it. And each time he inspected himself and found no blood, no wounds. There was only that force smashing into him, collapsing his lungs and muscles and blood vessels and organs into a squash. Like an accordion being compressed. Slowly, eventually, like an accordion, it all expanded back to normal. Only it never felt normal again. Not ever.

They had gone what seemed forever, a long distance, Kafak thought. He could see Cisterna, their objective, ahead. He guessed it was maybe a couple miles away yet. They could make it, he thought. They might make it. Then two men at the same time, one to his far right and the second to his left, though not so far, and both of them maybe thirty yards ahead of where he and his fellows were advancing, flew up into the air. Mines. One guy came back down a crumpled mess. He was dead. The other guy had lost a leg. He was shrieking from the pain of it. And from not being able to believe he no longer had a leg.

It was horrible, Kafak thought. Those screams. He wanted to help, but he couldn't do anything, and he knew it. A medic rushed to the guy. He had him quieted after a while.

Meanwhile, everyone had stopped pushing forward. They all dropped to the ground. The German guns pounded down upon them, the shells crushing and slamming them, the bullets whizzing around them. Everyone stayed pressed as close to the ground as they could. They would have crawled down into hell if they could have managed it to escape that heavy, unceasing fire.

He heard the lieutenant, about four bodies off to his left and a row or two in front, shouting into a radio. Asking for engineers to come clear the field. Or if not that, artillery to blow it all to hell, exploding the mines in the process.

"We're pinned down here," Dunphy said into the radio. "Under heavy fire." He got off the radio and hollered to everyone near enough to hear him. "Just stay put and keep your asses down. They'll send us help in a while."

Only they didn't. There was too much going on. They didn't have the men to send or the artillery to spend. Or maybe they just lost his request in a shuffle of paper back at HQ. Whatever the reason, they were stuck there, the minefield on their front, the Germans on both their flanks. They could no longer move if they wanted to. The German small arms fire pinned them down. It was terrible because they were sitting ducks, and more than a few guys were hit by well-aimed rifle fire. On the other hand, because the German troops were so close to them, it meant that the enemy artillery slowed down. They didn't want to take the chance of hitting their own people. That was a small relief because Kafak could breathe again even if it hurt his chest to do it.

He fired his weapon sporadically. It didn't matter where, in what direction, he fired. Germans were everywhere. He couldn't necessarily see them that well, but he knew they were there. He could feel and hear the results of their fire. Once or twice there was a tug at his clothing. Once on the back of his jacket, again on the back of his pant leg, near his calf. The second one stung quite a bit, so he figured a bullet had struck him. It didn't hurt terribly, though, so it probably hadn't gone in. Just streaked him.

He lay there, unmoving and hugging dirt for the most part, occasionally firing when he felt the mood strike him or some one of his comrades nearby started in.

The entire troop lay there like that, under heavy fire, waiting, pinned down, all afternoon. He could hear Dunphy cursing over the lack of response to his repeated requests. About four o'clock in the afternoon, one of the Germans realized Dunphy was the guy with a radio and he shot the lieutenant. Dunphy died with a bullet in his back. One of the sergeants took over.

Word spread, whispered from one man to the next. When it got dark, they'd move. Out of this depression and open ground and back to the closest Allied line they could find. They'd regroup and set up a defensive position.

Darkness couldn't come soon enough, Kafak thought. They all had to wait it out, though. One guy hadn't. He'd become overwhelmed by the fire and the tension of waiting to be hit and he'd gone a little nuts. He'd jumped up and begun running back toward the lines. He didn't make ten feet before a German rifleman brought him down.

Nobody tried it again. Nobody else lost it. Or, if they did, they stayed on the ground, shaking and hugging the earth.

Every so often Kafak heard someone shout very loud, curse. Sometimes cursing the Germans, sometimes the army, sometimes

God Himself. Kafak might've joined in if he could find the breath in him to do it, but he was still feeling compressed by the battering of shells.

Then it was dark. It didn't seem like it would ever happen, and then it just did. Word whispered down again. "Let's go." "Now." "Quiet as you can." "Watch your fucking asses."

Kafak rose up like the men around him. In a crouching run he began his personal retreat from the spot where they'd been pinned down all afternoon. He'd nearly made it out when the sky suddenly exploded into light. A German Kampfpistole sent up a flare. It burst high up, then rode down ever so slowly on its small parachute, illuminating everything as bright as day. Or nearly so. Enough, anyway, that the Germans could see them. They opened up again. The Americans stopped crouching and ran hell-for-leather. Kafak ran as fast as any of them. They all ran until they were out of that cross fire.

Once they had reached the safety of some rocks and a depression in the otherwise long, flat plain they had been on most of the day, the sergeant halted them and they regrouped. They prepared for any German attackers coming after their retreat. The Krauts didn't come, though. So they took the time to treat those wounded who could be treated and made makeshift slings to carry those they had had to drag out of the battle. They got their ammo squared away and started out again.

They moved back carefully now, looking for Germans they had bypassed during the day. They found a few of them, but these Germans were in no mood to fight anymore. It was dark, they were worn out right through, and most of all they had run out of ammo. They surrendered. The troop brought back half a dozen prisoners to the lines.

Kafak just wanted to fall into a stupor right there on the ground within the American lines. He knew he couldn't, though. He had to dig a foxhole for himself. He started in, bone weary and barely conscious of what he was doing. After about half an hour, he felt someone join him. He looked across. Marshak was digging, too.

"Willie," he said.

"You made it. That's a good fucking thing."

"You, too."

"I lost you there, somewhere along the way."

"I don't know what the fuck was happening half the time," Kafak said. "The other half, I didn't want to know."

"Fuckin-A right," Marshak agreed.

They finished their hole and fell into it.

While one of them slept a couple of hours, the other kept watch.

"And tomorrow," Marshak said just before he dropped off to sleep, "will just be more of the same fucking shit."

Kafak expected Marshak was right.

2

The next morning, well before sunrise, the Allied forces were once more formed up to make another push toward Cisterna. Marshak was indeed right, after all, Kafak thought. It was more of the same.

The Germans defended the town from well-fortified positions. Kafak had always loved to read, especially history and biography. And in that reading he had learned that a well-trained and entrenched army had to be outnumbered at a minimum of two to one for the offensive force to overcome such defenders. And right now it didn't feel to him as if the Allies outnumbered the Germans.

He'd come out of the previous day's struggle with nothing worse than a horrible, banging headache and a slight deafness in one ear. And a scratch on the back of his calf. Other than that, he was whole and complete, much better off than a lot of guys could say. He wondered whether he'd come out as well after another day of more of the same.

The Fifteenth Regiment advanced, pushed forward. The Germans held, then released. Then held again.

Kafak was part of a platoon, starting out.

"We're going to follow the footsteps of the main force," Sergeant Collins said. "Our job is to pick up any Kraut stragglers that the main force bypasses in order to keep moving forward. So be extra careful on account of these fucking Krauts will be behind our lines, and they'll know it, and that's gonna make them skittish and desperate. And ain't nothing fucking worse than a skittish, desperate enemy. So watch your fucking asses."

They moved out.

They found pockets of German troops here and there. The first five groups were in fairly exposed positions, hiding in ditches or behind rocks and the like. They put up brief firefights, doing some damage to the American platoon, but once a few of them were killed or wounded and they realized the overwhelming numbers against them and just how trapped they were, they surrendered. Kafak figured that half the Germans they came across in those encounters surrendered, while the other half got themselves killed or badly wounded. Some proved as desperate as Collins said. Others not so much. All of them, though, were skittish as hell. And that made them extremely dangerous.

The next encounter, the last of the day, was the worst. A squad of Germans with an MG42 had lain low while the main force passed them by. They had made themselves comfortable in a three-quarters-standing farmhouse. Once the main force had gone on, they popped out of hiding and applied harassing fire from behind. A squad had stayed behind to keep them cooped up in the house, but it was a waste of men. Those Germans weren't going anywhere now they were behind Allied lines.

When Kafak's platoon showed up, the squad left behind moved out to rejoin the main force. It was left to the wipe-up crew to eject the Germans from their squat.

Kafak was one of a group of the platoon put into position on a small rise that overlooked the farmhouse. They would supply cover fire for the group that would perform the actual assault. Collins led the attacking squad. He waved and the covering group opened up with everything they had. Rifles, a BAR, Thompson submachine guns, and a .30-caliber air-cooled machine gun the main force troops had had brought up.

As the group laid down a wall of fire to keep the Germans' heads down, the rest of the platoon leapfrogged forward, closer and closer to the farmhouse. But the Germans had superior cover and good weaponry. And they were experienced troops. They wiped out about half of the original assault squad, killed or wounded, before the rest of the men reached the walls of the house.

The cover group had to be careful now so as not to pick off their own men. A couple of the guys near the house tossed in grenades. They followed the explosions by bursting into the farmhouse, firing as fast as their weapons would allow. The sound of bullets flying, rolling out of the guns, smashing and ricocheting against the interior walls of the farmhouse, built to a mad crescendo. The cover squad moved down toward the farmhouse to provide closer support. All of a sudden the firing within stopped. The troops outside the farmhouse dropped behind cover or straight to the ground if they were in the open. Kafak was in the open. He had his rifle trained on the farmhouse door. Then he realized that was stupid if the Germans had won the firefight, so he quick switched his aim to a window. None of them knew who had won the battle within. They'd find out soon enough, though. Either their guys would come out or the Germans would start firing again.

A tense few seconds hung in the cold, wet air.

"Don't shoot, you fuckheads," Collins said. "We're coming out."

Kafak and the others relaxed. Stood up and waited. Collins came out of the house with four other men. They were all that was left. No prisoners accompanied them. No one asked about that.

Collins said, "Why'd you assholes let down your guard, for fuck's sake?"

"What do you mean, Sarge?" Marshak said. The guys all looked at one another. "We heard you telling us not to shoot at you. So we didn't."

"It coulda been a trick, yeah?"

Marshak frowned.

"I don't see how," he said.

"The fucking Krauts coulda made me say that just to fool you." Marshak paused, clearly thinking about this. Kafak felt suddenly guilty, exposed as a fraud. Not a soldier at all.

Then Marshak grinned. He said, "Not you, Sarge. The Krauts could never make you do something you didn't want to do. You're too tough."

Collins shook his head.

"Keep laughing, Marshak, you'll be dead soon. The rest of you, pay attention to what I'm telling you. It might keep you alive for a few minutes longer."

It was near to dark by this time, so Collins led them back to the lines. They were closer to Cisterna than they had been in the morning. Still, they weren't close enough. The German line, strong and seemingly unbreakable, remained standing between them and the town itself.

Even so, the Allies were digging in a good deal closer to the objective than when they started.

"Wonder if we'll make another push tomorrow," Marshak said.

Kafak found a foxhole to drop into. Marshak fell in right alongside him. They were eating their C-rations. Kafak had a can of stew while Marshak had one of beans. Neither felt much like talking. They were both bone weary and just wanted rest. They would trade off once more, couple hours' sleep, then a couple hours' guard.

Kafak said, "I don't know."

"We're getting close, but goddamn, every day we lose more and more guys. You know?"

"Seems like."

Later in the night, Marshak was asleep and Kafak was keeping watch when he heard someone approaching.

"Who goes?" Kafak said, hissing it through the darkness.

Only an occasional shell fell and nothing too close by where Kafak's hole sank in the ground.

A voice gave the night's password. "Crank." The Allies liked to choose words like that since Germans had difficulty pronouncing them without an accent. This voice gave out just fine with the password, and Kafak allowed its owner to approach. It was Sergeant Collins. He dropped into the hole.

"How's it hanging, Kafak?" he said.

Kafak found it amusing, in a way. The farther away a guy was from the front, the more difficulty they had in remembering your name. Back in Naples, he was mostly "Private" to every noncom and officer. Here on Anzio he became Kafak. During the assaults, he often became Bob. Kafak wondered whether it was something the army taught NCOs and officers or whether it was some simple trick of human nature.

Kafak said, "Seems quiet enough, Sarge."

"Good. Good. Get some rest. We've had a hell of a couple days."

"How'd we do?"

"You were fine, son, just fine."

Kafak felt grateful, but it wasn't what he had meant.

"What I meant," he said. "We close to Cisterna?"

"About two, three miles off," the sergeant said.

"We making another go tomorrow, then?"

"Not likely. Too many losses. We need to regroup. They just want us to dig in and hold what we've gained for now. We'll try again probably when we heal up some."

Kafak nodded.

"Sounds good," he said.

Collins slapped him softly on the shoulder and told him, "Keep your eyes peeled now, Kafak. Germans might be sending out patrols to probe our lines, find weaknesses, that kind of shit. A single German can kill you just as easy as the whole fucking Kraut army and sometimes easier. Don't ever forget that. Right?"

"Sure," Kafak said.

The sergeant slid out of the foxhole and moved on to the next one. Kafak waited, listening. It was tense at night because if the Germans were going to send out any probes, the darkness would be the time they'd do it. So you had to stay alert. He could hear things during the night. Other guys' voices, quiet but drifting along in the cool night air. And, of course, there were explosions occasionally blistering the quiet. Every so often you heard the *zzzinnng* of a shot firing or ricocheting, some German thinking he'd spotted movement in the dark. Kafak kept his head down so he could just barely watch over the lip of the hole. He tried not to move his head any more than he had to, just flicked his eyes. Constantly moved them. Once in a while a flare went up, either German or Allied.

Kafak tried to use the moonlight and starlight to keep his watch. He tried to memorize the shapes in front of him, the outlines of rocks and bushes. That way, if any of the outlines changed, he'd know something was going on. It wasn't easy, but he surprised himself. He'd never been especially observant back home, but when a guy's life is on the line, it makes everything a little sharper.

When Marshak woke up, Kafak took a crap in his helmet, then tossed it over the side of the foxhole. The entire line stank of men's shit. He thought it interesting that the army never taught a guy how to take a shit in a foxhole. After all, they spent so much time in their dugouts, you'd think the army would have thought of that, would have figured out a way to teach the troops to do it. Instead, they made do. Because you sure as hell weren't going to get out of your protection just to take a dump and risk being nailed by some German sniper with a lousy sense of humor.

The next day, they stayed put, like Collins had said. The Germans didn't, though. They counterattacked, trying to win back the ground the Allies had taken over the last couple of days. Now the Allies took the defensive and fought back. Kafak didn't see any Germans in his area, though, so he didn't have anything much to do except listen to the battle that was going on nearby, off to his front and left.

Midmorning, Collins came by and grabbed Kafak and Marshak and took them to another foxhole. This one was more in the center of the fighting, and there was a machine gun there that he gave to Kafak and Marshak to operate.

"Know how to work this thing?"

"Remember a little from basic."

"Well, you're all we got. The regular crew is all dead. It should come back to you quick enough once you start in working it."

"I sure hope you're right about that, Sarge," Marshak said.

Kafak didn't think he sounded too confident. Collins ignored him, his tone.

He said, "Hold this position and fire at anything German you fucking see. Got that?"

"Sure, Sarge," Kafak said.

"There's another machine gun to either side of you so you can cross your fields of fire. Keep everything under cover that way."

Collins moved off.

For the first hour or so they didn't see any Germans. Then they saw far too many of them. Germans everywhere in front of them. They started firing, Kafak pulling the trigger and swaying the gun in slow arcs to cover his entire front. Marshak fed the belts. They were under return fire, but they managed to shoot low and keep the Germans' heads down. Still, a couple times bullets singed by pretty close, once banging off the barrel of the machine gun. It didn't seem to do any harm to it, though, and Kafak kept firing.

Midafternoon, the Germans rose up as one and screamed, charging.

Kafak shouted. Marshak shouted.

"Fuck, fuck, fuck, fuck!"

Kafak pulled the trigger until his fingers ached and cramped. The Germans moved maybe ten or fifteen yards forward, firing every weapon they held, a hail of small arms fire swarming Kafak and Marshak. Kafak kept low but kept firing. He could hear bullets everywhere around him, kicking up the dirt in front of him, slapping against men's bodies nearby. Then the Krauts decided it wasn't going to work and retreated back behind cover. They continued harassing fire for the rest of the afternoon, and Kafak and Marshak, now switched off in their positions, kept firing at them, keeping their heads down. As night fell, the Germans pulled back.

The next day was similar, only Kafak and Marshak's position saw no action. They heard it off to their front and left and right but nothing ahead of them. They held fire and waited, tense and wondering. The entire day they never pulled the trigger on their machine gun. They never had to.

As night fell things once more grew quiet. Collins dropped into their hole.

"Good work, guys," he told them. "We think the fuckers have had enough, but we can't be sure, so stay alert. They might try a night attack. We got guys moved up ahead of you now in more forward positions. You guys hold here. If you see a red flare, that means the forward unit is going to retreat. Don't fucking shoot them! Let 'em through and then shoot anything that comes after them because that'll be fucking Krauts. Got it?"

"That sounds complicated, Sarge," Marshak said.

"It ain't complicated, asshole," Collins said. "Just shoot the right fucking people, is all you gotta do."

All night they waited for a red flare, but nothing ever came. Kafak guessed the Germans had had enough, just like the Americans had. They probably had to fall back and lick their wounds, try to reorganize for another time.

That suited Kafak just fine.

He'd only been on the line for a few days. Seemed like months, though. He stopped to think about it. It was January 29 when he came up to the front, and then they had attacked Cisterna, and then the Germans had counterattacked. Maybe four or five days total, for all of it. And yet he felt like he'd been fighting and shooting and getting shot at for his entire life.

That all seemed strange to him and somehow impossible. Yet there it was.

He felt he'd done all right. He hadn't run. He hadn't been a coward. When things had gotten hot, the training had taken over and he'd done what he was supposed to do.

Still, he didn't feel that sense of relief he thought he would once he'd undergone fire for the first time and held up against it. He figured after that he was a soldier. Done. And no one could ever take that away from him.

Only now that it had happened, he knew that wasn't the case. Not at all. Because each time you went under fire was a new time. Each time was the first time, sort of. All over again. Any single time you went into combat could be the time you broke and ran, turned coward. Even after you'd faced a dozen, a hundred times of people shooting at you, you could still find it impossible to face it the next time. The next time. That was just it. That was always the time that counted. The only time that counted.

The next time.

Kafak lay in his foxhole, trying to sleep and hoping he'd stand and do his duty the next time.

3

After that first five days of shit, things fell into a routine for a couple of weeks. A sometimes hellish routine, but a routine nonetheless.

Kafak sat in his foxhole with Marshak. Sometimes they would move up and dig a foxhole farther forward. Oftentimes they'd end up back in the same one they started from after the Germans began firing heavily toward the more forward position. Usually that fire came from artillery. Mortars and 88s. Other big guns firing down upon them from the Alban Hills. Sometimes it was snipers or other small arms fire, machine guns, burp guns, things like that. It wasn't worth keeping a foxhole twenty or thirty yards forward if it meant a guy was under constant fire. So they moved back.

Most of the time in the foxhole, Kafak was bored. It was boredom and waiting for the Germans to attack. They didn't attack. Not in those weeks, anyway. He and Marshak watched the German planes assaulting the harbor at night, attempting to disrupt the Anzio buildup of men and supplies that went on almost constantly. The Messerschmitts would come in right near dusk, with the dropping sun right behind them so that they could hide themselves as long as possible from the gunners' eyes. Then it would be dark. Kafak and the others would watch the tracers from the antiaircraft guns seeking out the German planes. Occasionally they saw a German plane get hit and go down. They didn't even consider chasing after the pilots any longer. They didn't think about leaving their foxholes at all now that the Germans would fire at any movement they saw. Or even thought they saw. No. Now, Kafak and the rest of them sat and waited, somehow bored and tense all at the same time. During the day, they watched the Allied planes, usually the Tuskegee Airmen, strafe the German positions in Cisterna.

It was trench warfare, the closest thing to World War I in the entire operations of the Second World War. That's what Kafak thought, anyway.

He sometimes felt afraid. No, not sometimes. A lot of the time. But he didn't say this to anyone. He only sat and kept it to himself and wondered if anybody else felt like he did. Wondered if the other guys were afraid. No one spoke about it. It wasn't a thing you wanted to talk about, admit.

It made him feel bad about himself, that he felt afraid. Afraid of getting shot, killed, wounded, sliced up by shrapnel. Maimed or disfigured. All of that terrified him. He kept it all locked up inside, though, and felt miserable for feeling that way, thinking about those things.

Then he figured that the important thing was to do what was expected of him. To fight when he was supposed to fight. If he just did that, he told himself, then the other stuff didn't matter. The being scared stuff. That would be OK just so long as he didn't let it stop him doing what he was there to do, what he had been trained to do.

And so far, he'd managed that. Once the fighting had started, the training had taken over. He didn't think so much about the fear then. He just fought.

That was good, he told himself.

That was all he needed to do.

The weather was miserable. Sunny Italy. They all had a laugh about that. Well, it was winter, after all. And at some point it had started to rain. And once it started raining, it didn't seem to ever stop raining. Everything turned into mud. Thick, viscous, boot-sucking mud. It was difficult to prop up the sides of the foxholes because the dirt turned to mud and rolled down into the bottom of the hole. Groundwater seeped through the sides of the holes. Rain puddled the bottoms of the holes as well. A lot of foxholes just caved in. Living conditions became more and more miserable every day.

Kafak thought he would never forget lying out in a foxhole all day in the rain. Not if he lived to be a hundred.

Of course, he didn't expect to live that long, truth be told.

Still, it was wet and cold and ugly and that made everything terrible and didn't even take into account the Germans shelling them and taking potshots at them every time they moved.

One day, Kafak came down with the shits. The diarrhea was horrible, and his guts cramped and he thought he would explode, and then the shit did explode out of him. He crapped into his helmet almost nonstop the entire day, tossing it out the side of the foxhole, whatever foxhole he happened to be in that day, he couldn't keep track any longer. He couldn't keep track of anything any longer. He didn't know what day it was or how long he had been here on Anzio now. He just knew he had the shits and felt miserable.

He knew, too, though, that it was no reason to be sent back to the rest area. Not that there was any rest area on Anzio. The Germans were shelling even the hospitals back at the beach. Doctors and nurses were being killed. Even if he could have been sent back, Kafak never would have asked for that. He wouldn't leave his position on the line for something as minor as diarrhea when other guys had much worse. That wouldn't be right. He wouldn't let down his buddies like that.

He stank and he knew it but he didn't care. Everybody stank. The entire front stank.

After two days, his bowels returned to normal. He felt better then. The Germans didn't seem to care, though, he thought. They increased their shelling that day for some reason. Every day on the beachhead the Germans delivered rolling barrages from one end of the Allied lines to the other. Those bombardments the guys all knew would be coming. They could surmise how long they would last and so could get through it. This was different, though. Kafak only remembered it happened that particular day because he knew it was the day after his shits ended.

At one point, the shells came so fast and furious that everyone along Kafak's line of foxholes had shoved themselves deep into the puddles of water and mud at the bottom of their dugouts, waiting out the damned explosions, cursing and screaming at the Germans, and praying to God to make it all stop.

It didn't stop, though. It went on for what seemed hours. Mud flew everywhere. It rained mud as the shells blew and erupted the mud out of the ground and then it fell back down again in sickening, wet plops that covered all the men with filth. Kafak figured some of his own shit was probably being thumped high up into the air and flying back down on him. And Marshak. And everyone else nearby as well.

Even though they knew that regular artillery was generally ineffective against well-dug-in troops, the bombardment was horrible. The noise of it, the shrieking and whistling of metal dropping through the air. The horrendous booming of the shells exploding. The screaming meemies that sounded like they were piercing your very eardrums with their shrieks. The Germans were expert at psychological weapons. Their guns, Kafak thought, often sounded worse than they were effective. But God! That sound. It drove you mad with terror because it sounded right on top of you.

Kafak wondered if he would get through it or if he would crack, and then he started thinking about baseball, playing baseball when he was growing up, he'd been a hell of a baseball player and he loved playing and had things been different, he might have gone on to play at a higher level, maybe college, he could have gone to college, he thought, no, he *knew* he could have, because when the army had drafted him and tested him they had told him he had scored high enough to become an officer, to go to Officer Candidate School, to lead men, but he hadn't wanted to lead men, Kafak hadn't, he only wanted to keep his fucking head down and survive this fucking thing, and so he told them thanks but no thanks and he was assigned to the infantry and now here he was sunk deep in the bowels of the wet muddy earth, shit dropping down out of the sky on top of him and nowhere to go to escape it, not even for a second, and the explosions battering his eardrums and smashing his head into splinters, or it felt that way anyhow, and he thought about a girl he had known in Naples, not for long because he hadn't been there long before they had shipped him here to Anzio, but he had met this Italian girl there and he had taken a picture with her and he still had the picture in which he looked like a tall, gawky, green American teenaged boy (all of which he was) and she looked like a pretty Italian girl (which she was; she wasn't a whore, in other words, just a regular girl, although the guys, a lot of the guys, said all the Italian women were whores nowadays, now that the Germans had ruined Italy and impoverished them all, but he didn't believe that, Kafak didn't think that was true, not at all) and he stood there in the picture, grinning like an idiot with his hands in his pockets, not even touching the girl, not an arm around her or anything because she wasn't a whore, she was a regular girl, a nice girl, and he had just wanted a picture to remember her by and he wished he could look at that picture now but he wouldn't try because all the mud and the rain and the shit falling down upon him would have ruined it, anyway, so he left it in his pocket where it was and while he was thinking about that girl the shelling stopped.

It was quiet then.

Deathly quiet.

All of the men scrambled into position, slipping and sliding against the muddy sides of their holes, readying their weapons over the lips of their foxholes, awaiting an attack. Because usually that kind of bombardment was the precursor to an attack.

When nothing happened after an hour or so, they started to relax.

And that was when someone down the row of foxholes shouted.

"Man on the end, let it go!"

Everyone laughed, the tension releasing.

They laughed because it was a familiar expression to them, an expression that had nothing to do with war. Or maybe something only tangentially to do with war.

The expression came from their being tested for venereal disease. It took place in the whorehouses in North Africa. In order to alleviate the spread of VD, the army had commandeered certain whorehouses to make them as safe as possible for US soldiers to visit. After a trooper had finished his business, an MP took charge of him. The soldier was forced to undergo a three-station treatment.

The first station consisted of the guy washing his genitals and pubic area very thoroughly with an antiseptic soap. It was green-colored. Then the soldier would move on to station two. There he would have his penis, the urinary canal, injected with a dark purple solution that burned and disinfected. But the solution wasn't just injected and let loose. Instead, the trooper had to hold the head of his penis, pinching it closed between thumb and forefinger. He stood before a urinal holding the disinfectant inside in this manner until a medical orderly shouted at intervals, "Man on the end, let it go." The guy would release, and the purple fluid would be evacuated from his penis. A minute later, the next soldier, the new man on the end, would be ordered to let it go. The final station consisted of spreading a white, gooey ointment on the head of the penis and covering it with toilet paper. The soldier would then be stamped as having received the prophylactic treatment required after a visit to the bordello in North Africa.

It became something of a joke for the men, the second part of the treatment, and that line turned into an oft-used expression that could relieve tension among the troops. Still, the treatment seemed to work in North Africa.

Later, in Italy, where such draconian measures were not put in place, the incidence of VD grew far higher.

One day another bombardment erupted, similar to the one the Germans had sent that day after Kafak had quit with the shits. This one, though, came from the Allied artillery joined by the Allies' naval guns. It started at 0430 one morning, waking everyone who might have been sleeping. The guns pounded for more than half an hour. Kafak could hear the *whoomp* of the guns going off behind the lines and hear the thunder of the explosions out in front of them, on the German lines.

"Something's up," he told Marshak.

"At least it's ours and not theirs this time," Marshak said.

"Fuckin-A right," Kafak said.

He listened to the shells exploding, feeling bad for the Germans. Well, in a way. He knew, they all knew, what it was like to live through something like that.

While the barrage went on, Collins came up with a couple of other guys from L Company. They dropped into the hole beside Kafak and Marshak.

"What's up, Sarge?" Marshak said.

"HQ got word that the Krauts are planning an attack this morning. So they opened up with everything we got to fuck with their lines and their formations. Once this is over, be ready, cuz the fucking Krauts will be coming."

"Sure thing, Sarge," Kafak said.

The five men crouched in the foxhole, staring out toward the German lines. Nothing obscured their vision. Everything here was fairly flat. Every piece of vegetation had long been blown away. There was nothing but mud and ditches and slit trenches and foxholes and some rocks. All the way to Cisterna.

After between a half hour and an hour, the shelling stopped, as suddenly as it had begun. A short silence ensued. One filled with tension.

"Get ready for it," Collins said.

"Fuck, fuck, fuck," one of the new men said.

Then the Germans' guns opened up, returning the favor. An incredible downpour of whistling bombs exploded all over the Allied lines. All the men ducked deep into the hole. The bombing went on and on. One of the new guys in the hole started shaking. He didn't say a word, just started shaking uncontrollably. The other new guy just hugged himself tightly and kept repeating, "Fuck, fuck, fuck!" Marshak howled a long, harsh, ragged scream and then fell silent, looking sheepish that the sound had come out of his mouth.

Collins moved to the guy who was shaking, and Kafak thought how the sergeant had brought these two guys along with him for a purpose, to keep herd on them, as it were. Collins, Kafak thought, must have seen something, realized something was up with them.

"Come on, Peterson, snap out of it," Collins said. His voice wasn't harsh, but strong and commanding. He wasn't yelling at Peterson; he was only talking. "You're all right," Collins said. Like he was insisting this would be true. "Snap out of it, son. You'll be all right."

Peterson didn't snap out of it, though.

Marshak said, "He OK, Sarge?"

"He'll be all right," Collins said, snapping the words out at Marshak. "Peterson's been with me since the Kasserine Pass. We've seen this before. We've seen worse than this, haven't we, Peterson?"

Peterson didn't answer, just kept shaking. But he glanced at Collins now, and Collins smiled at him. "Sure," Collins said, "you're gonna be fine."

Then Peterson's eyes cut toward the other new guy in the hole and Peterson's eyes somehow grew wider and Kafak said, "Oh shit!" and Collins spun around to look and the other guy in the foxhole shot himself in the mouth with his sidearm and dropped down into the bottom of the hole, dead.

"Son of a bitch!" Collins shouted. "Goddamn son of a fucking bitch whore fuck!"

Collins moved to the other soldier, but the guy was dead. They could all see that. Before any of them could even move, the guy had done the job. The shock of it popped Peterson out of his shakes.

"Shit, I'm sorry, Sarge," he said. He whispered it. He said it again.

Collins shook his head.

"Got nothing to do with you, son. Son of a bitch."

"He was with us at the Pass, too," Peterson said.

"I guess he just couldn't take no more," Collins said. "It all adds up on a fucker. You know?"

Nobody replied to that. What was there to say? Collins didn't expect any answer either. He kept them focused on the task at hand. Waiting out the bombardment. Then being ready for the German assault.

Kafak followed the sergeant's orders, kept crunched down, kept watchful. He started thinking, though, squatting and waiting in that hole. He started wondering if it would all add up for him at some point. And when that point might come. Especially in view of his earlier thoughts about his fear and what he needed to do to conquer that fear. He wondered would the fear at some point conquer him.

He hoped not. He prayed not.

"Lord," he said. He spoke aloud but in a mumble that no one else could hear with that horrendous pounding raining down all round them. He hoped God could hear over the explosions, though. "Lord," he said, "please watch over me and give me the strength to do my best. Don't let me let the guys down. Not now. Please."

Soon after, the shelling stopped, and out of the smoke and dirt still flying through the air rushed hundreds of German soldiers. Kafak saw them coming, and he readied to fire. He began firing. He took his time, aimed at the laundry. Just shoot at the laundry, they'd told him in basic, and never mind the guy inside of it. Kafak doubted it mattered much, though. The Third Division had positioned tanks and tank destroyers on the front line. They provided a withering fire that annihilated the lead assault companies of the German forces. Kafak didn't figure there was much work for his M1 to do, but he kept firing anyway, looking for targets and shooting where he saw any.

"Get those fucking Nazi bastard fucks!" Marshak screamed at the tanks. "Get them fuckers!"

Not that he could be much heard over the boom of the guns and the barking of the machine guns. Kafak said nothing. Just kept firing.

As the Germans fell back, the men cheered. The Third had maintained their positions in the face of the assault before Cisterna.

"That evens up the score some for what those bastards did to us when we attacked Cisterna," Collins said. He spoke in a grim tone. Kafak figured he was still thinking about the guy they had lost, the one who had shot himself. That had struck all of them hard, seeing something like that. Knowing it could happen. "Shit," Collins said then, mumbling more to himself than to the other three men in the hole with him. "They still owe us plenty, goddamnit."

Sporadic fighting continued on their front all day long, but there never appeared any danger of their breaking. Kafak didn't think so, anyhow. He kept firing when there was someone to fire at, and he kept his head down otherwise and let the armor do its job.

He wasn't scared now; he was just acting. His training had once more taken over.

They heard rumors as runners came to give messages to Collins that things were going harder on other areas of the front. Kafak wondered if they'd be pulled out and reassigned as reinforcements where there was more danger of a German breakthrough. But that order never came, and then night fell and the fighting slowed off.

Collins said, "Stay alert cuz they'll be sending out patrols and probes, trying to exploit any weaknesses they can find. Fucking Germans are good at this shit. Don't relax!"

"No, Sarge," Kafak said.

Collins left the hole, and Kafak, Marshak, and Peterson kept watch. One of them suggested a sleeping rotation, and the two others agreed. Marshak jumped at taking the first rest, and Peterson shook his head, amused at the little trooper.

"That fucker sleeps more than anybody I know."

"He don't sleep," Kafak said. "He only *wants* to sleep."

"That's right," Marshak said, chirping in quickly. "If I ever actually got the sleep I tried to take, I wouldn't need no sleep, and then I wouldn't be trying to sleep all the time."

"Whatever you said," Peterson said. "It's fucked up and makes no sense. You're the sleepingest fucker I ever seen."

"Sleepy-assed Marshak," Kafak said, grinning.

"Fuck you guys," Marshak said.

Marshak lay down and pretended to be immediately asleep. Maybe he was at that, Kafak thought. It was hard to tell with Marshak. Still, after that he was always Sleepy Ass to everyone in the company.

Peterson and Kafak kept an eye out for German infiltrators. With the tanks there, though, they felt fairly comfortable. Still, you could never know for sure, so they didn't relax, as Collins had ordered.

They were quiet for a long time, and then out of the darkness Peterson said, "Goddamnit, it's such a fucked-up piece of shit, you know."

"What's that?" Kafak said, not looking at him but keeping his attention trained on the area around their foxhole, the area through which the Germans would come if they were coming that night. Memorizing the shadows and the outlines of things.

"That shit with Jake."

Jake Czeshevski, Kafak had picked up, was the guy who had shot himself.

"Yeah. Hell of a thing," Kafak said.

Peterson fell quiet again for a few moments; then he said, "I don't know what the fuck came over me, you know, back there."

"Hell," Kafak said, "this shit is fucked."

"You got that right," Peterson said. Kafak thought he detected a note of relief in Peterson's voice. A thankfulness for being forgiven, Kafak expected. Something like that. Only Kafak didn't figure there was anything to be forgiven for. It could happen to anyone, Kafak thought. It could happen to him. He just wished Peterson would drop the subject. He didn't like thinking about any of that.

Peterson said, "You ever wonder what you're doing here, anyway, Kafak?"

"What do you mean?"

"You know. Here."

"In Italy? Anzio?"

"No. In this fucking war. This whole fucking thing. You ever wonder what the fuck you're doing in the middle of this fucking shitstorm?"

Kafak stopped to consider that, still staring out at the ground around them. Still on guard. Did he wonder what he was doing here?

He hadn't. Not really. Not until now.

His country was at war. He'd been drafted. You went to war for your country. That's how it worked. There was nothing else, nothing more to it, really. It wasn't anything a guy had to think about. You just did it. He shrugged internally over that. He couldn't see any other way about it.

Once you were in, of course, you did what you were told to do. You went where you were told to go. That was the point of orders. That was the point of a military structure. How else were you supposed to think about it?

Kafak knew, of course, that there were deserters. Every army, everywhere, every time, had its deserters. The thought of deserting, though, never occurred to him. He wouldn't ever do something like that. He might run; he might cower; he might shoot himself like Jake Czeshevski had done. All of those things seemed entirely within the realm of possibility in Kafak's mind. But the idea of deserting was not a thing he would ever contemplate. It seemed somehow dirty to him. A betrayal not only of your country but, more importantly, of your pals. The guys fighting beside you. He wouldn't let them down like that. They were his buddies. Sleepy Ass and Peterson and all the rest of them. He owed them. And he knew they felt the same way about owing him something. No, he'd never desert.

None of that, he supposed, really answered Peterson's question, though.

Kafak recalled when he'd been drafted. He'd been afraid, of course, there was that definite trepidation about what was going to happen. On the other hand, he'd been excited, too. He saw it as an adventure. The start of an adventure. There was a decided excitement playing within his mind and heart. He wanted to go. He looked forward to it, even, in some ways. The adventure every boy dreams about. The biggest adventure anyone could ever possibly face. Sure. It was *the* Big Adventure.

But after a few times in combat you understood that this wasn't any sort of boy's play. This wasn't playing army in the backyard, up and down the street. This shit was real. You learned that damned fast. It only took one bomb exploding close enough to rattle your skeleton. One bullet whizzing by like a bee in your fucking ear. After that you knew. You understood. Because then you realized you could be killed at any moment. Your life ended. All your hopes and dreams, everything you thought you wanted in the future, a future, maybe any future, could be ripped away from you in a moment. Kafak knew that. Understood it. Or thought he did, anyway. So, no, this was no boy's adventure any longer. This was real fucking shit, and he knew that now.

Of course, he was here now, too. So there it was.

Kafak didn't answer Peterson. He didn't feel able to.

Instead he said, "Well, why you here, Pete?"

Peterson shrugged. Kafak, even without looking at him, could hear the sound of his uniform rustling in the dark quiet.

Peterson said, "I wish to fuck I fucking knew."

They both were driven to silence by the pure agony of incomprehension expressed in Peterson's words, if not exactly in his tone. Then, after a couple of seconds, Kafak snorted a laugh. Peterson looked at him, and Kafak looked at Peterson for the first time, and then Kafak laughed out loud, but keeping it low, quiet in the night, and Peterson grinned and then they both shook their heads as if to say *What a couple of fucking assholes we are*, and then they both laughed until Sleepy Ass woke up and took Kafak's place and Kafak lay down and fell asleep in the mud.

4

Kafak and his comrades saw some more action over the next few days, some of it getting pretty thick, but they didn't get the worst of it.

Rumors abounded, and the company commander, Captain Cole, visited them several times over the next week, putting the wrong rumors right and letting them know as much as he knew about the bigger picture.

"We got a new boss," he told them one day as he squatted in their foxhole next to them. He traveled during the day through smoke to visit his men. Kafak thought that was a fine thing, that their leader would care enough about their welfare that he would risk death or wounding to visit with them, talk with them, keep their morale up. He thought a lot of Captain Cole. He knew all the guys did.

"Who's that, Cap?" Kafak asked him.

"General Truscott is taking over the Sixth Corps. Lucas has been relieved."

"Why'd they do that?" Kafak asked.

"Because we're sitting here instead of in Cisterna, I expect," Cole said.

"That's bullshit," Kafak said.

"What the fuck, Cap?" Jackson said. He was a corporal and had joined Kafak and Marshak in their foxhole over the last couple days. Peterson had been hit by a sniper and killed two days earlier. "Lucas did everything possible with what they gave him. We took the fucking beach. We're still here despite every-thing the Krauts could throw at us. What the fuck more do they want from the guy?"

"Hell, you got me, One-Eyed," Cole said. They called Jackson "One-Eyed" as in one-eyed jack. "Not up to me who runs the outfit. I just follow orders. But General Truscott's a good man. He cares about the troops as much as Lucas did, but he's probably more of a go-getter. And that's what Clark wants, I guess."

"Go-getter," Kafak said.

"Shit," Marshak said, using the same tone of resigned disgust that had sounded in Kafak's voice. "Hell, Cap, we all know what fucking go-getter means. It means we get to go and get our asses shot off some more."

"Your ass is so sleepy, Marshak," Cole said, "it won't know it's been hit for hours."

"Right," Kafak said, grinning. "Until it wakes the fuck up."

They all shared a laugh, even Marshak joining in. You had no choice but to laugh at yourself since they all took their turn being the butt.

"Shut the fuck up, you gawky-assed son of a bitch," Marshak told Kafak, still laughing.

Ever since he'd been tagged "Sleepy Ass" by Kafak, Marshak had been trying to tag Kafak with the name of "Gawky Ass" or "Gawky" since Kafak was six feet tall and skinny as hell and walked around with a kind of slouch. Some of the guys said it was just natural, but others said he had developed a permanent crouch so as to make himself less of a target. But somebody said he was too damned skinny to hit with a bullet and it would take a bomb to do him in. Kafak only grinned at them all and said, "I *hope* it ain't no fucking bomb."

Collins visited them shortly after Cole left.

"How's the feet, boys?" he asked them.

They all knew what he meant. They had seen what could happen.

Kafak remembered one of the guys from L Company named Preston. Preston had been around for a while. Kafak had met him back in North Africa. Here on Anzio, Preston had begun the whole thing with shaking his feet. Kafak clearly remembered that. How Preston would always be shaking his feet. Hell, they all did it. Lying there in your foxhole, unable to move all day because of the German snipers, the cold and the wet sneaking into your boots, all of them got numb feet now and again. So you shook them to get the blood going. Or you stamped them if you could stand up at all, like you sometimes could at night. Kafak recalled how Preston had begun stamping his feet. A little at first, then more and more as a few days passed. Then he started complaining about them.

"I can't hardly put my weight on them anymore, guys. They hurt like fucking shit."

"What's the pain like?" somebody asked.

"Like they're on fucking fire. I'm telling you. This is impossible. If the Krauts come through, I ain't going to be able to run away from the cocksuckers."

Everyone laughed and passed it off. But Preston was in true pain.

One day when he took off his boots to look at his feet, the stench of rotting flesh hit them all like a wave of shit from a sewer. Only worse.

"Son of a bitch, Preston," Marshak said. He sounded awed at the smell of Preston's feet, at the sight of them. "What you been doing to your fucking feet?"

"What the fuck?" Kafak said.

"It's the fucking cold," Preston said. "It's the goddamned water everywhere." He looked around. "Ain't your guys' feet just like this, too?"

The other guys looked at one another. They didn't say anything. They looked a little sick, all of them. Preston most of all. Then Kafak said, "You better talk to a medic, Pres."

Preston stared at Kafak. For a long moment. Finally, Preston looked back down at his feet and said, "Fuck," under his breath. With true fear. "Jesus Christ fuck."

Kafak and Marshak half-carried, half-walked Preston back to the nearest medical aid station. They wished him good luck, then returned to the front line and their foxhole there. They didn't hear anything more about Preston for a while and sort of forgot about the entire thing, and then one day Captain Cole was visiting them and told them that Preston would be going home.

Kafak, Marshak, and a couple of other guys who were there looked at one another. Then Marshak spoke to the captain. He said, "He gets out of this shithole because he's got sore fucking feet, Cap? Hell, my feet suddenly don't feel so hot neither. You know?"

"Preston got trench foot," Cole said. "They had to amputate most of his leg."

"Most of his leg?" Marshak said.

"Fuck!" Kafak said.

Cole nodded.

"Preston lost one leg to just above the knee, and the other one around the ankle," Cole said. "Way I heard it, anyhow."

"Jesus Christ," Kafak said. He shook his head, astounded.

"He just had sore fucking feet, Cap," Marshak said. "Fucking army doctors. Why'd they cut off his fucking legs, for Christ's sake?"

"I told you, trench foot, Sleepy Ass. The problem is, once it gets bad, gangrene sets in. That's what happened with Preston. He let it go on too long, and then it was too late. He had gangrene in both feet. The doctors start off by cutting off only as much as they think needs it. But they can't always tell how far the decay of flesh has set in, see. So with his one foot, they stopped at the ankle and that was the end of it on that side. But on the other side, they had to keep cutting until they went above the knee. But they finally got it all. Least, that's what I heard. So Preston's luckier than a lot of guys. A lot of guys they don't catch it even in that time, and those guys end up dead."

"Holy shit," Marshak said. "From fucking sore feet."

"He don't sound so lucky to me," Kafak said.

"He could be dead, Kafak," Cole said.

Kafak looked at the captain but didn't reply. He only shook his head. Dead. Or no feet and only half of one leg. He shook his head again, falling silent.

Cole said, "Anyway, Preston wasn't the only one, like I said. There have been others. Too many others. So the army's instituted a new procedure. New boots and socks. The shoepac procedure. And you're all going to follow it, because if you don't I'll be sent back to the States and lose my command. And I am not about to lose my command because of," and he paused and looked at Marshak, "a lot of sore feet."

Marshak nodded, but he said, "I was you, I wouldn't mind being sent back to the States, Cap."

Cole smiled at him.

He said, "I can't afford to let them send me back. If I left you guys out here on your own, I'd never overcome the guilt. You all wouldn't last a day without me and Collins on your fucking asses, now, would you?"

"Shit," Marshak said. But he said it quietly.

Kafak said, "You got that right, Cap."

Cole laughed and left the hole. Marshak looked at Kafak and said, "Kiss ass."

"What?"

"You're a kiss ass. I ain't alive cuz of Cole or Collins. I'm alive cuz I watch my fucking ass for myself."

"You're alive because you're too goddamned small for the Krauts to hit," one of the other guys said.

"Fuck you," Marshak said, but they all laughed. Then he looked back at Kafak. "Kiss Ass. That's what we should call you, Kafak."

Only that name didn't stick either.

So when Collins asked them, "How's the feet, boys?" they all knew what he meant, all right.

"'Fraid you're gonna get busted, Sarge?" Marshak said.

"Hell," Collins said, "I'd be glad to lose this job and not be responsible for a bunch of fuckups like you guys."

"Aw, Sarge, we love you, too."

"Shut the fuck up, Sleepy Ass, and change your fucking socks. All of you. Shoepac it right now."

"You gonna watch, Sarge?"

"Since I don't trust you half as far as I can throw your little ass, Sleepy Ass, yeah, I'm gonna wait and watch and make sure you all do it right. Get on with it now. And keep your dumb fucking heads down."

Kafak sank as low into the foxhole as he could. Sleepy Ass and Jackson crouched right beside him. Collins kept an eye out but half an eye on them as well.

Kafak had to scrape wet, sucking mud off his boots before he could even unlace them. He pulled off his left boot and pulled out the insole that had been added as one of the measures to combat trench foot. The piece of thick felt was sopping wet. Not from the outside water in the hole, because the boot he was wearing had been especially designed to keep that water out. The insole grew wet from the condensation of his own perspiration in the heavy socks and boots. He slipped a fresh insole into the boot. Well, fresh was a relative term, Kafak thought. It was the one he had used yesterday and then taken out to dry. It didn't dry completely in the rotten weather, but it was a lot less soggy than the one he was removing this morning. After that he removed the two heavy wool ski socks he had on and put on new ones. These, too, were not actually new, but the ones he had used yesterday. They were still damp and cold but not as wet as the ones he was taking off. There was no way to ever actually dry the stuff out because they couldn't light any fire. They lived cold. They ate cold. They slept cold. Cold and wet. Everything on the Anzio beachhead front lines happened cold and wet. Kafak tried not to think about any of that overmuch. Nothing you could do about it except hate it and curse it, and they all did that. And then lived through it.

Kafak put the boot back on and laced it up, tight. Then he performed the same ritual for his right foot. He silently thanked the Germans for not messing with them in the midmorning, the time when this shoepac discipline usually took place. The Germans' early rolling barrage had ended, and their patrols and probes wouldn't start until dark. The thought had no sooner floated through his brain than a single shot chinged off metal nearby. Everyone ducked.

"Anyone hit?" Collins said. "Call out!"

"I'm good, Sarge," Kafak said, checking himself quickly, though he knew there was no real need. He hadn't felt anything, and he'd heard it so he knew he wasn't hit. Still, he checked himself. Every time.

Marshak patted his body all over as well, making a show of it. Then he said, "Fuckers didn't get me." Then he turned his head a little and shouted out, "You didn't get me, you cocksuckers!"

"No, not this time," Collins said. "One-Eyed? How're you?"

Jackson didn't answer right away. Kafak and the others all looked at him. Jackson was sunk low in the hole and had his helmet off. He was rubbing the back of his head, near the top. He held his helmet in his other hand. There was a small dent in the metal.

"Son of a bitch," he said. His voice was colored with amazement. "Some fucker gave me a knot on my fucking skull you wouldn't believe."

But he was all right, and Kafak could see the relief on Collins's face. The sergeant shook his head.

He said, "I don't know if it was the helmet saved your ass or just your hard fucking head, but keep down from now on, will ya, ya stupid bastard?"

"Will do, Sarge, believe you me."

"That goes for all of ya."

"Sure thing," Kafak said.

"I ain't going nowhere," Marshak said.

"Tell me something I don't already know," Collins told him.

Things had fallen into a pattern for Kafak. He knew that the Allies were building up their forces, almost daily, because Captain Cole had informed them about that. Besides, they would still watch German raids on the ships in the harbor, and there wouldn't be ships in the harbor if the Allies hadn't been sending in more men and more equipment and more supplies. For Kafak, though, on a day-to-day basis, he didn't do much. He woke up in the morning. Pissed against the side of the foxhole while poised on his hip. Took a shit if he needed to. Ate a can of hash or stew or beans. Tried not to throw up. Drank some water. They mostly got their water from the drainage ditches. They scooped it up in their canteens or their helmets and then tossed in the tablets they'd been given that would disinfect the water. It tasted like shit, but it wouldn't kill you. At least that's what the army told them. Kafak was never sure he trusted it when the army said something wouldn't kill him.

After all that, he waited out the Germans' good-morning rolling bombardment. Then came the shoepac ritual, which Kafak followed religiously, with or without Collins's presence and prompting. He'd never forget that stench when Preston had removed his boots that day. That alone proved spur enough to make him self-enforce the discipline with his shoes and socks and insoles. Then it was a matter of keeping his head down. Then it was a matter of boredom and waiting.

The Germans wouldn't attack this late in the day. If they didn't come in at dawn, they weren't coming. Not in force, anyhow. In the dark, smaller groups of Germans oftentimes came. Or tried to. They were usually knocked back. Occasionally, on other parts of the front, rumor had it that their probes were more successful. The thing you didn't want happening was to get shot by one of these patrols. Or captured. That was the main thing you had to watch out for during those weeks after the Germans' big counterattack. When things had settled into this back-and-forth probing with these small pushes to extend one's lines.

The Allies sent out patrols as well. See where the Germans were at. Try to capture prisoners. Kafak had been spared that much so far.

During those long, boring hours, there wasn't much to do. Sometimes Kafak tried to zero in his rifle. That wasn't easy, though, because there was nothing much to shoot at. If he was in a foxhole farther back, he might shoot out to sea, but they were soon told not to do that because their bullets were reaching the ships in the harbor and annoying, when not actually injuring, the navy boys. And you couldn't shoot in front of you at the rear for fear of hitting your own guys. When he was in a foxhole on the front line, he couldn't fire either, because you had to stick your head up for that, and you were only asking for trouble then because the Germans would spot you and pull a One-Eyed on you. That's what it had become called if you got hit in the helmet. Most times, you weren't going to survive that the way One-Eyed Jackson had, though.

There wasn't much else left to do but daydream about home or something like that. Kafak thought a lot about the Italian girl. He wished he knew more about her. Once in a while he'd look at her picture, but he didn't like doing that because it might get ruined and also because the guys would rib him about it. Call her "his girl." Stuff like that. Yet he didn't even really know her but to say hello and one day ask for a photograph. Prove he had been there, in Naples. That's all it had been at the time. Now, it had become something more. Only he couldn't really say what.

The other thing they did was they talked with one another. Kafak thought Marshak could be annoying, but he liked him. Everyone thought Marshak could be annoying, but everyone ended up liking the little guy. He and Kafak had a lot in common. They were both from Detroit. They talked a lot about the city, where they'd grown up, the places there they hung out, liked to visit. They spent hours talking about the fate of the Tigers ballclub. They were both avid fans.

A guy named Pilotti was from Washington State. He said he intended to make his living following the horses when the war was over. He knew a lot about racing. He never tired of passing on his knowledge. Some of it Kafak even found interesting. He wasn't into gambling, though, so most of it he didn't pay much attention to. Still, Pilotti could make it all sound damned interesting, and Kafak enjoyed the hours spent with him.

Another guy named Chandler said he had a girl back home who was a Hollywood starlet. He showed all the guys a picture. The girl was a knockout, no doubt. A real looker. Chandler told them all her name and said, "Watch for her. You're gonna see her hit it big in the movies one of these days. And after the war, we'll get married. She's going to be a big star, and I'll manage her career." They all wished him luck. Marshak later told Kafak he didn't believe Chandler for a minute. "That picture probably came with the fucking wallet," Marshak said. Kafak thought Marshak was probably just jealous. The girl had been something, after all. And Chandler was a good-looking guy. Marshak hated that, Kafak knew.

There were other guys, too. They all had a story. They came from all over the country and had different experiences, and Kafak loved hearing about each and every one of them. All the differences between them. And all the similarities. That surprised Kafak the most. How much alike they all were in the end, despite how different their backgrounds and origins were.

Kafak especially loved talking to the guys from the South. Guys who had grown up on farms or in the country. Dirt poor, most of them were, so Kafak had that in common with them. But they had such interesting stories about hunting and living off the land, and just everything about their lives was so entirely different from his, him being a city boy and such. He enjoyed getting to know these guys and all the stories they told.

One day there were about five of them sharing a larger fox-hole, not at the head of the front line this day. They still had to keep their heads down, though. The Germans could see the entire beach, after all. So the five of them sat there in mud and puddles of rainwater, and Marshak said, "Bobby, tell these guys the story of how a pair of glasses saved your fucking useless life, buddy."

"Naw," Kafak said. "That's all right."

But the other guys had never heard the story, and they wanted to. They wouldn't let it go. So Kafak finally surrendered and told them the story.

"I'd just finished basic, and they gave us all a seven-day pass. So I went home for a visit. On the way home I somehow lost one of my pairs of glasses. The army gave me these glasses I'm wearing, right. The army gave me glasses, new teeth, more food than I've ever eaten in my life, better clothes, too. Sure, the army gives you everything. And all they ask in return is for you to put your ass on the line to get it shot off. Fair trade, right?

"Anyhow, I lost one of the pairs of glasses I was given on the way home. I lost the other pair on the way back. I could still see all right, but what the hell? You know how the army is.

"So, anyway, once I got back to my company, we all got shipped out to Camp Shenango. Now, Camp Shenango was a one-third camp."

The guys laughed quietly over that. They all knew from their own days getting prepared to be shipped overseas what a one-third camp was. One third of the men in the camp were AWOL, the second third were chasing them down, and the final third were waiting to be shipped overseas. Kafak was in that last third.

"Now, like you guys know, when you're in a one-third camp like Shenango, the first thing the army wants you to do is get all your fucking equipment up to snuff. All false teeth and glasses were to be replaced and reissued if you'd lost them. Well, I had my teeth, OK, but I had lost both pairs of my glasses. So they finally told me to go get my new glasses cuz they'd come in and were ready for me. So I went. When I got back to the barracks, all the other guys I had trained with had been moved out to another part of camp for disembarkation. The officer in charge there told me I was too late to join them. All those guys went on without me.

"Later I got a letter from a pal of mine. He told me they'd been shipped to England, so you know they're there to be used in the French invasion when it comes. I figure they're gonna get themselves ripped a whole lot of new assholes when they land against Fortress Europa. So, instead of that happening to me, I'm right here, happy and content in beautiful Italia."

The guys laughed.

"You should've stayed with the others," they told him.

"You'd be in nice sunny England now instead of wet and cold in Italy."

"You could be fucking some English cunt instead of humping mud."

"You could be in a decent camp instead of a foxhole with fucking Sleepy Ass."

"Hey, fuck you," Marshak said. Then he said to Kafak, "Yeah, you know, buddy, now I hear that story again, I don't think losing those glasses saved your life at all. I think they fucked your life up royal, and you're just too much a dumb fuck to realize it."

"Yeah," Kafak said, "well, I'll weigh it all up after the war."

"There you go," someone said, and laughed.

Marshak just shook his head, bemused.

Cole showed up then and greeted the men.

Marshak said, "Hey, Cap, you wanna hear how a pair of glasses fucked up Kafak's entire fucking life?"

"Love to hear it sometime, Sleepy Ass, just not now. I'm here for volunteers." Each of them shrank down in the hole a little bit more, except for Kafak. He had another story about how volunteering had likely saved his life once as well, so he never shirked from the stuff until he heard what it was about. Cole said, "I'm taking a patrol out tonight. Who's in?"

No one spoke up. That was one duty Kafak had never figured to volunteer for.

Marshak knew it, and just to be an asshole, thinking he was funny, he said, "Kafak'll go."

Kafak didn't say anything. He wouldn't say no because he didn't want to look like a coward, but he wouldn't say yes because he didn't want to get himself killed.

One of the other guys said, "Hey, that's right. Kafak's never been on a patrol, have you, buddy?"

"Kafak'll go," the other two guys immediately said, chiming in together and grinning.

Cole looked at Kafak.

"Nice friends you got, Kafak."

"Yeah, they're great fucking guys."

"What do you say?"

He couldn't say no.

So he said, "Sure, Cap."

Cole nodded.

Then he said, "Good. You and Marshak report to company HQ at oh–seven hundred for orders."

"Hey!" Marshak said. "What the fuck? I didn't volunteer for nothing."

"Yours was the first voice I heard when I asked for volunteers, Sleepy Ass. Wasn't it, boys?"

"Yeah."

"Sure was."

"You're right, Cap."

The others had grins on their faces and didn't hesitate to throw their comrade under the bus, just as they had done Kafak earlier. It was a game they all played. They found it amusing. But only if the guys they put forward actually came back OK from the patrol. Otherwise, they would feel terrible guilt. Both for putting the dead or wounded soldier in harm's way as they had and because they were glad, at bottom, it was not them but somebody else.

Marshak was still complaining.

He said, "Hell, Cap, I just went on patrol the other day. This ain't fucking fair. Somebody else oughtta be in the rotation."

"Sleepy Ass," one of the others said, "the last time you went on patrol was three weeks ago. That ain't *just* on patrol."

"But he's been sleeping since then," Kafak said, "so he didn't realize."

They all laughed, and Cole shook his head, amused at them all.

"You boys enjoy yourselves. I'll see you two later."

Then he left.

And that was how Kafak ended up going on his first patrol at Anzio.

5

Kafak and Marshak reported to company headquarters at the assigned hour. Even though it was dark and things were fairly quiet, they moved through the night in the crouched run that had become a way of life for everyone on that beachhead. In fact, it had a few names all its own. Kafak's favorite was the Anzio shuffle.

At HQ, they met the other guys who would go on the patrol. Besides Kafak and Marshak, there were three other privates, Henderson, McElvoy, and Goldstein. Cole was there, and a sergeant as well, but not Collins. Kafak didn't catch the NCO's name.

They were told the mission of the patrol was to capture German prisoners for intelligence purposes. After blackening their faces with burned cork and a few last instructions and words of encouragement from Cole, they were ready to go. They divested themselves of any gear that could make noise.

"We got an extra Thompson here. Anybody want it?"

Kafak raised his hand immediately.

"I'll take it, Sarge," he said.

"Ever use one before?"

"No, Sarge. But it sure seems like it'd be fun."

Cole chuckled.

"A regular all-American boy, huh, Kafak?" Cole said. "Give him the gun, Sergeant."

"Yes, sir."

The sergeant handed Kafak the Thompson submachine gun. He didn't seem to want to; Kafak noted a grudging expression on the NCO's face. Still, Cole and the sergeant already had tommy guns, and the others all had M1s. None of the others seemed all that interested in the submachine gun. None of them jumped forward like Kafak had done, anyway.

Cole led them out of the HQ in that low running crouch. They moved forward through the lines until they came to that spread of foxholes farthest forward in the Allied position. These were held by the Third. Cole motioned for the patrol to hit the dirt, and Kafak lay down in the squishy mud with everyone else. Mud covered him from shoulders to boots, front and back. The mud stank. He could barely tell the difference from how he had smelled before he sprawled in it. Everyone stank of filthy mud, sweat, shit, and gunpowder. It got so you didn't even notice any of that anymore. It was just the way things were. Nowadays, it took a really different smell, a really strong smell, to catch Kafak's attention.

Cole hung over the lip of the foxhole and whispered to the machine gun crew posted there. Kafak lay next to him, so he heard it all.

"We'll be coming back through this position in a couple of hours," Cole told the crew. "Don't shoot at us."

"You got the password, Captain?"

"Yeah. Shrank, right?"

"That's it. See you in a while, Cap."

"Bet on it."

Cole rose up to his crouch once more and hustled off. Kafak followed along with everyone else. The sergeant brought up the rear. Cole led the small group to one of the myriad drainage ditches, and they slid down the mud of the side of the embankment and into the water feetfirst. Kafak strolled along, the third man in line behind Cole and Henderson. Marshak crouched right behind him. The water in the bottom of the ditch reached up to Kafak's knees.

"Fuck," he heard Marshak whisper behind him.

For a guy Marshak's size, the water probably ran up to mid-thigh. It had been raining fairly steadily over the last few days. It seemed it was always raining, but it had come down especially bad in the last couple of days. And that rainwater that had gathered in the ditch was cold as well. It felt miserable to Kafak, even through his winter uniform clothing. The coating of mud actually helped to insulate Kafak a little bit. He knew everyone else in the line felt the same way.

It wasn't raining now, at least. Kafak thought that a good thing because it would have made the entire patrol more miserable. On the other hand, it might've forced the Germans to keep their heads down more, so that would have been all right, too.

Kafak moved like Cole and Henderson before him, observing them to see how this patrol stuff was done. Kafak held his crouch and moved painstakingly slowly. He understood they didn't want to rustle the water and make too much noise. He saw one man about to cough place two fingers on his Adam's apple to stop the action. He'd have to remember that trick. Quiet was the essential thing.

Marshak said something to Kafak, but it was so under his breath Kafak couldn't hear the actual words. Only sounds. Before he could even think about turning around and asking Marshak what he'd said, a hiss came down the line from Cole. Kafak knew that meant Marshak should shut up. Kafak left it alone. He kept moving at the snail's pace they all were using.

They stayed in the drainage ditch for some time. At some point the water actually lowered to about midcalf for Kafak. He had his shoepac-issued boots, worn some weeks now, the boots they'd been given to combat the trench foot, and the boots kept the cold and muddy water from leaking inside. They had rubber soles, and the rubber continued on up to about the ankles. Above that, they were leather. He had them laced tight with the gaiters pulled tight around them.

Every step he took, Kafak sank into the bottom of the ditch, into the mud hidden there. He never lifted his foot above the surface, just moved it along slowly within the cold, standing, silt-filled water. No plopping sounds. Fewer splashing noises. Cole finally led them out of the ditch and alongside some tall rocks. He gathered the men there and indicated a short rest, time to catch their breath. They'd gone miles already. Seemed like it to Kafak, anyway. After less than a minute, Cole led them on again. There wasn't much cover. Kafak saw Cole was leading them to another group of rocks about forty yards away. Kafak prayed the Germans didn't send up a flare just then. They'd all be sitting ducks, though they were spread far enough apart that no single burst could take them all.

Once they had all spread along those rocks, Cole motioned them forward once again. No rest this time. They moved at a walking pace, crouched low, keeping their eyes peeled. There was a little less than half a moon and some stars, so Kafak could see pretty well. His eyes had long ago adjusted to the dark. He looked at shadows and outlines, making sure they looked right. Making sure they didn't move. He didn't see anything. His adrenaline had been pounding inside him at the HQ and during the start of the mission. Now, though, now they were doing it, had been out here for a while, now he could control his movements and, he hoped, his reactions.

They used the pockmarks pounded into the land by the bombs of both armies. They moved from cover to cover as much as possible. Any depression in the ground would do. Kafak wondered if they were just patrolling aimlessly. He wondered if the captain was just hoping to run across some Germans. Or maybe Cole was just out going through the motions, hoping *not* to run into any Germans. Kafak didn't know and couldn't figure it. He just moved along with the rest of the patrol, ducking into holes and ditches and behind raised ground and rocks whenever he could. Once in a while they found some tall weeds or the remnants of a tree. Kafak thought it something like a game of musical chairs. You kept moving from one piece of cover to the next, hoping you would reach it before the music stopped. Before the firing started, in other words.

Finally, Kafak saw what Cole was up to. He understood. In the distance, a good one hundred yards away, he spotted a farmhouse. Or what was left of it. Maybe two-thirds of the place still stood, though the barn had been completely demolished. A chicken coop stood off to one side of the house. Once the farmhouse had been sighted, Cole motioned for them to spread out in a skirmish line for their approach. They leapfrogged from rock to depression to shell crater to abandoned foxhole. They were about twenty yards from the farmhouse when Cole signaled for them to stop and hit the dirt. He waved Kafak to his side.

"Bob," he said, surprising Kafak. Kafak didn't figure Cole even knew his first name. He supposed it one more example of how officers knew your name better the closer you got to the front. And here, tonight, they were well beyond the front. So he reckoned that was where *Bob* came from. "Here's what I need you to do. Get to that farmhouse. See if you can hear or see anyone there. If you do, fire a few shots, and we'll come to your support right away. Got that?"

"Yes, sir," Kafak said.

"Handle it?"

"Absolutely."

"Good. Look. Approach from the side where the barn used to be. The foundation there will offer you some decent cover. Then get to that side wall that's still standing."

"Got you, Cap."

"Good. Go on then. We'll be listening. Watch your ass, Bob."

"Bet on that, sir," Kafak said.

He smiled but didn't really feel it. It just seemed the thing to do. From movies he'd seen. Things he'd read. He felt afraid but not to any degree that kept him from doing what he had been ordered to do. He kept telling himself: This is what you've been trained for, Kafak, this is it, just do what they fucking trained you to do.

Kafak moved at a running crouch the fifteen yards to the outer stones of the barn's foundation. All that was left standing of the structure. He paused there a moment, gathering himself. He peered over the edge of the stones.

The farmhouse was dark. Soundless. He couldn't hear anything coming from it, but he saw it had a small roof, and if the Germans were anything like the Americans then they used it for protection from the cold and the rain. Buildings back at the beachhead were all overcrowded by soldiers. Anyone who could force a spot in one for their rest took it. Kafak never did. To him, a structure meant a target. Why not bomb a building and get plenty of the enemy instead of dropping your shell on empty ground where you might or might not get a single trooper laid out for the night? It only made sense to Kafak, so he avoided buildings on Anzio like the plague. He wondered if the Germans thought the same way, and hoped they did. That would mean this farmhouse would be empty.

His newly acquired tommy gun stuck out in front of him, Kafak circled the low wall. Reaching its edge closest to the house, he gathered himself once more, then dashed the few yards to the wall. The still-standing wall. He pushed his back hard against the rough stone of it. He waited. He listened.

He heard nothing.

Just his own breathing.

He quieted that down and listened some more.

Still nothing.

A window, its glass shattered out, cut the wall about five feet from where he stood. He eased toward it, careful with each step. He didn't want to make any noise. He didn't want to alert anyone if they were in that farmhouse. He crept along the wall until he came to the window, then paused, took a breath, held it, listened.

Nothing.

He slowly eased an eye around the side of the window to look within the house.

It was dark. Empty. Everything inside had been tossed around, beaten to hell. Most of the furniture had been used to make a fire at some point or another. But there was no fire now. No Germans, either.

Kafak let his breath out slowly. The place was deserted. He felt glad of it. He evened out his breathing, figuring that the thing to do now was to circle the house and see if there was anything else to note. He doubted it. Still, he kept careful. The tension still had him wound tight. He ducked beneath the window ledge. Just in case, he thought. Just in case. Then he crept along the wall toward the rear of the building.

He had closed on it, maybe ten feet from the back corner of the farmhouse, when he heard something. He stopped still. He gulped his breath. He listened. He listened as hard as he had ever listened in his entire life. Then he heard it again.

He thought it sounded like someone saying "Americush." Or maybe it was "Americanush."

He frowned. He thought he heard it again. He recognized they had to be Germans speaking, and if they were speaking about Americans, then that likely meant they knew he and the guys were around.

Kafak figured he'd better do something. After all, that's what he'd been sent here for. He lifted the barrel of the Thompson into the air and pulled the trigger.

A click sounded in the quiet night.

Nothing else.

Shit!

Kafak heard movement at the back of the house, around the corner. He whirled around and ran for where he had left his comrades. Behind him he heard the Germans. They were shouting now. He figured they were shouting at him. He kept running. The guys opened up, and bullets whizzed around him. Now everybody was shouting to their own guys, the Germans and the Americans. Kafak kept running straight so his own patrol wouldn't hit him. He hoped the Germans didn't open up, because running straight made him a ripe target for them.

He saw Cole and leaped into the shell crater right beside him. He rolled over, breathing heavily.

"Fuck!" he said through his ragged breath. "Son of a bitch fuck!"

"What happened, Bob?" Cole said.

Everyone else was firing at the farmhouse. They saw Germans running everywhere, but all of them had been behind the building, not inside it.

"This fucking gun jammed," he said.

"Did you try to fire it?"

"Yeah. Like you said. I heard a couple Krauts whispering. I was going to fire to alert you guys. Then it jammed."

"Here let me see."

Kafak handed over the gun.

He said, "That goddamned click was so fucking loud, I figure they heard it in fucking Rome."

It felt that way, anyhow, to him. Rome was dozens of miles away, but that click was loud in the quiet night. It gave him away. Made him a sitting duck. Sure, he thought, all the way to fucking Rome.

Cole cleared the gun and handed it back.

"Here," he said. Then he smiled. "You run pretty good."

"Think I just set a fucking record for the fucking twenty-yard dash."

"Think you did, all right," Cole smiled.

"Probably stand for a good long while, too."

Cole laughed, then started firing again at the farmhouse where the Germans had taken cover.

"How many you see?" he said, shouting over the combat.

"I heard at least two. Didn't see any."

Kafak started firing his own tommy gun. Now it worked, he found he liked it.

"Sergeant!" Cole said. "Anybody! We got a count on the enemy?"

"I'd say 'bout eight of 'em, sir. Three or four moved inside the house, another two are flat on the ground between the house and that chicken coop. A couple more dropped into the ruins of that barn."

"Sounds like we might get some prisoners tonight after all."

"We're gonna have to take 'em fast, sir."

Kafak understood that thinking. The longer they remained here, making this kind of racket, behind enemy lines, the greater grew the chance of German reinforcements arriving. And once reinforcements arrived, the entire patrol would be either dead or prisoners.

Cole started to give orders for Henderson and the sergeant to flank around to the barn foundation when the two Germans on the ground leaped up and darted to the chicken coop. They disappeared behind it. Cole yelled to the others.

"Keep fire on them!" he said. "Sergeant, take Henderson and Kafak and—"

His voice was cut off by the rip of a machine gun. Coming from the chicken coop.

"So that's why those fuckers wanted to get over there so bad," the sergeant said. "Fuck."

Cole frowned, thinking. After a few more seconds of that bonecutter battering toward them, he cursed.

"Fucking shit," he said.

"What say, Captain?" the sergeant asked.

"No way we can get to them now before they get help out here. Best thing for it, we skedaddle the fuck out of here. Shit. Come on, boys! Fall back!"

Kafak slipped out of the crater and ran hard in a darting crouch for a row of rocks. He jumped behind them. Marshak dropped in right beside him.

"Goddamn! It sure got hot, Bobby!" he said.

"Got that right. Fuckin-A."

"You sure did move your ass," Marshak said, and laughed, teasing Kafak.

"Yeah," the sergeant said. "Some dash, all right."

Marshak laughed some more, and Kafak said, "Your gun jammed with a bunch of Krauts on top of you, I hope you end up moving that fast."

"Got that right," Marshak said, grinning.

"Well get off your asses and start moving fast right now. We gotta get the fuck outta here. Now!"

The sergeant was up and running then. Marshak leaped up and followed, calling out over his shoulder.

"Let's go, Dash!"

Kafak figured he had a new nickname.

And he didn't mind it a bit.

6

They leapfrogged as they had done earlier, removing themselves from the firefight. They were halfway back to their lines, once more in the cover of the drainage ditch, water creeping up their legs, when Kafak knew the German reinforcements had arrived. He knew because a parachute flare had gone up, turning the darkness bright off in the distance where the farmhouse had been.

They were well and gone from there now.

They crossed back into their lines and didn't get shot. Kafak figured that for a plus.

Cole told him, "Good job triggering that ambush before they were ready for us, Kafak."

"Sure thing, Cap," Kafak said, only he wasn't sure that was exactly what he had done, but he felt grateful the captain thought it was.

He noticed, too, he had gone from "Bob" back to "Kafak."

He didn't mind that, though. It meant they were safe again, within their own lines.

Well. As safe as that could make them. It was all a relative thing when you were on Anzio.

More patrols followed that first one over the next weeks. Kafak still felt the adrenaline rush for the next couple times, but after half a dozen runs, patrols became a matter of course for him. Once they even captured a German. He'd been hiding in a hole, out of ammunition, his clothes barely rags, only the mud caked on them holding them together. He'd been happy enough to surrender. They took him in. He begged for food. Kafak always wondered if the guy had told the brass anything interesting. The only thing Kafak thought about him at the time was how hungry he seemed.

"He must've been lost out there for some while," Kafak said to Marshak.

"Yeah," Marshak said, "it don't seem like the rest of 'em are all that hungry. Except for our asses."

"They'd spit yours out anyway, raggedy as it is."

"Fuck you, Dash."

A couple of the patrols turned into firefights like that first one had. They were the bad ones. In one of them, Collins got hit. He didn't die, though. He had to be evacuated to the hospital at Naples. Kafak wondered whether he survived or not, in the end. Then Kafak forgot about him. They had a new sergeant then. A guy named Jerrigan. He only lasted eight days, and then he got hit, too. He died, though. They were running out of noncoms. One day Cole came to their foxhole. Kafak was sharing it with Marshak, Bentyne, and Stoddard.

"How's it hanging, boys?" Cole said.

They were all eating lunch out of the can. Kafak had stew today.

"Gotta have a cast-iron stomach for this shit," he said.

"I don' know," Stoddard said. "This shit's bettuh'n what I ate 'fo I's in the army."

Stoddard was from the Deep South; he had that accent.

"What, you were in fucking prison?" Kafak said.

"Nah, we was jus' po'."

"Hell, I was poor, but my ma could make something good outta nothing."

"Yeah, this ain't home cooking, that's for sure," Marshak said. Then he said to Cole, "When we gonna get a chance to get some real food, Cap?"

"Where you expect to get that, Sleepy Ass?" Cole asked.

"You know, back in Naples. Or Casablanca. Or New York City. As far away from here as you wanna send me."

"Nobody gets off this beach, Marshak. You know that."

"No R & R at all, Cap? That just ain't right."

"I know," Cole said. "I know it's not. Believe me. The top brass know it's a problem, too. It's just nothing much can be done about it. It's how things are." Then he changed the subject abruptly, making it clear this was not a thing he much wanted to discuss, and said, "Kafak, you're acting sergeant until we get some new NCOs up here from Naples."

"Me, Cap? What the fuck?"

"You, Kafak. Until further notice."

"Hey, let me be the sarge, Captain."

"What the fuck you think this is, Marshak? There's no fucking contest here. This is the goddamned army or hadn't you noticed the people shooting at you?"

"Aww, he gets that at home, too," Kafak said.

"Yeah, evuh Sat'day night," Stoddard said.

They laughed, and Marshak told them, "Yeah, that's what happens every time I'm with your wife."

That only made them laugh harder, and Bentyne said, "He ain't even married, you dumb fuck."

"Oh, maybe that was your sister, then."

They were still laughing and going back and forth when Cole motioned to Kafak to follow him. Kafak looked around. It was daylight. He didn't want to leave the hole during daylight. Cole tossed a couple smoke grenades, and they moved off. They found a small depression not far off from Kafak's hole and lay down next to one another.

"What's up, Cap?" Kafak asked.

"Those boys keeping up with their shoepac discipline?" Cole said.

"Sure thing, sir. We know better than to miss it. We seen too many black feet."

"Good, good. We just don't have the NCOs up here right now to keep things together. Too many getting killed or wounded."

And now you made me one, Kafak thought, but didn't say. Thanks a fucking lot.

Cole was quiet then for a while, and Kafak could sense he was thinking about something. So finally Kafak, not wanting to stay out here any longer than he had to since the smoke was already starting to be rained away, said, "Something else, Cap?"

"Yeah," Cole said. "Yeah, there is." He sighed and looked back at the hole they'd just come from. "I know things are tough for you boys, Kafak. The fucking weather, the patrols, being shelled every fucking goddamned day. And never knowing when some smart-ass fucking sniper's going to take a potshot at you. I get it. We all get it. General Truscott is very concerned about the fact that this shit, this tension of being near constant death and this depression over seeing your friends get shot up, and this fucking rain and this fucking cold and all the rest of it can destroy morale. Thing is, just not a lot we can do about it right now. We just don't have the men to let anybody off the beach unless they're dead or dying. You know?"

"Sure, Cap. I get it."

"So tell it to me straight, then. How's the morale with your folks, there, in your hole?"

Kafak shrugged.

"What you'd expect, sir. They ain't happy."

"How're they acting?"

"They're soldiers, sir. We're all soldiers."

"Which means?"

"We want to go home but know we can't. So we spend our days bitching and ducking."

Cole grunted. He seemed to like the answer, Kafak thought.

Then he said, "And patrolling. I want you to take one or two of the guys out tonight, Kafak. Make sure we got no infiltrators close by." Cole paused, looked at Kafak, said, "You do that for me?"

"You got it, Captain," Kafak said.

He'd taken it as an order, anyway. Cole might want to make it sound like a request, but Kafak knew better. Some general or colonel or someone who'd never seen the front, never stepped foot in the goddamned mud, wanted to send some men out and told Cole so. Cole passed it on to Kafak. Kafak knew he wouldn't be the only one. There'd be other guys on other parts of the line doing the same thing. He didn't hold it against Cole. He held it against the son of a bitch general or colonel who never set foot on the fucking front line. That son of a bitch he had no use for. That son of a bitch he hated more than the Germans.

That night Kafak took Bentyne. He wouldn't take Marshak because he didn't trust Marshak to respect his temporary promotion. Marshak and he had been together too long. Marshak only thought of him as Kafak, the guy he shared his foxhole with for what seemed like forever. Marshak wouldn't take any orders from Kafak, and Kafak knew it. So he took Bentyne. He could have taken Stoddard, too, but he remembered Cole had said one or two, and Kafak figured best not to chance two more guys besides himself. Only the one. Especially since he was in charge of the thing. He didn't want to be responsible for that, for seeing two guys killed or wounded. Or even one, for that matter, but he had no choice in that.

Bentyne told Kafak he'd been on patrol before. Kafak didn't know for sure. He'd only met Bentyne a week earlier. He took him at his word. They left all their noisemakers in their packs in the foxhole with Marshak and Stoddard. They were already at the front line, so Kafak passed the word along to the foxholes to either side of them not to shoot at them when they came back through the lines. They all went over the password. Before he left, Kafak smiled and told Marshak, "Now don't go shooting at me just cuz you're jealous I got made sergeant instead of you, you bastard."

"Hell, that don't worry me none, Dash. No way you could keep any stripes, even if they were given to you for real. Which they ain't, you'll notice, cuz the captain don't trust you any more than I do, pal."

"Green ain't a good color on you, Sleepy Ass."

"Tell it to the fucking army, buddy."

Kafak and Bentyne started off. They lowered themselves into one of the numerous fossas, those drainage ditches that sliced everywhere through the beach. The entire area had been just one huge swamp before the war. Mussolini drained it all to create this area as a demonstration of the good Fascism could do for the country. Kafak had heard the story. It was one reason the area was so tough on armored vehicles. Most of the ground, when not mud, still ran wet just below the surface. Get off the roads and you'd likely crunch through the surface ground and get yourself stuck. That's what the tankers said anyway, when Kafak had a chance to talk to them at the rear, once or twice. The ditches came in handy now for the Allies to move about. The Germans, too, come to that. Kafak and Bentyne walked along first one, then another, then another. About six inches of water filled the bottom of the ditches this night. Not so bad as some other times. They still had to be careful not to rattle it, not to make too much noise slopping through the stuff. They'd gone miles and miles in the ditches. It felt that way to Kafak. They hadn't seen or heard anything German the entire time. They would stop every so often and listen for what they could hear above them on the ground surrounding the ditch they happened to be in at the time. They heard only the sounds of the night. Quiet. An occasional shell exploding, lobbed by one side or the other just for the hell of it. No other reason than that. Once in a while they might hear a single bullet, a sniper's call, but those were always far off in the distance. Twice the Germans sent up flares. Kafak and Bentyne ducked low in the ditch. They waited out the light. Nobody shot at them, and that was a good thing.

After a couple of hours of this sneaking around in the ditches, Bentyne said, "You figure we oughtta go topside, see if we can see anything more that way?"

"Why?" Kafak said. "You think we should?"

"I don't know. You're the sergeant."

"Fuck that."

"Well, sure, then. I think it might be a good idea. Really get an idea of the lay of the land, you know?"

"How fucking long you been on Anzio, Bentyne?" Kafak said.

"Not so long as you, Dash, that's for sure."

"All right," he said at last. Feeling resigned. "Let's crawl out of this muck. See what we can see."

Bentyne nodded and smiled. He seemed really to want to leave their cover, Kafak thought. The guy had to be crazy. He'd take Stoddard next time, he thought to himself. If there were a next time.

They scrambled out of the ditch, slipping in the mud a little but keeping as quiet as they were able. Up on the lip of the ditch, they lay flat. Kafak looked around. He noted the shadows, the formations of rocks and trees around. He looked for anything unusual in the outlines. He didn't see anything. He waited to see if they had been noticed. He waited to be shot at.

When he wasn't, he said, "Come on," to Bentyne.

Bentyne started to get up, and Kafak slammed a hand onto his back, forcing him back down into the mud.

"What the fuck?" Bentyne said.

"That's what the fuck, Sarge, to you," Kafak said.

"Well, what the fuck, Sarge?"

They spoke in low, hissing whispers. Kafak still worried they carried too far in the night. Better not to talk at all, but sometimes a guy had to.

"Let's just crawl for a while," Kafak said.

"What? In this fucking slop?"

"You wanna be dirty or you wanna be dead?"

". . . Right then," Bentyne said.

They crawled farther away from the drainage ditch. They reached a low row of rocks. Kafak looked around. Not a German in sight. Not a messed-up shadow around, either. He figured it safe to move in the usual manner, and he patted Bentyne on the arm and motioned him up. They moved in that crouching walk then, covering ground more quickly than in the watery ditch, but still moving carefully, slowly. Eyes open.

After nearly forty minutes of this and finding no infiltrators, no Germans even moving toward the Allied lines, Kafak suddenly stopped. He put up his hand. Bentyne stopped. Bentyne looked at Kafak. Kafak frowned and pointed to what he was looking at, what had halted him. Kafak saw two figures. They were a good distance away. In the darkness, they were just two shadowy figures in a ditch. But Kafak could see that they were moving carefully, sneaking about. He thought they might be infiltrators. Germans.

Bentyne raised his M1, started to draw a bead on the men. Kafak put a hand on his arm.

"Wait," Kafak said.

"What?" Bentyne said.

"Give it a second."

"They'll be on top of us, Dash. I don't need them shooting back at me. We need to shoot now."

There wasn't enough light from the crescent moon to see the men clearly. They were only outlines of men. Men carrying guns, that could be seen. But the uniforms couldn't be made out.

Kafak said, "They could be our guys."

"I don't want to find out they ain't once they're already on top of us."

"Just let's see."

"Fuck that, Dash. It's like deer hunting, you know? You fucking shoot the deer when you fucking see the deer. Cuz you might not get another chance to shoot the fucking deer."

"Just fucking wait," Kafak said.

"But—"

"That's a fucking order, Bentyne."

They waited. They lay down in the mud, and Bentyne drew a nervous bead on the two approaching soldiers. Kafak could tell Bentyne was nervous. He could feel the jumpiness in Bentyne's body lying next to his own. Kafak wondered if Bentyne really had been on a patrol before. He had seemed all right until now. He'd done everything else right. And what the hell? Kafak asked himself. Maybe Bentyne was the one doing things right now as well, wanting to shoot those soldiers before they alerted, before they reached a position where they could shoot back effectively at Kafak and Bentyne. Kafak sure as hell didn't want to get into any firefight all the way out here. Alone. Maybe Bentyne was right and Kafak was wrong.

"Shit," Bentyne said then.

He stopped being nervous. Kafak could feel the tension drain out of Bentyne. Kafak saw why. The uniforms could be made out now. The helmets were telling. They were US. Their own guys.

Bentyne started to rise up, and Kafak grabbed him and pulled him flat.

"Don't move," he said, a low whisper.

Bentyne looked at him, curious.

"What's up, Dash? Those guys are ours."

"Yeah, they are," Kafak said. He even recognized one of them now. A guy called Riggsby. Still, Kafak didn't move.

"What's going on?" Bentyne said.

"Just wait."

They did. They waited until Riggsby and his partner had passed by their position. Kafak still made Bentyne wait until Riggsby and the other guy were out of sight. Even after that, Kafak waited another ten minutes or so.

Then he rose up and started off. Bentyne didn't say another word. Kafak headed back to their lines.

Once they had reached their foxhole, they lay down to sleep. Since they had taken patrol, Marshak and Stoddard took the first watch. Sprawled there in the mud, nothing but a misting rain to wash off the filth, Bentyne turned to Kafak and whispered.

"Why didn't we hook up with those two guys, Dash? We coulda come back together. Safety in numbers, right?"

"Because," Kafak said. He spoke quietly. Tired. He only wanted to sleep, not explain things to this new guy. He said, "I didn't want them to see us and start shooting in the dark the way we were going to shoot at them."

Kafak said "we" even though he hadn't had any intention of shooting. It had just been Bentyne. Only Kafak wouldn't say it that way. He didn't figure it did any good to point out something like that. He didn't figure that's what a good leader did. Only an asshole would do something like that.

Kafak knew he had to act like a leader now. He didn't want to. The captain had given him no choice, though. He would be a leader. At least until they got more noncoms up to the front.

Bentyne paused for a moment, and then he finally said, "Thanks, Dash."

"For what?" Kafak said, curious. He thought Benytne was thanking him for bringing them safely back to the foxhole.

Only that wasn't what Bentyne meant.

Bentyne said, "Thanks for not letting me shoot those guys." Bentyne paused. Then he spoke again. "I don't know how I woulda lived with myself if I had shot my own guys." Another pause. "You know?" he finished.

Kafak didn't reply right away. After a time, he did.

He said, "Fuck it."

Bentyne grunted in the darkness of the bottom of that hole. "That's all?" he said. "Just fuck it?"

"It didn't happen, Bentyne," Kafak said.

"I know. Because of you."

"Don't waste time thinking about things that didn't happen," Kafak said.

"But that would've been really fucked up. You know?"

"If you want to survive this fucking shit," Kafak said, "you don't think about the past. You put it out of your head. You got to think about the future. About what happens next, you know? That's what'll keep you alive and keep you from going crazy."

"So when do you think about the past?"

"I don't know," Kafak said. "Maybe when the present's over. Or maybe never." He paused, he sighed, then he added, "Or maybe just in another life."

7

Kafak was a sergeant for a week. Then a bunch of new NCOs arrived at the front lines. Kafak didn't think much of them. They were coming from the States. From home. What did they know? He didn't even care to learn their names. Maybe they stuck around a while, he would. But not right now.

Still, he was glad he wasn't a sergeant any longer. He didn't like the responsibility. Cole offered to make the stripes permanent, but Kafak told him, "Fuck that. With all due respect, sir."

Cole could have taken it another way, but he didn't. He laughed and said, "You're probably smarter at that, Kafak."

Kafak figured he was. The way they were bleeding noncoms on this fucking beach, he didn't like the odds.

Besides, despite what he had told Bentyne, he couldn't stop thinking about things that had happened. Friends who had died. Been killed. He wondered why it was them and not him. He wondered was he not doing enough, not doing as much as they had done? Was that what had gotten them killed and kept him still here, alive?

He thought then about the men he had killed. Or might have killed. He couldn't be sure, after all. In all the combat he'd seen, he'd always been firing when other guys were firing right next to him. So even if he pulled his trigger and saw a guy in his sights go down, a German soldier, that is, he still couldn't say for certain that he had killed the guy, that it had been his bullet that knocked the guy down. It was the same sort of premise as a firing squad. The one rifle with a blank cartridge. The one rifle that could alleviate every conscience. Because all the members of the firing squad could believe it was they who had fired that one rifle. It was all the others who had killed the guy, and you had fired a blank. They all had that thought to hold onto. If they needed it. And even beyond that, even if it had been true, even if it had been his bullet and nobody else's that had knocked the enemy soldier down, it still didn't mean he, Kafak, had killed the guy. Not necessarily. Because the guy might only have been wounded. He might not have been killed.

Kafak remembered the time with the machine gun. Others had been firing then, too, to his left and right. More machine guns. Still, those Germans right in front of him. He figured they had gone down from his bullets, his machine gun. But it didn't mean he had killed them. They could have been wounded, all right, or they could have just been ducking. He didn't know they were dead; he didn't know it for certain.

He believed he had killed some. He thought he had.

Only he didn't *know* it.

And that made a difference. A big difference. That he could tell himself that. That he could believe in that, hold onto that. It made a huge difference.

To him, it did.

He had to stop thinking about that, though. He had to stop it and start thinking about what happens next. You can't dwell on all the shit, he told himself. That will drive you crazy. That will break you. In your mind. You've got to only think about what happens next. Just get through what happens next. And then you just get through what happens next after that.

That's how you make it through something like this.

That's how he had to do it, anyway. That's how he forced himself to do it.

They made another push toward Cisterna. It was to be a night attack. An assault in force but not anything like they had done at the end of January. Nothing that grand. They were hoping more for surprise to carry the day than force. Kafak thought it a damned fool's idea. Only nobody asked him what he thought. They just ordered him to be ready one night because they were going to move up and take the town.

Like hell, they were, he thought.

One second lieutenant told Kafak and Marshak, "We don't really figure we'll take the entire town."

"Then why we doing this shit, Lieutenant?" Marshak said.

"The brass is hoping we can move up far enough to settle into those burned-out buildings on the outskirts of the town. Be a better spot for our front line. Be a better jumping-off point for the next assault."

"That sounds like shit to me," Marshak said.

"We got orders, son," the lieutenant said then.

Marshak looked at the second lieutenant. The guy was a pure shavetail, couldn't be anything more than right out of college. So what? Maybe twenty-two or something, tops? That's how Kafak had it figured. He could tell from Marshak's face that Marshak thought so, too. And while Kafak was only a little over nineteen himself, Marshak had gone in older, was nearer thirty than twenty-five. So Marshak didn't much care for being called "son" by some young rooster just out of ROTC or OCS. No, Marshak didn't like that at all.

"Goddamned ninety-day wonder," Marshak said after the second lieutenant had moved off to the next foxhole to keep the soldiers there informed about what was going on. "Can you believe that fucking idiot is gonna lead the platoon into a night battle, Dash? What the fuck is the fucking army coming to?"

"Don't mean nothing, Sleepy Ass."

"Like hell."

"We'll be back in this hole by morning."

"Or we'll be fucking dead."

Marshak spat over his shoulder, the moisture lost in the mud. Kafak said nothing, but turned away and knocked lightly on the stock of his tommy gun. He wasn't superstitious. Not really. He just couldn't take the chance, was the thing.

That night, after full dark, they moved forward. They crawled out of their foxholes and moved up the road behind some armor. Two tanks and a couple of tank destroyers. The vehicles had to stay on the road. Kafak wondered if the Germans would send aircraft to try to knock them out. They were sort of sitting ducks, having to stay on the road like that. They had no choice, though. One tank had tried the ground next to the road and immediately sunk in. A gang of GIs was now working feverishly to get the tank unstuck and moving. Otherwise it would be lost for sure come daylight. If not before.

Kafak ignored them as he passed them by. He continued on forward with the rest of his company. It was heavy slogging with all the rain and mud, even on the road. Marshak was next to him. Flares went up, a bunch of them. The entire battlefield was lit up. Kafak hit the dirt. Everyone around him hit the dirt. Shells started dropping. Mortars mostly. But Kafak heard the shrieking whistles from the fins of Nebelwerfers as well. The shavetail second looey came running forward, shouting.

"Let's go! Let's go!" he said.

Kafak leaped up and followed. He didn't see if anyone else did, and then he took a chance and looked around. About half a dozen guys were running along with him and the platoon leader. The rest of the guys were much slower in getting up.

Kafak ran up behind a tank. He moved along in a crouch behind it. It fired a couple of times, but he didn't see if it hit anything. Then there was a huge force slamming into him and an incredibly bright light. Kafak felt himself flying through the air. He landed off to the side of the road in mud. He sank in. A soft landing, at least, he thought. He shook his head and checked himself. Nothing. No wounds. His bones felt rattled and his lungs burned. Only the force of the explosion. He looked for its source. The tank he'd been walking behind was on fire. It had been hit by an antitank gun.

"Shit," Kafak said.

"Ain't nowhere safe in this fucking war," Marshak said. He laughed, helping Kafak to his feet.

"Goddamned tanks."

"You're just asking to draw fire. Stick with me, Dash."

They moved on in their crouches. More mortar shells were blowing but nothing close enough to make Kafak hit the deck. Then he thought he heard one, and he went flat in the mud, just the side of the road. He was looking up from under the lip of his helmet when the shell exploded. He saw the new lieutenant go up in pieces and come down in smoke. Wisps of the stuff curled off his uniform in the cold, wet night air.

"Jesus Christ," Kafak said. "Fucking cocksuckers."

"Well," Marshak said, "that fucker didn't last long."

"They never fucking do."

Kafak stood up and ran forward. Marshak followed him. They stopped and started duckwalking when they came to the back of a pack of men. They didn't know if these guys were any part of L Company, their company, but they tagged along with them. It all ended up the same, in the end, Kafak figured. They were all moving toward their objective.

Another tank got hit, and then the infantry Kafak was with had outdistanced the armor. They were moving across the open field, the burned-out buildings within sight. This area had been thoroughly shelled already and kept under fairly constant cover, so Kafak didn't worry overmuch about mines. He couldn't see where the Germans would have had the time to re-mine the area. He kept moving steadily forward.

Small arms fire opened up on them then. They all dropped to the ground. MG42s ripped the air apart just above them.

"I hate those fucking Kraut machine guns," the guy next to him said. "You can't even hear a pause between the fucking shots."

"They go quick, all right," Kafak agreed.

"Fucking Germans," the guy said.

Kafak crawled through the mud, moving forward. He hoped other guys were as well. It had gone dark again now, though, so he couldn't be sure. The rain and the clouds splintered the moonlight so you couldn't see more than a few yards in any direction. He heard shouts, though. Shells exploding. Guns firing. More shouting. He figured, from the yelling he could hear, that he was moving in the right direction. He'd lost all contact with Marshak. He kept crawling forward. The mud sucked at him, tried to hold him in place, but he elbowed and kneed his way through it. Some of it plopped onto his glasses. He didn't bother trying to clean it just then. It made no difference to him right now, the little he could see anyway in the darkness.

Some more flares went up; he saw their comet tails. He waited for it, hiding his eyes, sinking as low into the ground as he was able. Then everything turned bright, and the German machine gunners let loose an even stronger barrage of fire. A guy right next to Kafak grunted and stopped moving. Kafak pushed on his shoulder. The guy fell back. He didn't move. His eyes were open. Kafak knew the guy was dead. Kafak crawled forward.

In the fading light of the flare, Kafak could see one of the buildings, one of their targets, nearby. The building stood maybe forty yards away. Mortar shells were still dropping, but most of them were blowing behind where Kafak sprawled now. There were plenty of Germans in the building, though. Kafak could feel the intensity of the small arms fire coming from them. He kept low and hoped nothing hit him.

He wasn't alone. About a dozen guys were scattered around him. They all hugged the earth as well. They were all screaming. Not in terror, maybe not even in anger. Just screaming. "Fuckshitcocksuckersonofabitchgoddamnedfuckingshiteatingfuckercocksuckerbastardfucks!"

Kafak's voice blended right in.

Then some sergeant Kafak didn't recognize dropped into the mud between Kafak and another guy. He yelled to the nearby troopers.

"On my three we rush that fucking building!" he told them.

"What the fuck? You crazy?"

Kafak heard someone say that. It sounded, he thought, like Marshak's voice.

"On my three!" the sergeant said again, sounding more stern about it.

Then he counted it off. On three Kafak leaped up, figuring everyone else would as well. He could feel the other guys around him. They all ran.

"Fucking cocksuckers!" Kafak said.

He fired his Thompson as he ran forward, shouting.

He felt a guy beside him drop. Others nearby were falling as well. Kafak didn't actually see them get hit or get knocked down. He more sensed it. He just could tell it was happening, was the thing.

He kept running. He ran hard. He knew now the only safety was to reach one of the still-standing walls of that building and press himself flat against it. Then the German guns couldn't reach him. He ran harder. Shouted harder. Fired and emptied his clip. Without a break in his steps, he dropped the empty clip and inserted another. Started firing that one as well. He didn't know if he hit anyone. Didn't know if he hit anything at all, really. He just fired through the darkness.

Then he heard the whoosh and saw the comet tail, and he said "Oh fucking shit!" and threw himself forward and down upon the ground. He was maybe ten yards away from the building and realized once that flare went off he was dead meat. He tried to get back up, realizing he'd made a damned stupid mistake in dropping to the ground. He felt something sting him and spin him around, and then he fell again. This time, not his idea. He fired toward the building as he dropped. On the ground, breathing heavily and feeling like a bullet would smash into him at any second, he pulled out a grenade, popped the pin, threw it toward the house. He threw it high. Didn't want it bouncing back at him off the wall. He tossed it over the top of the wall where the roof had been burned away. He heard the explosion even as he was throwing another one. The second landed within the building as well. He jumped up and started running again. Other guys were tossing their grenades, too. Firing. He was firing. There was a lot less fire coming from the building now.

He reached the wall. Fell against it. The sergeant stood just the other side of a window from him. He nodded at Kafak. Together they flipped a couple more grenades into the building, ducked back as they blew. Then the sergeant climbed through the window. Kafak jumped in right behind him.

Inside, all the Germans were dead. Some had been shot but most had been hit by shrapnel from grenades. Kafak saw two machine guns and their two-man crews. Another four Germans with burp guns. No rifles. That probably saved their asses, he thought. The machine guns all sprayed their loads, but a rifleman could have drawn a bead on a particular guy. Maybe Kafak.

Kafak didn't want to consider that.

That didn't happen, he told himself.

What did happen was, they had taken the building. The objective. Kafak felt elated.

The sergeant started preparing their defensive positions within the building. One of the guys there somehow knew how to use the MG42. The second one had been destroyed by a grenade's explosion. The sergeant had the working machine gun turned around to face for the inevitable counterattack.

"Think they'll be coming?" somebody asked.

Foolish question. Had to be a new guy. First battle.

"They'll be coming," the sergeant said. "Just a matter of when."

"Maybe our artillery can keep them off us," Marshak said.

"That's wishful thinking," someone else said.

"Sure," Marshak said, "like a fucking Christmas present."

"Christmas is long over," Kafak said.

"Fuck you, boys," Marshak said. "Get a little optimism, why don't you?"

They all had set up in positions facing Cisterna and the German lines. They couldn't see a goddamned thing in the darkness.

"Fuck," Kafak said.

"I wish we had a light," Marshak said.

A few minutes ago, they had dreaded the German flares; now, they prayed for one.

They knew the Allies wouldn't send anything up just now because their attack was predicated on the darkness. On surprise. They wouldn't give away their own positions.

The sergeant was moving back and forth behind the men as they knelt or stood in firing positions. He kept telling them to be ready, stay alert. Like they might do anything else. Kafak understood, though. He was bucking up their spirits. Good leadership. Kafak felt the sergeant stop next to him.

"Soldier," the sergeant said.

"Yeah, Sarge?" The sergeant nodded toward Kafak's biceps. His jacket there was drenched in blood. "Shit," Kafak said, a surprised mutter. "What the fuck?"

He pulled off his jacket, quickly. The sergeant helped him. He tore off a piece of Kafak's shirt and wiped down the arm. There was a bullet crease beneath all the blood.

"That ain't so bad," the sergeant said.

Kafak thought, Sure, it ain't your goddamned arm.

But he said, "Don't mean nothing, Sarge."

"You did a good job out there, Private," the sergeant said as he was tying a wrapping around the arm. "Get that looked at by a medic once things calm down a little. Right now, we need you to fight."

"Sure thing."

"By the way," the sergeant said, just before moving off, "nice arm."

He meant about the grenades, Kafak understood, throwing the grenades.

"Thanks," Kafak said.

"You play some ball?"

"High school."

"Yeah, didn't figure you to be much older than that, Private."

A captain arrived then with a half dozen more men. He and the sergeant talked quietly for a few moments as the captain looked over the preparations. He added the new men to the wall and said to everyone, "We hold this position. There are four other buildings we want to take tonight, and our troops are moving toward all of them even as I speak. But this one we got. And this one we hold. Understood?"

Everyone said their "yessirs," though some were louder than others. Most were mumbles, truth be told. Only a few of the newer guys shouted theirs out.

The captain took what he could get and turned away to talk more with the sergeant.

Kafak watched the darkness out in front of them. He wondered when the Germans would be coming. Occasional rifle fire zinged off the bricks of the wall. Nothing close to him, though.

Then the Germans sent up another flare. In seconds, it exploded, turning the night to day.

And Kafak screamed out loud.

"Goddamn son of a bitch!" he said.

Because dozens of German troops were advancing and were now about twenty yards from the building. All the Americans opened up. The Germans gave as good back. The firefight was fast, harsh, intense. Bullets whizzed everywhere around Kafak. He felt a smack in the head, and it knocked him down. Dizziness flowed over him, through him. He lay there for a few moments, wondering what the hell had happened. He shook his head to clear it. He had a ferocious headache. He felt his head, but no blood came away in his hand. He realized his helmet was missing. He looked around the ground for it, found it. He saw a bullet had smashed a dent into it, on the front right side. The slug hadn't gone through, had caromed off. Kafak whistled.

"Son of a bitch," he said. "They fucking One-Eyed my ass."

The sergeant genuflected beside him.

"You all right, soldier?" he asked.

"I guess so, Sarge," Kafak said, not really sure, in fact.

"Then get off your ass and fight before we get overrun, goddamnit."

"Sure thing, Sarge," Kafak said.

He took back his position and started firing again. The German fire was lessening now, though. The American troops kept theirs up, steady, strong. Suddenly, the sergeant was yelling at them.

"Hold fire! Hold fire!" he said.

Kafak stopped firing, wondering why. Then he realized: no more fire from the Germans.

"We beat those fuckers," Marshak said.

"They'll be back," the sergeant said.

"We need some heavier weapons," somebody else said.

But there was no radio to call for anything. They couldn't afford to send anyone back as a runner either. Of the fourteen men that had started their defense, only eight remained. Six had been killed, including the captain. Four of the eight were wounded, including Kafak. But he thought he wouldn't even count himself as wounded. One of the others was in a similar situation, but the two other guys who'd been hit had taken it pretty hard. One guy had a gaping hole in his chest. He was on the ground, a couple of the others trying to help him. Kafak didn't think there was too much help for the poor SOB, though. The other wounded man had been hit in the leg. He'd bandaged it up, but he looked pale from loss of blood, and he couldn't put any pressure on the limb.

Marshak moved up beside Kafak and whispered to him.

"We're all fucking dead," he said.

"Shut the fuck up, Marshak," Kafak said.

"If we fucking stay here, Dash, we're all fucking dead. Don't you get that, pal?"

"Don't matter, Marshak. We were ordered to stay here. That's what we gotta fucking do, right?"

"Hell, that captain gave them orders is dead, buddy. Long dead. We ain't gotta follow a dead man's orders, do we?"

"Until better ones come along."

"Ain't nothing or nobody coming along here, Dash. It's just us. It's just us against the whole fucking Nazi fucking army."

"Fuck that."

"Get back to your post, Private," the sergeant said, barking the order at Marshak.

Kafak wondered if the sergeant heard what Marshak had been saying. He felt embarrassed that the sergeant might have. He hoped the sergeant hadn't.

Then they all heard it. The low, whining growl of a Panzer making its way through the thick mud.

"Oh Christ!" Marshak said.

"Goddamnit," Kafak said.

"We're fucked now," one of the others said.

Kafak glanced at the sergeant. The sergeant frowned, looking around. Kafak knew he was assessing their chances. Kafak could tell the sergeant didn't want to give up this building because it was one of the night's objectives and they had taken it and they had paid a high price to take it and to hold it this far. So, no, he didn't want to just walk away from it. On the other hand, they all could see it was futile. If that many German troops attacked again, with a tank in support, there was no chance that the seven men who could still fight were going to hold onto that building.

"Son of a bitch," the sergeant said.

Kafak knew he'd made his decision.

"We getting the fuck outta here, Sarge?" Marshak said.

The sergeant said, "You and you," pointing at Marshak and another of the unwounded guys, "you carry Bryce there back to the lines."

Bryce was the soldier with the chest wound.

Another guy said, "Bryce just died, Sarge."

"Fuck!" The sergeant shouted that. Frustration and anger echoed against the building's walls. He took off his helmet and ran a hand over his sweating head. Even as cold as it was he was sweating. Kafak was, too. A lot. The sergeant plunked his helmet back on his head and said, "All right. You," again pointing to Marshak, "you help him," pointing to the guy with the wounded leg. "Get back to the lines. The rest of us will fight as we retreat." He looked around. "Got that?" to everyone. They all nodded and mumbled their agreement. Then he looked at Kafak. "You might want to take one of the dead guys' helmets, soldier. You could use a new one."

Kafak nodded and found one with netting, grabbed it, tossing his own onto the ground.

Then they all fell back, leaving the house, fighting as they retreated. It took them a long time before they reached any US troops. And then the front line wasn't much farther behind them. The German counterattack had been very successful.

They fell, exhausted, into their foxhole.

"Well, that was classic FUBAR," Marshak said.

And Kafak said, "Sure, that didn't go so well."

Stoddard said, "Right back where we fuckin' started from."

"Told you," Kafak said.

Marshak sighed.

"What a way to fight a fucking war," he said.

8

They didn't get any sleep after that because the Germans weren't about to give up their morning rolling barrage just because the Americans had tried another attack. In fact, Kafak thought the barrage was even more nasty and relentless than usual, probably because of the attack. As if to say, *We'll show you since you want to go and try something like that.*

The thing of it was, the rolling barrage was an annoyance. It increased tension. Kept you from getting any rest while it lasted. Banged through your ears, smashed against your brain. Still, you knew it wouldn't likely hurt you. It was a fact of war, and they had all been told about it time and again: artillery can't really hurt a well-entrenched force. Now if they caught you out in the open, forget it. They'd tear you a new one. But if you were well entrenched and kept your head down, and there were no air bursts, artillery couldn't physically hurt you unless a direct hit. But it could mess with your head, well enough. The noise of it, the thunderous, unceasing, earth-rattling horror of the overpowering noise of it, could make you want to crawl right back into your mother's womb. Or, failing that, ten feet deeper into the mud and gunk that surrounded you.

And then there was always the tension, the fear, that one day they just might get lucky and make that direct hit.

One of the guys in their foxhole that morning was a new guy, one of the new guys from the building last night. They found out his name was Acker. He was with G Company.

Kafak had told him, "You best wait until tonight when it's dark to get back to your own folks, Ack-Ack."

They'd already nicknamed him.

Acker thought that a sound idea.

Kafak saw the way he seemed to shrink into himself when the bombing started. He could tell Acker was afraid, but he didn't want to make a big deal about it.

Marshak said, "You OK there, Ack-Ack, buddy?"

"Sure," Acker said. "I'm OK."

"You don't look it."

"I'm fine."

"Pale as a fucking ghost, buddy."

"Let it be, Sleepy Ass," Kafak said.

Acker looked at Kafak.

"Don't this shit bother you guys?" he said.

"We been on this beach too long for anything to bother us," Marshak said.

"Fuck you, Sleepy Ass," Kafak said, laughing at him.

"What?" Marshak said, pretending to be hurt. "I'm a fucking veteran, I'll have you know."

"So's he," Kafak said, nodding toward Acker. "After last night."

"Yeah," Marshak said, acknowledged, "that was some shit, all right."

Stoddard said, "These fuckin' 'splosions cain' hurt ya none, Ack-Ack, on accounta they blow up 'n outwards when they hit the ground. So's all ya gotta do is git low 'n they blow right over ya."

"That's why we're in fucking foxholes, see," Marshak said.

"I know all that," Acker said.

"What you really got to worry about," Marshak said, going right on, "is the treed bombs and shit like that. When those bombs hit a tree and explode above ground level, that can tear you to pieces, all right. And then there's the delayed fuse bombs. Those'll sink right into the mud and then they blow, and they can take your fucking head off, you don't watch out."

"Shut the fuck up, Sleepy Ass," Stoddard said.

"I'm telling you, guys," Marshak went on. "One time, early on, it was, wasn't it, Bobby? Me and Dash here, we were in a hole, a nice one, too, big, we'd made it a real home away from home, hadn't we, Dash?"

"Shut the fuck up," Kafak said, shaking his head.

"Anyhow, we had a perfect little holiday getaway there, and then the fucking Krauts had to go and drop a delayed fuse bomb on us. It landed not far off, and when it blew, brother, I'm telling you, it caved in the sides of our foxhole until we were buried in fucking mud. Me and Dash were digging out of that mud for weeks. Ain't that right, Dash?"

"No fucking way," Acker said. He clearly didn't believe this story. "That never happened."

"You'd better check around, pally," Marshak said. "There's been guys buried alive that never dug out from that kind of thing. I was walking by a foxhole once when a bomb with a delayed fuse went off right next to that hole and cut the two guys in the hole right in half. Both of them. Turned them into four guys. One way to get reinforcements, I suppose."

"Now that's a load a hosscrap," Stoddard said, "'n I kin prove it."

"Prove it, then," Marshak said.

"If the fuckin' Nazis was droppin' bombs like that delayed fuse one you talkin' about, old Sleepy Ass would nevuh be walkin' 'round neah any foxholes. He'd be right smack dab in the bottom a one. Now, ain't that right, Dash?"

"You got that one, all right, Country."

"Now, that's a hell of a thing, don't you think, Ack-Ack? A guy's pals telling stories like that on him. I'm just trying to give some information might could save your life, and these boys here don't want me to help you. You ought to ask yourself the reason why that's so, my friend."

"I don't believe nothing you said," Acker told Marshak.

"Dash," Marshak said. "Tell this boy about the bomb that caved in our nice foxhole we had. Tell him how that was true."

"It's true, all right," Kafak said.

"Really?" Acker said.

"'Fraid so. What Sleepy Ass said about delayed fuse bombs is true. You got to watch out for them."

"See? I told you so, Ack-Ack."

"But he was lying about the foxhole."

"It was a piece a shit, wan' it?" Country said, grinning.

"They always are," Kafak said.

Later that morning somebody laid down some smoke, so the boys in the frontline foxholes like Kafak and the rest knew something was up. Somebody was coming for a visit. They'd just finished their shoepac regimen when a supply sergeant arrived. He was dragging a mattress cover along with him. It looked filled to bursting and lumpy.

"Hot damn!" Marshak cried. "Fresh bread!"

The sergeant dropped into the hole with his corporal right beside him. Denny and Batarski. They occasionally brought bread to the troops in these mattress covers.

"Here you go, fellas!" Denny said. "Have at it!"

He handed out a loaf to each of them. Marshak started right in eating his. Kafak put his aside until he ate his C-ration.

"Hey, Sarge," Marshak said. "I always wanted to ask you something. How come you use them goddamned mattress covers to bring us bread in?"

"What?" Denny said. "You got a mattress in here you need it for?"

"Naw, I don't mean that."

"Ain't nobody using mattresses up here in this war, Sleepy Ass, case you hadn't noticed. Might as well use them for something worthwhile, like feeding your scrawny ass."

"You're missing the point, smart-ass," Marshak said.

"That's Sergeant Smart-ass to you, Sleepy Ass. So what's the point I'm fucking missing, then?"

"You fuckers use the same fucking mattress covers to take corpses back to HQ."

"They ain't the same bags, you fucking idiot."

"They sure look like the same bags."

"My only question is," Country said, joining in teasing Denny, "do ya use 'em fust fo' the bread 'n then the bodies, o' fust fo' the bodies 'n then the bread?"

"Which you figure it is?" Denny said.

"Knowing the army," Marshak said, "it's the bodies, then the bread."

"You don't want no more bread, you just tell me so."

"We just want you to bring us the bread in something other than these goddamned mattress covers, Sarge," Marshak said.

"Yeah, well, that ain't gonna happen."

"See how it is, Dash?" Marshak said, trying to get Kafak involved in the ribbing. "These supply guys just don't care about us boys in the rifle companies."

"Hell," Kafak said, "nobody cares about us boys in the rifle companies."

"I like that," Denny said. "Me and Batarski risk our lives crawling around the fucking Anzio Bitchhead to bring you boys fresh bread, and this is the fucking thanks we get."

"I'm only wondering," Marshak went on, "why it is we always seem to get fresh bread right after a battle. You know, when there's all them fresh bodies around."

"Well, that do seem to ansuh the question, though, don' it, now, Sleepy Ass?" Country said. He laughed. "The bread comes fust, then they use the bags to take back the bodies."

"See?" Denny said. "So it ain't all that bad, is it?"

"Fuck you, Sarge. That's still the shit." Marshak turned to Kafak. "What'd you say, Dash? You figure it's bodies first, then bread? Or other way around?"

"I don't give a fuck," Kafak said. "S'long as it ain't bread and bodies in the bag at the same fucking time."

"And there you have it," Denny said. "The voice of reason."

He grinned and slid out of the foxhole to pay his visit to the next bunch of soldiers.

Acker said, "They don't really use the bags for both, do they? I mean, not the same bags?"

"Hell," Marshak said, "you never know with the fucking army, pal. You just never know."

They settled in and ate the rest of their breakfast then. Kafak had cold beans. The bread worked well with them. He was glad he saved it. After that they all used their helmets to bail water out of the foxhole because it had gotten deep from the rain that had been falling all morning. Up to their ankles. They bailed until there was only soupy mud left. Then Kafak went to sleep. The sound of a bullet damned close startled him awake a few hours later. He looked around and saw Marshak hovering over Stoddard.

"Son of a bitch!" Acker said.

Kafak thought he sounded near hysterical. He spoke to Marshak.

"What the hell happened?"

"Sniper," Marshak said.

"I can fucking see that. How?"

"Goddamn idiot Stoddard wanted another loaf of bread. I told him Denny wouldn't give it to him, anyway, but he insisted. He wanted to crawl out and find him. He didn't get but halfway out of the hole before some fucker nailed him."

"He dead?" Kafak said.

"Yeah," Marshak said, "he's fucking dead."

"Holler for a medic, Ack-Ack," Kafak said, thinking to give the new guy something to do.

Acker started hollering. His hysteria sounded in his voice for the first few shouts, but then, as he got more and more hoarse from the continued yelling, he seemed to calm himself down. A medic finally came and checked Stoddard.

"He's dead, all right."

"Figured."

"You didn't need a medic for that."

"Hey, it's your fucking job," Marshak said.

Kafak spoke quickly.

"Sorry for making you come out in the daylight, pal."

"Sure," the corpsman said, staring hard at Marshak.

"Don't mind him," Kafak told the medic, pulling him aside. "He's just upset about our pal getting hit and all."

"I get it," the medic said. He calmed down a bit.

Kafak said, "I suppose you ought to look at this while you're here."

He showed the medic his arm. The corpsman put some stitches in it, threw on some disinfectant that burned like hell, then wrapped it up in a new bandage to keep it from getting infected.

"Keep it clean," he told Kafak. "It'll heal just fine. You'll be all right."

"Why should he be all right now?" Marshak said. "He wasn't never all right before."

"Fuck you, Sleepy Ass," Kafak said.

Marshak laughed, and the medic said, "I'll send someone to get the body. Soon's it gets dark."

The corpsman left, and Kafak spoke to Marshak. "You hear that, Sleepy Ass? Someone'll come for the body soon as it gets dark. Right?"

"What the hell?" Marshak said. He shook his head, a disgusted look on his face. After a pause of no more than a moment, he shook his head again and smiled. "What the hell?" he said again. "Let's just have Denny bring back the bread bag."

"Fucking idiot," Kafak told him.

Then he went back to sleep, listening to Marshak having a conversation with Stoddard. Later, when Kafak woke up

again, he asked Marshak, "Why you wasting your time talking with Stoddard when you got a perfectly good Ack-Ack
right there?"

"Cuz Stoddard's more interesting than Ack-Ack."

"Fuck you, pal," Acker told Marshak.

"Hell," Kafak said, "he only prefers Stoddard cuz Stoddard
can't talk back and tell him what a fucking asshole he is."

"That's another good reason," Marshak said.

That night their Top Kick, Sergeant Barnes, came with the
two men who'd arrived to take Stoddard's body back to HQ.
He waited for the body to be retrieved, watching Marshak watch
the retrieval unit.

"What the fuck's up with you, Marshak?" Barnes said. "Why
you so interested in their work, all of a sudden?"

"Nothing," Marshak said.

"He's just trying to find bread crumbs in the bag."

"They use different sets of mattress covers for the two things,"
Barnes said.

"I know that, and you know that, Sarge," Kafak said, "but
Marshak don't believe nothing the army tells him."

Barnes snorted, then told them he'd send some more guys
up to share their hole that night. Acker had already returned
to his own comrades. Then Barnes told them, "Here's the good
news, the brass has finally seen fit to send us some galoshes."

"Wow," Marshak said. "I guess they finally realized this rain
ain't just a passing summer storm, huh?"

Barnes grinned.

"Bet you wish you were back in North Africa now, complaining about the heat, don't you, Sleepy Ass?"

"Hell, I'd give my left nut to be back in the fucking desert,
Sarge."

"Yeah," Kafak said, "the desert wasn't so bad."

Then Marshak said, "Wait."

"What?" Barnes said.

"You can still fuck with one nut, right?"

Kafak and Barnes laughed.

"What the fuck?" Kafak said, shaking his head.

"Well," Marshak said, "I just wanna know the bargain I'm making, is all."

"Well, don't worry about it, Sleepy Ass," Barnes told him. "You ain't gotta give up anything for the desert on account of you ain't going to no desert. Ain't nobody getting off of Anzio."

"Except in one of them bread bags," Kafak said.

"Don't I know it," Marshak said.

Then Barnes said, "Anyway, when the two new guys get up here, you two head back. The supply guys dumped them galoshes behind the church back in Anzio. You got a nice moonless night to travel by, so you shouldn't get shot. Still, watch your fucking asses."

Barnes left then. Within an hour Martinson and Pizzoli arrived. They both wore new galoshes.

"Like 'em?" Pizzoli said. "I got a fucking discount."

"Yeah, free if you're in the fucking army," Marshak said.

"What a life we got, eh, boys?" Pizzoli said.

"Three meals a day and a nice mushy bed," Martinson said, and Kafak told Marshak, "Come on."

They crawled out of their foxhole and kept crawling through the mud until they'd gone a couple hundred yards from the very front of the front lines, and then they rose up into a running crouch and ran the rest of the way back to the beach. They found the pile of galoshes behind the church. Dozens of guys were there, going through the galoshes, trying to find their sizes. Some of the guys had one rubber boot on, two more in each hand, and were staring down at the pile for a potential match. Boots were flying everywhere as soldiers dug through them. Kafak and Marshak jumped right in.

"I can't see shit in this dark," Marshak said.

"Just take anything close to fitting," Kafak said.

They couldn't afford any light. German artillery wouldn't allow for it.

They took about half an hour, but Kafak ended up with one boot that fit pretty snug while the other banged about loose upon his foot. It would be the best he'd do, he figured. He looked for Marshak. Sleepy Ass was still digging for a pair of boots that matched.

"I ain't found nothing yet," he told Kafak.

"I guess they don't make them in girls' sizes," Kafak said.

"Yeah, fuck you, pally."

"Come on, Sleepy Ass. We got to get back."

"Fuck it, Dash, longer we're here, longer we're out of the firing line, right?"

"Hell, Pizzoli'll figure us for dead and start going through our stuff."

"I got nothing the army can't replace," Marshak said. "Ha!" he said then. "Lookee here, lookee here!" He found a pair of boots that looked to be a matched set. He tried one on. "Fits perfect!" he said. The next one didn't. "Fuck!" he said.

"Come on," Kafak told him. "It'll have to do. I'm going."

"Go without me. I'll be there later."

Kafak returned to the hole alone. He went to sleep. He woke up when he heard Marshak scrambling back into the mud.

"Well?" Kafak said, half-asleep. "How'd you do?"

"Came close, but no cigar. They'll do OK, though."

"Good," Kafak said. It was raining. "I'll take the next watch."

Marshak and Martinson slept, and Pizzoli kept up a running, albeit quiet, commentary on everything he could think of. From baseball to movies to weather to how he wanted to come back to Italy and see it as it really was once the war was over and "my fucking home dagos clean the fucking place up a bit." Kafak said nothing, just listened. He lit a Lucky with his battered Zippo, hiding the flame, and cupped the burning end of the cigarette in his hand. When the cigarette was done, he tossed the butt and drew his blanket tighter around himself against the rain, but it did little good.

When Marshak and Martinson woke up to take their turn on watch, it was still raining. Kafak tried to sleep. He tossed and turned a bit. The blanket was so wet it only made him colder. And the galoshes kept tangling his feet. He kicked them off and threw the blanket aside. He shoved his gloved hands beneath his armpits and curled up in the bottom of the foxhole. He felt exhausted, but he couldn't drop off. "Fucking rain," he said.

He fell back asleep.

9

The next morning when Kafak awoke, his ear was on fire. It ached and throbbed and burned all at the same time.

"Shit," he said.

He touched it, and that made it shoot pain.

"You don't look so good, pally," Marshak said.

Pizzoli said, "You look like shit. You know," he said, "more shit than you usually look like."

"My fucking ear," Kafak told them.

He looked down where he'd been sleeping. A puddle spread there. The water was cold and his side and back were sopping wet.

"You'd better get a medic up here," Marshak told him.

"I don't want some guy risking his life cuz I got a fucking earache, Sleepy Ass."

"Here, lemme feel your temperature."

Marshak pulled off his glove with his teeth and reached for Kafak's forehead, under his helmet.

"Don't," Kafak said.

"Shut up and gimme your fucking head," Marshak said. Kafak did, looking sheepish about it, and Marshak said, "Fuck, pal, you're on fire."

"It's just your fucking hands are cold."

"Hell, a hot meal would feel cold to you right about now, Dash. You need a medic."

Kafak shook his head no, but Pizzoli hollered for a corpsman, and one came within the hour. He looked at Kafak, felt his forehead, and said, "Come on, let's get you back to the rear. Have a doc look at that ear."

"I'll take him, buddy," Marshak said, volunteering quickly. "So's you can stay on duty up here where the troops need you."

The medic frowned at Marshak. He told him, "Go ahead, but there ain't no dames back there, you know. It's too dangerous for female nurses on Anzio nowadays. Even at the rear."

They saw how that could be true, too, Kafak and Marshak, when they reached the beach where the hospital tents had been set up. One had been blown to hell. They were using some of the ruined buildings for hospital work as well, but mostly those were used as headquarters along with the huge underground system they had built. Engineers had sunk the large red-crossed tents a few feet into the ground and surrounded them with walls of sandbags. Random shells exploded nearby, but nobody seemed to notice; they all just went right on working. Even with the huge red crosses painted on the tents, the Germans didn't stop bombing the area. Doctors and the male nurses were often killed. It was exactly because it was so dangerous that the army didn't want to allow female nurses to be stationed on the beachhead any longer.

"Shit," Kafak said. "I'd've been safer staying in my hole up front."

"Fuckin-A right," Marshak said. He was peering around the compound, searching desperately. "Shit," Marshak said after a time. "There ain't no women here."

"The corpsman told you that, Sleepy Ass."

"Who fucking believes those bastards, anyway? They'll say anything to keep a guy on the goddamned line. And keep the dames to themselves."

Kafak reported to one orderly, a corporal, and the guy told him to get into line. Marshak stayed with him in order to help him stand. Kafak felt incredibly and increasingly weak. His ear hurt more and more. Marshak stood on his left side. Kafak waited at the back of a line of about forty guys. He noticed none of them had any bullet or shrapnel wounds. They weren't being treated for wounds; they were being treated for illnesses. Like Kafak.

Guys went into the tent, one at a time, then came back out the same way. Some of them reclaimed their equipment from the orderly station and headed back toward the front lines. Others skipped the orderly station and walked toward a tent nearer the bay. They sat or lay down there on cots under the open-sided tent. It, too, had a big red cross painted on it, which meant nothing.

"Hey," Marshak said, his voice sudden and urgent. "Look there, Dash! It's a dame. A bona fide female nurse."

"Bullshit, Sleepy Ass. You're seeing things."

"No, I'm telling you. I saw one."

"They told you there weren't any female nurses here."

"That corpsman was full of shit. I'm telling you, Dash. I saw one. A real looker, too."

"Sure," Kafak said, "she would be."

"What's that supposed to mean?" Marshak said.

They argued like that for a time. Kafak figured Marshak was trying to keep his mind off things. He wondered, though, if Marshak really had seen a female nurse. Kafak didn't see any.

Kafak still waited on line, maybe a dozen guys before him now, more men constantly filling in behind him, when four soldiers came running in carrying a man on a blanket. The man had a wound in his neck. Blood was pouring out of it. Medics applied pressure to the wound, but it was doing no good. Blood covered his entire shoulder and chest area.

"Looks like a sniper," Marshak said.

"Yeah," Kafak said.

He watched the man be rushed straight ahead and into the tent, bypassing the line.

"What the fuck is with that?" Marshak said. "We been waiting here."

"That guy needs a doc way more than I do," Kafak said.

"Jesus, Dash, a fucking fever can kill you just as good as any fucking Kraut bullet, you know."

"Thanks for the reassurance, you fuckhead."

"I'm only telling you how it is, pally. You're looking worse by the fucking minute."

"I'll live. I can wait."

By the time Kafak got into the tent, he saw a couple of doctors still working on the wounded trooper. The line had fallen into a slower pace once that soldier had been carried into the hospital. Kafak saw now it was because there were only two other doctors available for the injured and sick. One of them approached him and said something.

"What?" Kafak asked.

The doctor repeated what he had said. At least, Kafak figured he did. Kafak saw the doctor's lips move, but he couldn't really hear anything but a blurred mumble. Then he realized the doctor was standing on his right-hand side, talking to his right ear, the ear that hurt so bad.

Kafak pointed to the ear and said, "I can't hear."

The doctor frowned and stepped to Kafak's left-hand side.

"Can you hear me with this ear?"

"Yeah," Kafak said. "Sure."

"You're having problems with that ear, then?" the doc said, pointing to the right ear. Kafak nodded. "What happened?"

"I woke up this morning and it was on fire. Hurts like a son of a bitch, doc. If you could just give me something for the pain, I can go back up to my hole."

"Sit down," the doctor told him.

Kafak sat. The doctor took his temperature.

"How's it look, Doc?" Kafak asked.

"Bad, but not too bad." The doc paused, thinking, then grabbed a pad and wrote something down on it. "Here," he said, ripping off the top sheet and handing it to Kafak.

"What's this?"

"Three-day pass to the rest area."

"Oh," Kafak said. "All right."

He handed him another sheet of paper. "And here's a prescription for some medicine. Give both of these to the orderly over at the rest area. Right?"

"Sure thing, Doc."

But the doctor was already calling in the next guy.

Kafak stood up and nearly fell over. His equilibrium had been impacted by the infected ear. He hadn't noticed before, with Marshak holding him up. He grabbed onto a nearby cot to steady himself. He had to make his way to the exit from the tent by lurching from one piece of furniture to another. The doctor saw him and stared at him. Kafak smiled at the doc. The doc turned away, frowning, already examining the next patient. Kafak figured the doctor must have thought he was faking the stumbling routine. Kafak only wished he was. He felt like he was going to puke.

Marshak met him just outside and said, "Well?"

"Three-day pass at the rest area," Kafak said.

"Rest area?" Marshak said. He sounded disbelieving. "There ain't no fucking rest area on goddamned Anzio, Dash."

"I know that," Kafak said. "You know that. But I figure that doctor don't know it."

"Son of a bitch. You gotta be fucking dead to get off this fucking shitass beach. It ain't fucking right, pal."

"Don't I know it," Kafak said.

He stumbled toward the rest area with Marshak supporting him. The rest area consisted of some tents, some cots, and some radios playing big-band music piped in from somewhere. He handed the orderly the papers the doctor had given him, and the orderly pointed him to a cot. Marshak humped him over to the bed, and Kafak plopped down on it. Kafak lay down in the same filthy clothes he'd been wearing for weeks now. Maybe two months. Ever since he'd been on Anzio, anyhow.

"You be all right, Bobby?" Marshak asked.

"Sure," Kafak said. "Sure."

He was already falling asleep.

"I'll be by to see you soon's I can," Marshak said.

"OK."

"Take care of yourself, Bobby."

"Sure," Kafak said, smiling. "Why the fuck not?"

Then he fell asleep.

Kafak woke the next day to the smell of bacon frying. He almost fainted from the beauty of it. His mouth watered. He hadn't had a hot meal in weeks, the entire time he'd been on Anzio, really. He couldn't wait for the breakfast to be served. Even if he didn't feel much like eating because of the pain in his head and the queasiness in his stomach from his fucked-up equilibrium. A doctor had entered the tent. A different guy from the one who had seen him yesterday. He moved from cot to cot, checking on the patients. They all seemed to be getting better. At least that's how it looked to Kafak, judging by the doctor's expressions and words of encouragement. Then he came to Kafak. He looked at the papers the last doctor had made out, that the orderly had taken and then pinned to a board that now hung at the end of Kafak's cot.

"How we doing, son?" the doctor said.

"I feel fucking great, Doc," Kafak said.

He smiled. The doctor smiled back. He put the chart back on the end of the cot.

"Let's take that temperature, shall we?"

"Whatever you say, Doc. You're the doctor."

Kafak laughed at that, and the doctor frowned. He took Kafak's temperature. The look on his face scared Kafak, but the doctor erased it quickly. Then he said, "You're up a couple of degrees from yesterday, son. Are you still deaf in that ear?"

"Not deaf, exactly, Doc. Just like underwater. It's all right, though. Cuz now I only hear half the fucking Kraut bombs, you know?"

Kafak giggled at that, too.

The doctor said, "I think you're suffering from delirium, son. Or maybe it's just a bad sense of humor." He smiled. "Either way, you're going back to Naples."

Kafak's turn to frown at that.

"What?" he said.

"You're off the beach. Until you get better, anyway."

"I can't leave, Doc," Kafak said. "Didn't you know there's still Germans here?"

The doctor smiled. "Yeah, but your friends'll have to fight them for a while. Just until you get back."

"I can't leave my friends, Doc."

The doctor pointed to his lapel.

"See these bars, son? That means I outrank you. I'm ordering you to Naples. Have a good trip, and get better quick. I'll look for you when you get back."

Kafak was carried to an LCT. He lay there, sleeping on and off, until the craft had been filled with the day's transports back to Naples. It was full up. It finally took off, lurching through the waves. Kafak puked from the waves adding to his unsettled stomach. He tried to vomit into his helmet, but he missed more than he made, what with the tossing of the craft.

"Sorry, fellas," he said to the guys around him.

Most of them didn't hear. They were puking, too.

In Naples, Kafak was transported to the Forty-Fifth General Hospital located near the Bagnoli racetrack. The weather in Naples was better than at Anzio. It was a little warmer, and there was a lot less rain. Anyway, he was inside a tent. They laid him down on a cot. He looked around. All the cots surrounding him were full as well. A couple of guys had wounds. One guy had lost a leg up to his knee. Kafak figured it was trench foot, but he didn't know. It could have been an explosion or something, too. A couple other guys looked OK, so they must be recovering from their illnesses or wounds.

"Who you guys with?" Kafak asked them.

They told him their units. Some came from Anzio, but he had never met them there. Some of them came from the line up north, near Cassino.

"How's the action there?" Kafak asked them.

"Fucked up. How was your Anzio?"

"It's a fucking beach. Sunshine and goddamned lollipops. Why, what have you fucking heard?"

Everyone laughed hard at that. Some other guys chimed in. Pretty soon they were all talking shit and laughing loudly. A nurse came in. Kafak saw her. An honest-to-god female nurse. She must have been about fifty or more and built like a Panzer, but Kafak thought she was fucking beautiful. She spoke in a harsh tone.

She said, "You boys will need to quiet down. You're disturbing our other patients."

Kafak said, "Sorry, beautiful."

The nurse scowled and shook her head. The other guys laughed, and that was the last thing Kafak remembered.

10

When Kafak woke again he found he had been shaved, cleaned up, and put into fresh pajamas. He felt fine. He was hungry as hell. He looked around and saw the sides of the tent had been rolled up. Sunshine burned bright outside. A nice warmth with a sweet breeze flowed through the opened tent. It felt wonderful. Everything felt wonderful. Kafak could hardly believe there was a war going on. That he had been in mud and blood and gunfire just a few hours ago.

A nurse came by with some breakfast. Kafak sat up. He felt famished and couldn't wait to dig into the food. Bacon and eggs and coffee and juice and toast. And all of it hot. He couldn't believe it. Maybe this was heaven, he thought. Maybe he had died and now he was in heaven.

The nurse smiled at him.

"Hungry, aren't you?" she said, noting him wolfing down his food.

He chewed, nodding. Then he swallowed and paused in his attack long enough to look at her. She was younger than the nurse he'd seen last night. And much, much prettier. Kafak smiled. He felt stupid, figuring she got that dumb look all the time, but he couldn't help himself. She was the first really pretty girl he'd seen in nearly three months. He'd all but forgotten such things existed in this world, outside of pictures and conversation.

He said, "I'm real hungry, all right."

"How do you feel, Private?"

"I feel great."

"Well, that's good. You sure look a lot better."

"Who shaved me, by the way?"

"That was me, actually."

"Well, I appreciate it."

"Oh, that was doctor's orders, Private. We wanted you to look good in case we had to send you up to Saint Peter."

She laughed; Kafak grinned.

"Ha-ha," he said. "It wasn't that bad," he said.

"Actually, it was, Private. We thought we'd lost you there for a while. But you look like you pulled through OK."

"I just went to sleep, and now I feel fine."

She looked at him. An odd expression on her pretty face.

"What day do you suppose it is, Private?"

"What?" Kafak said. "Today?"

"Yes. Today."

"It's the day after yesterday," Kafak said.

He shrugged.

The nurse shook her head.

"You've been out for three days, Private. You fell asleep the other night, and we didn't figure you were going to wake up again. We did everything we could to keep you with us. And it looks like it worked out just fine."

"Except you shaved me. Just in case."

"We didn't want to take any chances," she said, and laughed again.

She moved off, and soon a doctor arrived.

"How you feeling, son?" he asked.

"I feel fine, Doc. You can send me back any time."

"You in a hurry to get shot at again, Private?"

"I miss my pals. You know how it is."

"They'll still be there when you get back. We want to keep you with us a few more days, make sure you're fully recovered from that infection. You hear me all right?"

"Yes, sir."

The doctor pressed a hand over Kafak's left ear. Applied firm pressure. Then he said, "Can you still hear me all right?"

"Clear as a bell," Kafak said.

"Good, that's good. We were worried you might lose your hearing in that ear. We would've had to send you home."

"Well, I screwed up that test, then, didn't I?"

The doctor laughed.

"You'd have missed your friends, though, right?"

"Well, I wouldn't mind missing them from back in the States, I guess."

"No, son, I guess you wouldn't."

The doctor moved on to the next patient.

Easter came and went. They gave all the men candy, and the nurses put on a little skit. There was a High Mass held outdoors on a hill that Kafak attended. He took Communion, then wondered if he should have. He might have killed people, after all. He stopped himself thinking about all that. It would do him no good right now. He buried all that away to think about it later. After the war. When he was back home. That way, if he never made it back home, he would never have to think about stuff like that.

One nurse told him, "If you'd have gotten here a few weeks earlier than you did, you'd have seen quite the explosion. Mount Vesuvius erupted. First time since 1906. The guys got to see the show nearly every day there for a while."

"I heard some guys talking about that," Kafak said. "It sounded beautiful."

"It was. We could see it even this far away."

"I guess it wasn't so great for the people who lost their homes, though."

"Yeah, not so great for them."

"Lots of people losing their homes nowadays," Kafak said.

"Don't think about that now, Private. You're in Naples now. Relax and get your rest. When you go back, you'll be glad you did."

"Sure," Kafak said. "I don't mind if I never sleep in mud again."

"Well, the weather's getting better. Spring is here."

"Hope it's getting better on Anzio, too."

"You think it's different there than here?" the nurse asked, smiling.

"Everything's different on Anzio," Kafak said.

A couple days later, the doctor was visiting with Kafak and told him, "You're nearly fully recovered, son. I figure there's no danger of that infection returning now. Not to say you can't get a new one, so you be careful."

"Tell it to the Krauts, Doc."

"Sure will, Private."

"Say, Doc. Something I been wondering."

"What's that, Private?"

"I know there's a lot of guys been moved off the line on account of trench foot. But I don't see that many guys here with the stuff. What happened to them all?"

"Oh, we keep them in a separate tent, separate location. The stench is not good for anyone, especially not other troopers trying to recover from their own wounds or illnesses."

"Makes sense, I guess."

"You wouldn't believe the smell, son," the doctor said.

"I've smelled it," Kafak said.

"Have you?"

"A guy in our hole. He got evacuated here, to Naples."

"Oh, I see."

The doctor waited. As if, Kafak thought, Kafak might ask about the guy he knew who had been taken off the beach with trench foot. Kafak didn't ask, though. He didn't want to know anything more about what had happened.

Instead Kafak said, "So, is that the hospital for trench foot?" He pointed to another huge hospital tent not very far off from where he lay in his own cot.

The doctor shook his head.

"That's not trench foot over there," he said. "That's something else."

"Yeah? What's that?"

The doctor looked at him, raised a brow. Finished writing the latest information for Kafak on the chart. Then he said, "That tent is filled with VD patients."

"VD?" Kafak said. He sounded amazed. He felt amazed. The tent was huge, filled to overflowing with GIs. "What the fuck?" he said.

"You've got that right," the doctor said. He sounded grim. "Enough men over there suffering from venereal disease to fill out an entire division. And all lost to the army due to a highly preventable situation."

"Yeah, but they're gonna be OK," Kafak said. "They'll be back up to the front soon's they're cured, right?"

"Some of them, certainly. Others, well, they might never be cured."

"Never?" Kafak said. He couldn't believe it. It was only VD, after all. Hurt like hell, right, but it was treatable. He thought so, anyway, despite what the army's scare films showed.

"Some of those men will never be healed, will die from their disease," the doctor said, "because they waited too long to seek treatment. They hid the disease. Because they knew whatever time they lost to VD is tacked on to the end of their enlistment, would keep them in the service longer. So they hid it, hoping to treat it themselves or hoping it would just go away. It doesn't just go away, though."

"Except none of that matters anymore."

"Right," the doctor said. "Because now you're in it for the duration. But these guys caught it before that was the case. And even now, you can lose rank for it."

Kafak had heard about that. One of their platoon sergeants had been demoted because he'd been discovered to have VD.

"Some of these guys've kept it secret a long time, seems like."

"Exactly. And that's why some of them are going to die of it now."

"Why don't you just fill 'em all up with this penicillin stuff, Doc?"

"Well, for one thing, there's not enough to go around. Wounded men get preference for the use of penicillin."

"Well, that's only right."

"As they turn out more in the States and get it to us, we'll use it more for the VD cases and so on. For now, we have to use it for wounds first, then other infections after that."

"Did you use it on me?"

"You were nearly dead from your infection, Private. We had no choice."

"Well. Thanks, then."

"Don't mention it." The doctor paused and rubbed his chin, staring off at the tent filled with patients laid low by venereal disease. "The other problem with using penicillin on those guys," he said, "is that it just doesn't always work. This strain of VD these guys have caught in Naples is a particularly tough one. It's one of the worst I've ever seen. We don't really know what to do with it."

"Wow. Tough town, Naples, huh?"

"It's a fairly dangerous place, all right, even without Germans shooting at you here. So I'd suggest you stay away from the whorehouses when you get out of here, Private. Or at least take the proper precautions."

"Will do, Doc. Say, that must be the same strain that Columbus's guys got in the New World, brought it back to Europe. Looks like it's still here."

The doctor looked at Kafak.

"Just might be," he said. "You know your history, Private. You a college man?"

Kafak looked suddenly sheepish.

"No, sir," he said.

"They drafted you right out of high school, huh? You sure look like it, anyway."

"Something like that," Kafak said.

He dropped the subject. He was poor, from a poor family. Nobody in his family ever thought about college. It was not something someone like Kafak did. You grew up, you worked in an automobile factory if you were lucky. Steady job, good pay. If you weren't lucky, maybe you went into business with your old man, a handyman, like his old man. Something like that. Kafak didn't see much future beyond that when he was growing up back in Detroit. Now he didn't see much future beyond the day after today. Guys talked about their futures all the time. It was a way to get past the present since the present often felt so terrible. Kafak didn't bother with all that, though. He loved to listen to other guys' plans; only he didn't make so many of his own. He figured he'd wait the Germans out on that.

The next day Kafak was given a three-day pass to leave the hospital, see the sights of Naples. Kafak dressed in a uniform another guy in the hospital lent him. That guy was a supply guy in Naples and had caught the flu, bad. He was in a bed a couple over from Kafak's. He didn't need his dress uniform any time soon, so he let Kafak wear it. It was in perfect shape. All the guy's uniforms were. He hadn't seen any combat. The dress kit was a bit small since the guy was a good deal shorter than Kafak, but it worked well enough.

Kafak checked out with the corpsman in charge. He received the usual allotment of three condoms for leave, and the sergeant told him, "Make sure and use 'em. You don't want to end up in that other tent."

"Sure thing, Sarge."

"You need more, you let me know."

"You already gave me three," Kafak said.

"There's some pretty girls in this town," the sergeant said. He winked.

Kafak toured the streets of Naples. He saw plenty of whorehouses but remembered what the doctor had told him about the venereal disease here, and so stayed away. He didn't really trust the rubbers. He spent most of his day just wandering the cobblestones and back alleyways of the city. He knew he wouldn't find her, but some part of his mind hoped he might run into the girl from the picture again. Maybe this time, he could actually get to know her a little bit more. He journeyed back to the neighborhood where he'd met her. He hung around there for hours. Of course, he never saw her. Toward midafternoon, he found a café and ducked into it. It wasn't crowded. Maybe half a dozen guys there. Kafak ordered a beer. They didn't have beer. He ordered a glass of wine. It came to him in a clay cup only a little chipped. He'd drunk about half of it when a couple of Negroes came in. Kafak had never seen Negro soldiers before. He'd seen plenty of Negroes back in Detroit. Thousands had come up for work in the factories when the South went bad during the Depression. Even earlier than that, Kafak knew. He knew that Detroit had owned a really strong Ku Klux Klan movement as far back as the twenties. They'd tried to recruit his father during the Depression, when things were bad for the entire Kafak family. His dad had sworn at them in German, sent them flying out of the house. Kafak still remembered the pair of KKK recruiters leaping off the porch, running. Kafak didn't blame them. He knew his old man's anger. Better than he cared to admit. After the way his father had reacted to them, Kafak had always believed there was something wrong with those Klan folks. Whatever it was his father didn't like about the group, that was good enough for Kafak.

The two Negro soldiers ordered wine right off and sat at the bar. Kafak figured from their order that they had been here before. All the other soldiers that had been drinking there quick finished their drinks and left. They shot looks at the Negroes, but the two soldiers at the bar didn't look their way. When everyone was gone, it was just Kafak and the Negroes. A couple of times some other white soldiers stuck their heads in, but they took one look at the bar and then turned around and found somewhere else to drink. It never

occurred to Kafak to leave the bar. He didn't know why it
didn't. It just didn't.

Once a second lieutenant came in, and the two Negroes
and Kafak hopped up to attention. The lieutenant looked at
the two men at the bar. He told the owner of the place, "You
shouldn't serve coloreds here, mister. You won't get any white
men to come in here anymore."

The owner, an elderly Italian man with wispy white hair and
clothes that hung too big on his bony frame, shook his head.

"I no unnerstan'," he told the officer.

The lieutenant looked at Kafak.

"What're you doing here?" he said.

"Drinking this wine, sir."

"Why here?"

"First place I come across while I was walking around."

"You here before them?"

The lieutenant jerked a thumb over his shoulder toward the
two at the bar.

Kafak shrugged.

"Didn't see when they come in, tell you the truth, sir. I just
been concentrating on this wine."

The officer looked at him.

"You shouldn't be drinking wine with coloreds, Private."

"I ain't, sir. They're there and I'm here, sir."

"Why don't you just get the hell out of here?"

"They got some good wine here, Lieutenant. Want some?"

"No," the officer said. "Not with them. You wouldn't either,
if you had any brains, peckerwood."

Kafak shrugged. The second lieutenant scowled at him once
more, then at the two Negroes for good measure, and then he
spun on his heel and left, calling over his shoulder to the bar
owner.

"Remember what I said about these goddamned coloreds,"
he said.

The owner looked at the three men in his place.

"What this mean, 'coloreds'?" he asked.

Kafak didn't say anything. He heard the men at the bar mumble something, but he didn't catch what they told the Italian. He sipped some more of his wine.

One of the men at the bar turned on his stool and looked at Kafak.

"How come you didn't leave?" he said.

Kafak looked around. He remembered he was the only one in the place besides them. He smiled awkwardly, a little embarrassed that he'd forgotten that.

"They got good wine here," he said.

"Yeah, they do."

"But what I really want is a beer."

The second Negro laughed, and the first Negro said, "Then how come you don't find some place that's got beer?"

Kafak shrugged.

"First place I seen. I got to get back soon."

"You got time for dinner?"

"What the fuck you doing, Lester?" the second Negro said. "Leave the motherfucker alone."

"He's all right," Lester said. Then to Kafak, he said, "They got real good spaghetti here. S'why we come in. The wine's OK, but the food is better'n a motherfucker."

"Sure," Kafak said. "Spaghetti sounds good."

Lester ordered three plates, and he and the other man came to the table where Kafak sat.

"This here's Orville," Lester said.

"Fellas," Kafak said, nodding to them both. "Have a seat."

"You don't mind?" Lester asked.

"S'long as you don't try eating my food."

"All right, then."

The two men sat down.

"You guys're Red Tails, ain't you?" Kafak said.

They both nodded, smiling. Happy to be recognized.

Lester said, "We're with the 332nd Fighter Group."

"I thought so," Kafak said. "Tuskegee Airmen."

"That's us," Lester said, still smiling broadly.

"You know us?" Orville said.

"Seen you guys hitting the Germans over to Anzio."

"You on Anzio?"

"Until a couple weeks ago."

"Shit, man. That place is hell."

"If hell is made up of mud and rain," Kafak said. "And Germans trying to shoot your ass."

"Well," Orville said, "motherfucker got that last part right."

Kafak looked at him, frowning.

"What's that?" he said.

"What?"

"That word. Motherfucker. I never heard that word used that way before."

The two Negroes looked at one another for a moment. Then Lester spoke without looking directly at Kafak.

He said, "Just something we all say, the Negro troops, you know. It comes from all these white soldiers over here. They meet up with these Italian women around here who got them some kids but ain't got their husbands no more on account of they either dead or off fighting somewhere or in some POW camp or something. So these white boys fuck these mothers, see. So that's where it comes from."

Kafak smiled. He thought about it, then nodded.

"I like that," he said. "Motherfucker. Hell, yeah. That's good. Got a ring to it, all right."

"We like it," Lester said, looking back at Kafak, smiling.

"So what?" Kafak said. "It's only white boys fucking these mothers? You boys don't do that?"

"Shit, motherfucker," Orville said, "a black man get caught with one of these Italian women, they'd string the motherfucker up. We don't go near the Italian women, friend."

Kafak didn't believe that for a second, but he said, "Good. More for me."

Lester laughed.

"Mother-fucker!" Orville said, then laughed, too.

They ate their spaghetti and had another glass of wine and talked about the war and how long it might last, and they both had big plans afterward. Lester was going to open a pizza parlor with recipes he was collecting here in Naples. Orville was going to go back and run a photography studio. He had some photos he'd taken around Naples. He showed them to Kafak while they ate. Kafak was no judge, but he liked them well enough.

Kafak headed back to the hospital. The next day he went into the town again, but this time he just wore an old uniform of his own. He didn't see the use of getting himself up in the dress uniform. His A bag had been sent from Anzio to the hospital. The mud-caked uniform he'd come to the hospital in had been taken off somewhere and shot. That was what one of the nurses told him, anyhow. He wasn't ever going to see that thing again. He didn't mind. It had been torn up, soaked through, worn out. He felt glad it was gone. In fatigues and helmet, he toured Naples once again. His glasses had been broken and were taped together. He'd lost the backups somewhere. He strolled about, heading always toward the neighborhood where he'd met the girl. The one in the photograph. He again spent a couple hours just sitting on the edge of a dead fountain, waiting. Wondering if she would pass by. He smoked half a pack of cigarettes while he waited and watched. He stopped a couple of people and showed them the picture, asked them if they knew the girl. None of them spoke English. All he got was a lot of headshakes. Whether those meant they didn't understand him or that they didn't know the girl, Kafak couldn't figure. It didn't matter, really. Either way ended up the same thing. He thought he might go back to that little place with the spaghetti, but he didn't bother. He stood up, ground out his latest cigarette, and started back toward the hospital. Nearly there, he found a small place and ate some more Italian food. It was very good. Homemade stuff. The building was really somebody's home, but they had turned it into a kind of small café while the Allied troops were around. Try to get a stake to start themselves up again. Kafak finished the meal and walked back to the hospital. He lay in bed that night, thinking. Thinking about the girl. He wondered why he hadn't found her. He thought maybe he'd gotten the neighborhood wrong. Then he started wondering whether she might be dead. Or something. He didn't like thinking about that. She couldn't be dead. That would ruin everything, he figured. He stopped thinking that. He decided he didn't want to find the girl. He wouldn't go looking for her anymore. He didn't want to find out she had been killed. Or something. Beyond that, though, he didn't want to run into her again because it might ruin the memory he already had. Of that other day. That first time in Naples. Before Anzio. Before the war, really. Because, until Anzio, he hadn't really been in the war. He could say he was. A soldier. There was North Africa. Then there had been Naples. But there really hadn't been any war. Then there had been Anzio.

Kafak sighed.

No, he wouldn't look for the girl anymore.

He fell asleep.

11

Kafak spent his last day of leave helping out around the hospital. He tagged after the nurses and did whatever chores they needed done. Things they didn't want to do themselves, or things they'd been wanting to do for some while but just couldn't find the time. The day flew by. The next morning Kafak reported to the Bagnoli Repo Depo. All his equipment was replaced or repaired. He got a couple new uniforms. Nice and clean and fitting right. He liked them. New underwear as well. They even gave him new boots. Ones that didn't leak. They gave him a new bayonet and M1 and some grenades, and all the rest of the stuff he'd need as well. He asked them for a Thompson instead of the M1.

"Fuggedaboudit," the supply sergeant said. He was from Brooklyn, Kafak could tell from guys he'd talked to in his foxhole, other guys from Brooklyn. The accent was telltale. "The M1's a good fuckin' weapon."

"I like the Thompson."

"We ain't got no tommies. What the fuck's wrong with the M1? Ah, don't tell me. You're another one don't like it cuz the stripper clip makes a loud noise when it pops out, right? Give your position away, right?"

The M1's stripper clip made a metallic pinging sound as it automatically ejected.

Kafak shook his head.

"That don't bother me," he said. "If they don't already know where I'm at from me shooting at 'em, I don't figure the ping'd give me away."

"Well fuggedaboudit then, what?"

"You can't reload the clip. You gotta take all eight shots before you can reload."

"So what?"

"So I don't like walking around holding a gun with only one or two bullets ready to fire. That scares me."

"Why?"

"Cuz I'm usually gonna have to shoot at more than one or two guys."

"Fuggedaboudit, soldier, you're getting the M1. I'll give you some extra clips. Don't worry 'bout nothin'. Fuggedaboudit."

After that, they replaced his glasses, which kept him at the replacement depot for another day. He didn't mind. They had decent food there, and a couple of English soldiers had ended up there somehow and they had a nice talk, and the English guys had some rum that they shared with Kafak. He'd never had rum before. He didn't much like it, but he liked the way it made him feel.

"You could really get through a war on this shit," he told the English troopers.

"Why d'you suppose they give us our ration of the bit?" one of them said.

"The English sure know how to fight a fucking war," Kafak said.

"We've been at it a long time," one of them said.

The next day, it was the very beginning of May, Kafak was loaded on another LCT, a different one than the one that had brought him to Naples, and headed back for the beachhead. The LCT was packed tight. New guys as well as returnees, like himself. Some of the new guys seemed nervous, asked questions. Kafak didn't listen to the answers. Some of the returning troops had expressions on their faces that Kafak couldn't stand to look at. Defeated expressions. Faces awaiting death. As if they just knew that, in going back after they had thought they had escaped, they were somehow tempting fate. They knew they were going to buy it this time around. They just knew it. Their faces told that story.

Kafak turned away from all of that. The guy packed in next to him started in on a conversation. He was a corporal.

"Brother," he said, "the Germans don't need to spy on communications to know what the fuck we're doing."

"How's that?" Kafak said.

"All they got to do is watch the hospitals. The hospitals get cleaned out of every available trooper once the big boys are getting ready for a push. You notice that?"

Kafak had. He had noticed how packed the LCT was.

He said, "There's that English girl, too."

"What English girl?"

"You know, the one in that comic."

He meant "Jane."

"Oh yeah, her. What about her?"

"The closer we get to a big push, the more naked she gets."

The corporal laughed.

"I hadn't noticed that," he said.

"Check on it. You'll see."

"I guess it's one last treat before we hit the shit, huh?"

"I suppose it's something like that," Kafak said.

There were more indicators on the beachhead. Things were hopping. Everywhere you looked, Anzio was crowded. Even the foxholes were crowded. Kafak had just arrived and been sent to a reassignment tent. He asked to be sent back to L Company, Fifteenth Regiment. The lieutenant there nodded and grunted an OK. Then he looked up at Kafak and said, "Unless you want to volunteer for the boat teams?"

"Boat teams?" Kafak said. "Hell yeah. I'll volunteer for that."

The lieutenant smiled at him.

"Great," he said. "That's just great, Private. We need some experienced soldiers for that duty. They'll be glad to have you. And it'll keep you off the line, too. Leastways, for a while. So that's good news, right?"

"Sure," Kafak said. "Just tell me where to go, sir."

He reported to an area well to the rear, near the beach, in fact. A sergeant fresh out from the States was in charge of the boat team to which Kafak had been assigned.

"I'm Staley," he said. The sergeant looked at the orders Kafak handed him. Then he looked at Kafak. "You volunteered for this?" he said. He didn't sound like he believed it. He sounded like he thought Kafak was crazy.

At least, that's how it all sounded to Kafak.

Kafak shrugged.

"Sure," he said. "Why not?"

"You know what this is all about?"

"Not really, Sarge. What's up?"

"Some higher-up got the idea from the Russians. They do this on the Russian front, apparently. See those?" The sergeant pointed to what looked like a couple of water heaters that had been cut in half, lengthwise. They were chained together in a series of six rows of two each. A metal bar was welded to the two in each row, connecting them fast. "All of that is gonna get hooked up behind a tank. Then a guy climbs into every one of those sleds, and the tank takes them into battle. We're supposed to lead the attack when the breakout comes. It's such shit duty we can't get enough men for it. Hardly anybody's volunteering. So Command has ordered every unit to supply us with troops. They all got a quota. Well, you can guess the kind of guys they're throwing at us. All their green boys or the goldbricks or the guys they got no use for. It's not the best crew I've ever seen, I can tell you that."

Kafak eyed the sergeant.

"You're new to Anzio, ain't you?" he said.

The sergeant looked back at him.

"Yeah. So what?"

"If a guy ain't a goldbricker on this motherfucking beach, then he's already dead."

"That right?"

"That's right."

"Then why you volunteer, soldier?"

"Well," Kafak said, and smiled. "That's kind of a long story, Sarge."

"I got the time."

Kafak shrugged.

"All right, then." He threw a thumb over his shoulder. "Back when I was in North Africa, they needed volunteers for what they called a boat team. So I volunteered. What that was, that boat team, was loading barracks bags onto a boat for shipment to Italy. Easy duty, see. We spent the whole day loading that shit. It worked out for us, too, because the boat we otherwise would've been on got sunk. I'd've likely been killed if I'd've got on that boat. Instead, volunteering for the boat team saved my fucking life. So when they asked me to volunteer for this boat team, I remembered that and volunteered."

"Well, this boat team is more likely to kill you than save your ass, Private."

"I kinda see that now, Sarge, but I guess I'm too late."

Kafak turned away, but the sergeant called him back.

"By the way, what happened after that? With your boat team?"

"Well, that's another long story."

"I still got time."

"We stayed on the boat, it was a barge, supposed to take us somewhere, probably Italy. Used to ferry folks between North Africa and Marseilles before the war, I heard. Anyway, we shared it with a bunch of French native troops. These guys really knew how to go to war. They had their fucking women with 'em. The officer in charge, though, he told us not to even glance at those dames on account of these African troops would cut our throats. They were good with knives, and they didn't like nobody looking at their women, see. So we looked the other way and just went to sleep. It started raining, though, like hard, and it wouldn't stop, so we couldn't make the crossing. The next day they put us on a Liberty ship, and we started to head for Italy. Next thing we know, we get rammed by another Liberty ship. We had to go back to North Africa. We heard later that ship that rammed us? It was loaded with high explosives. Lucky for us, it didn't go up, right?"

"You seem to get a lot of luck, soldier."

"Sure," Kafak said. "That's why the fuck I'm on motherfucking Anzio."

Kafak figured it all balanced out, one way and another. He tried not to think about it. It was no good jinxing something like that.

"How long you been on Anzio?"

"Two months or more. You lose track of time when the days all run together in mud and shit."

"Yeah, I can understand that. Well, I'm glad to have someone like you aboard, a guy with your experience. I may be relying on your help."

Kafak shook his head.

"I'm a private," he said, "I just follow orders."

"You could be an NCO, Kafak."

"No thanks. I don't want the responsibility. See, I *like* being a private."

"Yeah? So what's that about?"

"The more responsibility a guy gets, the more he's got to do. The more a guy's got to do, the more he's got to run around. The more a guy runs around, the more likely he's gonna get his ass shot off. So, no thanks to the responsibility, Sarge."

"Right. Goldbricking, huh?"

"You just got here, Sergeant," Kafak said. "You can call it whatever the fuck you want."

Kafak walked away then.

They trained for the next three weeks with the boat sled teams. Getting into the sleds. Traveling behind the tanks. Jumping out once they reached a point of action. They used smoke created by huge smoke-fog generators to hide their training from the Germans. Once in a while, an artillery shell or two came close, but no one got hurt. Anzio Annie paid a call one day. It left all their ears ringing but didn't kill anyone. Kafak took a small piece of shrapnel in his wrist. It didn't mean anything. He got it disinfected and wrapped and went right on. One day General Clark and General Truscott and some other general Kafak didn't know came by to observe the training. See how things were coming along. They seemed impressed. To Kafak they did, anyway. But he figured you could never tell what a fucking general was thinking. They weren't to be trusted half the time. The other half of the time, you didn't want to listen to them at all, if you could help it.

One day they had a ball game, just to relax. The beach made running hard, but it was a good time. Kafak played first base and hit a double. His side won 6–5. That night, a bunch of the guys sat around in a pretty large dugout, eating and talking. They heated up their cans of rations with Sterno disks. These were pinkish-colored wax disks of flammable material. About the size of a silver dollar and a quarter-inch thick. You ignited them and they burned hard and fast for about five or six minutes. Just long enough to heat up a guy's field rations. Well, heat them up some, anyway. Kafak never used the disks at the front. He'd seen guys try to ignite them and next thing they knew they were shot by some German sniper. Or shot at, the very least. Kafak didn't care to be shot at any more than he had to be, so he never even bothered taking the chance with the disks up front. Back here, nearer the beach, he figured it was safer. German observers might see something, but they'd have to try and shell them, and Kafak didn't worry overmuch about that in the dugout.

"So since we're all gonna be dead soon," one guy, Kafak thought his name was Bielchuck but everyone called him Upchuck, was saying, "you guys been laid yet?" There were grunts all around from the other guys, but that didn't suit Upchuck. A guy could hide in a crowd of grunts like that. "How about you, Dash?" he asked Kafak directly. "You look like you're about sixteen going on forty. How old are you, anyhow?"

"I'm nineteen," Kafak said. "Though it ain't any of your fucking business."

"So you been laid? Or what?"

"That ain't none of your fucking business neither."

"Ha, ha! That means you ain't."

"Fuck you, Upchuck," Kafak said. He was smiling and shaking his head.

He'd been laid. Twice. Once when he'd been stationed at Fort Wolters in Texas. Right after basic, a bunch of the guys had taken him to a local whorehouse and got him initiated. It had been fine. The whore had taken extra good care of him because his buddies had told her he was a first-timer. The second time had been while he'd been stationed at Camp Shenango in Pennsylvania. That time had been miserable. He'd felt like one of the cars passing through the assembly line at Ford. It was in and out and over with before he could barely take a breath. Besides which, the whore had been ugly as shit. Kafak figured the first whore he'd been with had probably been ugly, too, but he could hardly remember what she looked like, so in his mind she had become beautiful. A whore with a heart of gold. Like some fucking storybook. He knew better; it was just something he liked to hold onto.

"Fuck you is right, Upchuck," Marshak told Bielchuck then. Marshak had received word from Kafak that Kafak had volunteered for the boat sled teams, so Marshak had joined him. "Dash just got back from fucking Naples. You think he didn't get laid in Naples? Everybody gets fucking laid in Naples."

"Not me," Kafak said. "They got VD there that'll kill you. Docs can't figure out how to cure it."

"Fucking sulfa cures the clap," Upchuck said.

"Not the Naples clap," Kafak said.

"That's bullshit."

"No, he's right," Marcowicz said. "I've heard that same shit. That Naples clap is hell on wheels, they say."

"Clap's the clap," Upchuck said, insisting on that fact.

A corporal named Higgins shook his head.

He said, "I was in the hospital there, and I was pretty well healed up so I helped out some for the docs, and I went into the VD tent over there. I saw this one guy had the clap so bad that the head of his cock was the size of a fucking lemon."

A couple guys whistled at that; a few others put down their food.

"Fuck," Marshak said.

Kafak said, "Holy shit."

And Upchuck said, "Bull-fucking-shit, Higgie."

"I'm telling you what I saw," Higgins said. "And you don't even wanna know what they were gonna do to that mother-fucker to fix him."

"No, we don't," Marshak said. And said it quickly.

"How'd we get on this shit, anyhow?" Upchuck said. "We were talking about getting laid. Let me tell you guys a story since you're all a bunch of fucking virgin motherfuckers anyway."

"Fuck you," several of the guys said at once.

Kafak just shook his head, and Marshak said, "Go on then, since you won't leave us alone until you do."

"See, there was this guy I knew," Upchuck said.

"It's always some guy somebody knew," Higgins said.

"Which means it was you," Kafak said to Upchuck.

"Fuck you guys," Upchuck said. "You gonna listen or you wanna tell the story?"

"Tell your fucking story," Marshak said, grinning.

Upchuck told them:

"This guy I knew, this was back in the States, we'd just got done with maneuvers for basic so we'd been out in the hills for a week, ten days or so. When we got back to base, we all got a twenty-four-hour ticket, so me and this guy, let's call him Stan, so me and Stan, we went into town for some R & R. Well, of course, we wanted to get laid, so we went to the local whorehouse. Only everyone from the goddamned camp was there before us and just back from a week in the wilderness and so they all wanted to get laid, too, so the place was too crowded for us to get in. We knocked on the door and that little window they always got slid open and the madam's face showed and she told us they were all filled up. Her name was Beulah, I think."

That drew a chorus of howls.

"Beulah, for Chrissakes," somebody said.

"What the fuck, Beulah?" Kafak said, and laughed.

"Who's telling the fucking story, goddamnit?" Upchuck said.

"Go on, go on," Marshak said.

Kafak looked at Marshak. He seemed to be really interested in Upchuck's story now. Kafak couldn't fathom it.

Upchuck went on:

"Anyway, Beulah told us all the girls were busy, to come back later. So Stan and I went across the street, had a beer, and then went back. But Beulah told us she was still busy so go have another beer and try again. We did that. We did that like five times and still none of the girls were available on account of the whorehouse was so busy. Now by this time, with about seven beers under our belts, we were getting a little woozy. Stan was getting crazy to get laid. He was so fucking horny, I thought he might start humping a telephone pole or something, he needed it so bad. So he went and begged Beulah to let us in, but she said she still didn't have any girls available. So, finally, seeing how bad off Stan was, she offered him something else. She told him she could see how hard up he was, and she could offer him something special she kept in the back room, just for emergencies such as this one. Stan asked what that was, and she told him if he really had to get laid, he could fuck Bubba in the back room."

Groans and hisses of disgust accompanied this. Upchuck waved them all down.

"I know, I know," he said, "and my pal Stan told Beulah the same thing. He told her, 'Now, Beulah, I don't go for that kind of crap. You're just gonna have to find me a gal.' Well, Beulah told us again there weren't any gals available so go have another beer and come back. Well, this happened a few more times, a few more beers, and by now Stan was pretty fucking drunk, see, and so that time when we went back and asked Beulah if she had any girls available and she told us no but she still could offer Bubba to Stan, Stan asked her, 'Well, if I took you up on this offer, even though I don't really go for that kind of crap, who would know about it?' So Beulah told him, 'Well, Stan, it would be just you, me, your pal there, Bubba, of course, and the six other guys.' Stan was upset with that. 'Six other guys?' he said. 'What the hell you mean, six other guys? What six other guys?' 'Well,' Beulah told him, 'the six other guys holding Bubba down. Cuz see, Bubba don't go for that kind of crap neither!'"

"Oh, fuck you," somebody said.

"You're so full of shit," somebody else said.

"You son of a bitch," Marshak told him.

Kafak guessed Marshak was hoping for a better story. One with more sex stuff in it.

Kafak said, "That's a load of horsecrap. A friend of mine stationed in England wrote and told me the same exact story happened there, except for the names."

"Naw," Upchuck said, "that ain't possible. This happened to my friend Stan. Out on the West Coast, back in the States. I was there with him."

"Bullshit," Higgins said. "I heard the same story in North Africa from a couple of guys."

"Well," Upchuck said, shaking his head, "I guess old Stan gets around, is all I can think."

During the extended training, Kafak had gathered quite a few weapons, picking them up here and there. At one point, he carried an M1, a Thompson which he'd been given by the tank commander for his squad of boats since the guy had an extra one, a Springfield .03 rifle for launching rifle grenades, two Molotov cocktails for attacking tanks, and four rifle grenades. When Sergeant Staley saw Kafak in his sled, he said, "How the hell did you get in there with all that stuff?"

"I just did," Kafak said.

"You really need all that shit, Kafak?"

"I like to be ready, Sarge."

"Well, you look more than ready now, Kafak."

"I feel good about it, Sarge."

"Christ," Staley said, and walked away.

A few nights later, a bunch of guys were resting in a dugout, falling off to sleep. One of them had a radio receiver. He had it tuned in to Axis Sally. Sometimes she was about all they could pick up on Anzio. Once in a while they could get an Armed Forces radio broadcast, something like that, but mostly it was Axis Sally. She played music they liked, trying to make them homesick. She told them stories about what their girls were doing back home, fucking the 4-Fs behind their backs while they were over here in Italy getting their asses shot off. None of it bothered Kafak. He didn't have a girl back home. This time, Axis Sally had a very personal message for the US troops.

"I hear you boys are planning on attacking our brave men with a bunch of toy sleds. Like little children. Sliding into your deaths. You're a great bunch of fools, if you try it. If you try something like that, you'll all be killed. Annihilated. Listen, though, we know it's not you, it's not the troops who have to actually do the fighting. This is not your idea. This is some fool general's idea. Someone who's never been shot at in his entire life. No, but he's willing to throw your lives away on a foolish plan like this. Battle sleds. That's funny, when you think about it. I laughed so hard when I first heard about it. You'd laugh, too, if you didn't have to be in those sleds. Instead, you won't be laughing. You'll be screaming in pain and terror as you all die."

It went something like that, anyway, best Kafak could make out. A hell of a thing.

"I thought this unit was supposed to be secret," Marshak said.

"Can't keep anything secret from the Krauts on this beach," Higgins said.

"Fucking Sally."

"She really knows how to hurt a guy."

"Well, it don't make anything worse for me," Marshak said. "I was already expecting it to go like shit, anyhow." A few of the other guys laughed and agreed. "What d'you think, Dash?" Marshak asked then.

"Fuck it," Kafak said, rolling over on the ground. "Don't mean nothing."

One night Staley came back from HQ and told all the men in his squad to report to the rear supply area for their PX ration.

"Shit," Marshak said, "that means we're going soon."

"The next day or so, I'd guess," Kafak said.

"Stuff the chatter," Staley said, walking past them.

Marshak glared after the sergeant and waited for him to get out of earshot and then said to Kafak, "I hate these guys just out from the States. That fucker's never been under live fire a minute of his life. And they put him in charge of us. We're gonna get fucked, Dash."

"Naw," Kafak said, looking after the departed Staley, "I figure he'll be all right."

"You like that guy?" Marshak sounded like he couldn't believe it, Kafak thought.

Kafak shrugged.

"Better than some second lieutenants I've known," he said.

"Well, hell," Marshak said, "anyone's better than a goddamned second lieutenant."

Down near the beach behind some headquarters buildings they received their PX rations. Beer, cigarettes, candy bars, and Barbasol shaving cream. Kafak took the stuff and walked off with the others.

"Hell of a lot of Barbasol on that beach," Marshak said.

"Enough for all Naples to shave for a year," Kafak said.

"They might as well. We sure as hell don't need to."

That night Kafak got himself ready. He cleaned and prepared his weapons. He was down to the tommy gun and the Springfield for the rifle grenades. He'd handed off the M1 to another guy who had busted the stock on his own. He drank the beer, smoked a couple of the cigarettes and stashed the rest away. He kept the candy. It was hard stuff, but it gave a guy a jolt of energy. All the troops knew when they were handed that candy that they were going into battle soon. Kafak figured it for the next day. Kafak left all his other gear behind. So did everybody else.

"Hell," he told a guy they all called Izzy, "you wanna supply an army, all you'd have to do is follow a unit going into battle."

"Sure," Izzy said. "Everything gets left behind."

"Except for the important shit," Kafak said, tapping his Thompson.

They moved up to relieve the Forty-Fifth Division. It had rained earlier in the morning, but the sun was shining now. It poured down on them, bright and warm. The Third Division band was playing "Dog Face Soldier."

"There's a hell of a thing," Kafak said to Marshak.

"What's that?" Marshak asked him.

"Such a beautiful day," Kafak said, peering up at the sky.

"Sure," Marshak said. He grunted. "A beautiful day to die," he said.

Kafak grinned at him. He slapped him on the back. He figured that was probably what all the guys were thinking.

"Move out," Staley said.

12

The battle sled team hurried up to wait.

It was May 23, 1944.

The first day of the Anzio Breakout.

They could hear the sounds of shells and scattered gunfire ahead of them. There'd been an intense artillery barrage earlier, prior to the attack. The sky was still dark at 0630 when the attack began, and the air was already suffused with the smoke and dust and smell of cordite from the thousands of shells that had been dropped. Kafak waited in a house near the front with the rest of the battle sled team. The tanks and sleds were camouflaged outside the house, nearby. Kafak glanced over at Staley. The sergeant looked calm enough for someone who'd never been in battle before. Kafak thought that a good sign. Then he figured it only meant Staley didn't yet know what he was in for. The lieutenant in charge of their team stood a few guys over. Kafak had never learned the lieutenant's name. He didn't figure he needed to know it. If the guy lasted any length of time, Kafak would learn his name then. In the meantime, why waste the effort.

"I thought we were supposed to headline this motherfucker," Marshak said.

"Thought so, too," Staley said.

"So what the fuck happened, Sarge? Why we sitting back here holding our dicks while they're fighting up there?"

Staley looked at Marshak.

"Never figured you for the blood-in-his-eyes type, Sleepy Ass," he said.

"I ain't. No, don't get me wrong, Sarge. I was only wondering, is all. I'm content to spend the entire war hanging around back here. You, Dash?"

"Hell, I just follow orders, Sleepy Ass."

"Fucking soldier."

Staley walked back to the company commander, held a short conversation. When he came back he said, "Some genius at HQ figured out it would be better if the division attacked, and when they hit a strong point, then we'd come up to break it."

"Sounds good to me," Marshak said. "Maybe they'll cut through the Krauts like a hot knife through warm butter and we won't have to see a single minute of action."

"Now you sound like the Marshak I'd expect."

"Hey, Sarge, we been here. We seen enough action to last a lifetime. Ain't that right, Dash?"

"We'll see," Kafak said.

They were ordered up around noon. All of them felt thankful for the hours of carnage they had been spared. A lot of guys had already been killed or wounded. Their reprieve was over with now, though.

Kafak hopped into his sled and waited. The tank finally started moving. He kept his head down. He was protected on the sides and front and rear. The top was wide open, though, leaving his back prey to any shell that might explode in a treetop. Or the shrapnel from a shell that hit the ground and that arced into his sled. As long as he kept his head down, though, Kafak felt pretty safe in the sled. Only he couldn't see where they were going. The tank kept moving, first up the road, then turning this way and that. Then it stopped. They'd hit some fossas they couldn't cross in the sleds.

"All right," Staley told them. "We've been ordered to abandon the sleds and move forward. Let's go, let's go, let's go!"

Kafak rolled out of his sled. He lay hugging the earth. Marshak crawled up right beside him.

"All those weeks training with these fucking things," he said, "and now we ain't even gonna use 'em."

"Fucking army," Kafak said.

"Get us killed, they're so fucking fucked up, these mother-fuckers."

"Fuckin-A right," Kafak said.

"Where the fuck are we, anyway?" Marshak said.

Kafak didn't know. All he could see was a field of what looked to be wheat. Kafak kept himself buried against the ground. German machine gun fire was snipping the shafts of wheat apart just above his head. He started to crawl forward. He could feel Marshak right behind him, crawling as well. Kafak suddenly stopped.

"Shit," he said.

"What?" Marshak said.

"We're in a fucking mine field," Kafak said. He pointed. "Look."

Wooden antipersonnel mines. The rain had run off the dirt around them so they were visible. That didn't mean they all were, though.

"We got to get the fuck out of here, Dash," Marshak said.

German artillery was zeroing in on the abandoned sleds. Mortars and 88s. They would be pounding them, slicing them to shreds soon. They couldn't stay out in the open ground where they were. Moving forward, though, held its own perils. Kafak didn't want to be blown to shit by a mine. He didn't mind getting killed so much. At least, he told himself so. Something fast and if he never knew what hit him, he thought that might be fine. Good enough, anyway. What he feared, though, was being wounded. Maimed, specifically. He didn't want to lose an arm or a leg or something else. He'd seen a picture once of a World War I vet, a French guy, he thought he remembered, and the guy had somehow lost his nose in the fighting. He had to wear a leather patch over the empty space where his nose should have been. It was just a hole there. Kafak didn't think he could live with something like that. A fucking hole in his face. No. No, he would rather just be dead.

He started crawling forward because there was nothing left to do. The Germans were marching their artillery fire toward his position. He couldn't see anyone else but Marshak right off to his side and slightly behind him. Letting him go first. My buddy, Kafak thought. Only he didn't hold it against Marshak either. He completely understood the thinking. He'd have done the same if Marshak had been in front to begin with. Kafak didn't know where he was, where they were. He knew where the front was, though. He could hear the fucking German MG42s spitting out their constant barrage.

Kafak just kept crawling forward. Looking for mines. Keeping his ass down as low as he could make it go. Until you heard a bonecutter slicing the air right above you, you didn't know what it meant to hug the ground, Kafak figured. He knew, though. He saw a few more of the treacherous mines that had been washed clear of the dirt. Those were the easy ones to avoid. He hoped he didn't come across any that were hidden. Kafak had slung the Springfield and carried the tommy gun. Mortars kept dropping and exploding but nothing too close, now he was moving. Kafak came out of the wheat field, and there was a patch of ruined ground, so he knew any mines that had been there had been blown already. Or mostly, anyhow. He leaped up into a running crouch and darted forward. He reached a drainage ditch and slid down into it. Kafak saw a group of US soldiers there, in the ditch, hunkered down. Their faces were grimed, and they had smoke and the acrid smell of gunpowder all over them. He knew he wouldn't smell that difference between them for very much longer since the same odor was beginning to cover him as well.

"Hey, Smitty," Kafak said, recognizing many of the faces. "Hey, Barstow. Guys," he nodded. "What're you doing here?"

One of the guys said, "We're all that's left of the Third Battalion of the Fifteenth, Dash."

That had been Kafak and Marshak's battalion; their regiment. Kafak and Marshak exchanged a look. If not for the sleds, they might not even be here now. Volunteering saved my ass again, Kafak thought, but he didn't say anything about it. That kind of thing caught up with you, he knew. He stopped thinking about all that.

"That's all?" Marshak said. "Just you fuckers?"

"It ain't been easy," another guy told them.

"Well," Marshak said, "we're here now."

"Good fucking luck with that," somebody said.

Marshak grinned.

"Hey, I'm just saying we're here to keep you company, Mac. I don't plan on winning the goddamned war for you, or anything."

Some guys laughed. It eased the tension in the ditch, but only a little. Kafak saw Staley slide down into the ditch further along. Some of the other guys from the sled team had arrived there as well. They had maybe a hundred guys or so in that ditch. Kafak wondered what they were supposed to do now. The ditch was taking heavy fire, though they were safe as long as they kept beneath its lip. Kafak watched as the company commander told Staley something. Staley frowned but then crawled up the side of the ditch facing the enemy position. He gingerly stuck his head up above the lip to see what they were facing. Kafak saw a flamethrower erupt. The fire shot forward, toward Staley. It fell a good ten or twenty feet short of him, but he ducked back down, quick. He wiped his face. He felt the heat, Kafak knew. He felt bad for Staley, hoped he'd survive. He was OK, Kafak thought. Kafak took his own peek then, just out of curiosity. He saw a terrain that had been wrecked by months of shelling. A broken farmhouse, some ruined trees. Pockmarked earth everywhere. He thought he saw the German position, a trench, maybe forty yards away.

A couple of slugs skidded in the dirt nearby. Kafak dropped back down. Quick.

"Curiosity satisfied?" Marshak said. His voice sounded mocking. He was hunkered down with no intention of moving.

"Sure," Kafak said. "Good enough for now."

"Just so you fucking remember what that fucking shit did to the goddamned cat, right."

"I'll keep it in mind."

Kafak waited for orders. He didn't intend to do anything until somebody in charge told him he had to. No use taking chances, he figured. He saw a guy he barely knew, one of the men from the battle sled team, push himself up over the edge of the ditch and begin crawling forward. Kafak figured he must have gotten orders to do it. No one would have done something like that without being told to. So Kafak followed him. He assumed they were moving forward, attacking the German position. He kept crawling along, firing his tommy gun at nobody, just trying to keep the Kraut heads down. Machine guns were firing, but the slugs were ripping the air above his head. Some splashed up dirt a few yards ahead of him. He heard Marshak yelling something, couldn't make it out. He kept crawling, fast as he could. He figured if he made it to the German ditch, he could stop those machine guns from rattling his ass. Of course, he'd have a whole different set of things to worry about then. Still, he kept going. Right behind the guy from the team. He figured everyone else was right behind him, but he didn't know. He couldn't take the time to look back. Forward, he thought, keep moving forward. He reached the German trench and poked his Thompson over the edge. Shot a burst. This section of the enemy position held no troops. He slid down into the ditch. Looked both ways. Every ten or fifteen feet, the trench made a turn. Germans could come at any time from either side. He'd lost sight of the other guy, the guy he had followed. Kafak crouched in the trench, catching his breath, keeping himself ready to fire in either direction. Long seconds crawled by and nothing happened. No Germans attacked. But then, no help arrived either. Where were the other guys, Kafak wondered. They should have been here, in the trench, with him, by now. He took a chance and looked back over the lip of the trench. The ground was empty. No one was coming. Kafak ducked back down. A tremor ran through him.

"What the fuck?" he said in a low mutter.

He kept looking for Germans to attack him. He wondered what he should do. Going back didn't seem a likely alternative. There was still gunfire coming from every direction, both from the Germans manning another trench line forty or fifty yards farther on as well as from his own fellows who were shooting toward the Germans. He'd stuck himself in the middle of a cross fire without realizing it. He thought about the guy who'd gotten him into all this. Where was that fucker now? What was he doing?

"Fuck me," Kafak said.

Out loud but in a hissed whisper.

Kafak thought he might wave to his own guys, let them know he was here in the German trench line and still alive. That might alert the Germans, though. They could converge on him. He'd be in the shit then. Hell, he was already in it, for that matter. Kafak heard some feet scrabbling in the dirt of the trench, off to his right. He swung the tommy gun in that direction. He plopped down on the ground. Flat. A guy came around the bend in the trench, firing a machine gun of his own. The slugs cut a line in the side of the trench, right where Kafak had just been standing, crouched and waiting. Kafak nearly pulled the trigger to fire back, but held up.

"I'm American," he said. Shouted. His voice raw and edged. "Stop fucking shooting at me, goddamnit!"

"Holy shit," Staley said. "How'd you get here, Kafak?"

"Same's you, I suppose," Kafak said.

He got back to his feet. That's the second son of a bitching GI's life I've saved, he thought. Maybe I am doing some good in this goddamn war. A couple more guys followed Staley into this section of the trench. There were five of them total now. Kafak felt better about things.

"You OK?" Staley asked. He sounded worried that he might've accidentally killed Kafak. It wouldn't be the first casualty of friendly fire in the war, nor the last.

"Yeah," Kafak said. "Thank God you shoot for shit."

Staley grinned.

"Thank God for small miracles," he said.

"Yeah." Kafak paused. He looked back over their shoulders. "Anything back that way?"

"It's all cleaned out," Staley said. He nodded behind Kafak. "What's there?"

"You got me," Kafak said. "I ain't looked yet."

"Well, let's take a gander now, shall we?"

"You're the boss, Sarge."

Kafak fell in with the rest of the guys, and Staley led them through a couple more turns. Staley shot a German in one of them, lacing the guy in the back with his tommy gun. They all passed the man by, and Kafak paused to make sure the soldier was dead and then plucked the soldier's Luger from him. He stuck it inside his field jacket. Lugers made the best souvenirs. He followed just in time to curl around another corner in the trench, right next to Staley and another guy. A German with a burp gun was there and fired at them. He fired too quickly, though, and his bullets all dug into the ground at their toes. Kafak opened fire with his Thompson. A reflex. Staley and the other guy pulled their triggers at the same time. Bullets went everywhere, a bunch of them kicking up dirt in front of the German, a bunch more pocking holes out of the sides of the trench to either hand of the German, and a bunch more stitching new lines into his chest and stomach. The German jerked around from the impact of the slugs that hit him, banging back against the side of the trench, and then just dropped straight to the ground once the bullets stopped hitting him and there was nothing left to hold him up.

"Fuck," Kafak said.

"Son of a bitch, that was too fucking close," the other guy said.

"Shit," Staley said, a mutter.

They moved forward again. Kafak noticed that Staley had searched the latest dead Kraut for a Luger. He figured Staley must've forgotten with the first guy he'd killed. Too much adrenaline or something. This time, though, he remembered. In the end, though, Staley passed on this German's pistol because it was covered and sticky with blood. One of the other guys didn't mind so much. He picked up the gun and wiped it clean on his pant leg, then tucked it into his belt. They crouched along, and more of their fellows were joining them now, sliding down into the trench, the American line moving forward. They came first in dribs and drabs and then, all of a sudden, a slew of guys dropped into the trench all at once, up and down the line. Staley gathered up all the men so they had some semblance of organization. A captain jumped down into the trench and took command. He led the entire group up over the top and on toward the next line of defense. They took heavy fire for a minute or so, then peppered the Germans with grenades and small arms fire, Thompsons, M1s, BARs. It took only maybe a minute and a half, and then they saw a Kraut raising his arms, holding up a white handkerchief. Dozens more hands followed in the same way. One of the Americans hollered something in German. It must have been an order to come on out because the Germans climbed out of the trench. The captain assigned Staley and some others to take the prisoners back behind the lines. Staley didn't take Kafak or Marshak with him.

"Fucking bastard," Marshak said. "We coulda been out of this shit, Dash."

"Well," Kafak said. "Staley is."

"Fucking Staley. A newbie like that and he's out after an hour or so. We've been in this fucking hell for months, and we get stuck with more of the same. Always more of the motherfucking same."

"Fucking soldiers, is what we are," Kafak said, and grinned.

"Aw, fuck you, Bobby," Marshak said, but he smiled back.

Kafak saw the captain speaking rapidly into the radio. Then he cleared the line and ordered the men to follow him. He led about fifty guys or so down the trench line, heading east, mostly. Marshak, always wanting to know what was happening, skittered up close to the officer and said, "What's going on, Cap? Where we headed?"

"There's a farmhouse near here. It's holding up the advance. We've been ordered to remove that obstacle."

"Attack a farmhouse, huh? A dug-in, fortified position." Marshak looked at Kafak and all he said was, "Fucking Staley."

Kafak heard the machine guns then. Sounded like maybe four or five of them, overlapping. And then he heard one of the worst sounds any GI could hear coming from a German position. The sound of their 20 mm gun. The 20 mm flak wagons. Machine guns sort of *rat-a-tat-tatted*, with just the smallest of pauses between shots. But the 20 mm, belt fed, fired so fast that it just sounded a *brrrrrrrrrt* because all the shots sounded as if rolled into one long shot. Every GI who'd ever heard one recognized the sound immediately. And hated it. The huge slugs were devastating. Kafak had seen guys torn up by them before. One guy took one of the bullets high in the bicep, and his entire arm went flying off behind him. The guy actually took a few more steps before he understood what had happened and fell to the ground screaming in horror and pain. Kafak didn't think he'd ever forget that. One of those 20 mms hit you in an arm or a leg, and you could count that limb gone, and gone for good. Hit you in the body full, you were just dead meat. Kafak had seen one guy who'd taken a 20 during the first assault on Cisterna. The soldier had been lying in a field as Kafak duckwalked past. The man had been hit in the belly. A hole the size of a fucking softball. Kafak could actually see the ground underneath the guy, through the hole. It had rattled him at the time.

"Fucking twenties," he said then to Marshak.

"Fucking Germans. They got more and better ways to kill a guy then anybody I know."

"Inventive sonsa bitches, you gotta give them that."

"I ain't ready to give 'em nothing but a bullet up the ass."

"Let's do that, then."

The farmhouse stood about twenty yards from the edge of the trench where the line drew nearest to it. That's where the captain set up for the assault. He pointed to five guys, including Kafak and Marshak. "You guys go left," he ordered them. "Flank that house."

The five men all nodded simultaneously and looked at one another.

"We go up together," Marshak said. "Right?"

"On three."

"Wait," Kafak said. "Let me shoot these first." He still had his rifle grenades. He unslung the Springfield and loaded it with the blank cartridge that would explode the rifle grenade out of the barrel without blowing it to hell at the end of the gun, sending Kafak and everyone near him straight to hell. Kafak rose up to fire over the lip of the trench, but German machine guns pushed him back down. "Shit," he said, "fuck." He held the gun just above the edge of the trench and fired it. "I hit anything?" he asked.

"What the fuck?" Marshak said. "None of us are gonna stick our asses up to take a look."

"Your grenade missed the house," the captain said. "Try looking when you aim."

"Try go fucking yourself," Kafak said, but under his breath so the captain couldn't hear.

Marshak heard, though, and said, "You got that one right on the money, partner."

Kafak grunted, then reloaded with a second grenade. He moved along the trench to his left, in case the Germans had zeroed in on his position. He took a deep breath, got himself ready. Then he popped up, placed the gun on the house, and fired. He jerked back down without getting shot at.

"That one was a hit, soldier. Good shooting," the captain said.

Kafak grunted to him, then said to Marshak, "Yeah, blow it out your ass, you asshole son of a bitch." Marshak laughed, and Kafak repeated the action with his last grenade, moving down the trench to a new firing position again. This one, too, hit the farmhouse. Kafak didn't know if any of them did any damage. Other guys were firing rifle grenades at the house as well, but there weren't that many guys who had the Springfields along with their main weapons. Only a handful besides Kafak. When he'd finished with the rifle grenades, he abandoned the Springfield in the trench. It was useless to him now. He looked at Marshak and the others. "OK," he said. "Now we can count this fucker off."

Marshak nodded, then counted it off, and they all sprang up over the edge of the trench. Marshak immediately flew backward, back down to the bottom of the ditch. Kafak slid back down after him.

"Marshak!" he said. "Marshak!"

Kafak tossed down his weapon and knelt on both knees beside Marshak. Marshak's helmet was gone. So was part of his head. He'd taken a slug from the 20 mm gun. It had split his head like a meat cleaver, had cut his skull wide open. Kafak stared at him, wide-eyed. He couldn't believe it, was the thing. All blood and brains and bone where once there had been a guy he knew. Kafak knelt there for what seemed a long time, hours maybe. But in only seconds a sergeant he didn't know came over and genuflected next to Kafak.

"That fella's bought it, soldier," he said to Kafak.

"What?" Kafak said.

"He a good friend of yours?"

"What?"

"This guy, he a friend of yours?"

Kafak paused. He frowned. He stared at Marshak. Then he shook his head and picked up his gun.

"Aw fuck," he said. "Fucking motherfucker."

Kafak stood up and vaulted over the lip of the trench and moved forward with about half a dozen other guys. He didn't know where they were going or what they'd been ordered to do. His first group was well out of sight by this time. He just followed these other guys and figured to do whatever it was they were supposed to do. After advancing about halfway to the farmhouse on their bellies, Kafak came to a tree with no leaves and only a few limbs. It had a nice thick trunk he could get behind, though. He rose up and peppered the farmhouse with his Thompson. He was screaming.

"Motherfuckingsonsofbitchfuckingbastardmotherfucking-cocksuckers!"

Guys around him were shouting as well. The same things. And all of them laying down a hard fire on the farmhouse. Tossing grenades. The Germans were giving as good as they were getting, but Kafak thought that at least a couple of the machine guns had been silenced. He still heard the hot sound of that 20 mm, though. Luckily, the 20 was firing at the trench line, trying to keep the rest of the Americans' heads down, keep them trapped in the trench, while the machine guns mowed down the troops who had made it closer to the house. Kafak saw a few potato mashers flying through the air as well. The Germans must have had a radio inside that building because, all of a sudden, mortar shells started dropping. A spotter was walking them toward the trench line. It was dangerous because one wrong shot could have hit the German position itself, but they were desperate and knew they'd eventually be overrun without the artillery support. This way, they might still be over-run but they'd take a hell of a lot of folks with them. And if the mortar fire became effective enough, they might halt the Americans in their tracks.

Kafak kept firing. It seemed hours. It definitely lasted at least a couple of minutes, which was a hell of a long time to be out here like he was, attacking a fortified position. Kafak was taking his chances all right. He didn't care. He couldn't think about anything but firing his gun. Not killing Germans, not taking the farmhouse, not staying alive. He thought about nothing but the mechanical act of firing his Thompson. He emptied two clips and had just put in a fresh one. He was still swearing, making up words as he went along. Just saying anything. Anything that came out. Because he wasn't actually thinking about it. It was all reflex. Training. He just fired. The third clip must have been halfway gone as well when Kafak felt something smash him in the back and send him flying. He thought someone had come up behind him and slammed him across the back with a baseball bat. Some good hitter at that, too. He lay on the ground, feeling dazed and woozy.

"What the fuck," he said. A whisper to himself. He tried to look around but found it difficult to move his head. He lay facedown in the dirt. For a while he couldn't hear anything, not even his own voice when he said, "What the fuck?" again, but he knew he had said it because he had said it and he could sort of hear it in his head, in his own mind, but not in his ears. Then, gradually, his hearing came back. Muted booms at first, as if he were listening from underwater. Then they grew more and more clear, well-defined. Pretty soon he heard them clearly, and then the small arms fire as well. The firefight, he understood, was still raging around him. He wondered what the hell had happened. He tried to look around again and did a little bet-ter this time. He saw his tommy gun. He'd dropped it when he catapulted through the air. It had leaped out of his hands and now lay maybe five yards away from him. He thought to crawl to it but couldn't get his legs to move. He tried to push himself up with his arms, but the abrupt pain of that movement made him woozy again, and he dropped back down flat on the ground, panting for breath, fighting to keep conscious. He felt someone beside him rather than saw them. He hoped it wasn't a German. Then he thought that was a stupid thing to think. Still, it might have been, he told himself. He felt hands on him, then a voice spoke.

"Lie still, buddy. You been hit. You with me?"

"I'm here," Kafak said. "But where the fuck are we?"

"You remember the farmhouse?" the guy asked.

"Sure," Kafak said. "How'd we do?"

The guy started doing something to Kafak, but Kafak couldn't really feel it, couldn't tell what was happening.

The guy said, "They're clearing out the farmhouse now."

"We took it?" Kafak asked.

"Yeah. A nice job, soldier."

"Sure," Kafak said. "We're making some fucking progress now, ain't we?"

The guy laughed, then said, "I'm going to give you morphine."

"Great," Kafak said.

"You're gonna be all right, soldier."

"Easy for you to say," Kafak said.

"Just stay with me, pal."

"Sure," Kafak said. "Why not?"

His eyes were closed; he felt immensely tired.

The guy told him, "You stay with me, you hear me, son?"

"You ever been dead?" Kafak said then.

"No," the guy told him, "and you ain't dying neither, soldier. That's a goddamned order."

"All right, then," Kafak said, a mumble.

He smiled.

And then he passed out.

13

Kafak once more awoke in a hospital bed.

He lay on his stomach, and his jaw hurt from the way it pressed against the mattress beneath him. He realized there was no pillow. That was the first thing he realized. The second thing was that he couldn't hear any bullets or bombs. He figured that meant he had to be somewhere safe or else in heaven. Or maybe hell. But no, he decided, hell would definitely have bullets and bombs going off. This had to be heaven.

"Well, welcome back to the living, Private," a voice said.

It was a female voice. Sounded like an angel's voice. Wait, though. She had said "the living" Kafak realized. That meant he wasn't dead, after all.

A sudden terror gripped him. He could barely keep his voice in check when he spoke.

He said, "Am I crippled? What the fuck? What the fuck's going on? Am I fucked up?"

The nurse made soothing sounds.

"Calm down, soldier," she said. "Calm down. You're all right. You're going to be just fine."

"You mean I'm alive, but that's not what I'm asking," Kafak said. His voice still rising despite his best intentions. "What I'm asking is, am I gonna be a cripple?"

"No, Private, no, you're not crippled. In fact, they'll probably send you back into combat in a few months' time."

Kafak paused, digesting this. It took him more than a couple of moments. He filtered her words through his brain. His thought processes seemed sluggish, tortuous. Finally, he thought he understood. If they would be able to send him back into combat in a couple of months, that meant there would be no lasting damage. He'd be all right. He was OK. He laughed. Out loud.

"Thank God," he said.

"Well," the nurse told him, "I've never heard of anyone being so happy to know that they were going to be sent back into combat."

"Sure, you don't understand," Kafak said.

"So tell me, soldier."

"It means I ain't dead," Kafak said.

"That's right," the nurse told him. "Otherwise, you couldn't be talking to me."

"Unless you were dead, too," Kafak said. He frowned, thinking this one over. Then he added, "Maybe. I'm not really sure how all that stuff would work."

The nurse laughed.

"Well," she said, "I'm not dead, Private. Leastwise, not the last time I checked."

"Good. That's good," Kafak said.

"Yes, I suppose it is. For the both of us."

"And that means, too," Kafak said, "that I ain't crippled up."

"No. You're not, soldier."

"Thank God," Kafak said again.

"You get some rest now. The doctor will want to take a look at you in a bit. OK?"

"Sure," Kafak said. "Sure thing."

Everything was all right now.

He fell asleep.

He woke when he felt hands pressing on his back. No pain, just pressure.

"Healing nicely," he heard a voice say.

This time a man's voice. The same female voice replied, though.

"I thought so, too."

"Hey," Kafak said, his own words still dripping sleep, "what's going on back there?"

The male chuckled, and the female said, "He's a lively one, Doctor. I've already found that out."

"Good," the doctor said. "That shows his wounds haven't affected him mentally." He came around to stand where Kafak could see him. "I'm Dr. Gibbs," he said. "I've been your surgeon, and I'm in charge of your case." He waved a hand to the woman standing beside him. Kafak thought the girl beautiful. And not just because she was female. And not just because they had earlier determined that she was alive and that meant Kafak was alive as well. She was truly beautiful. Like a movie actress or something. The girl that played the ingenue. That sort of looker. Kafak fell halfway in love right then. The doctor introduced her. "This is Nurse Madeline Sullivan. She's in charge of this ward, and I wouldn't advise crossing her."

"Make life tough for me," Sullivan said, "and I'll smack you across the back."

"See what I mean?" Gibbs said, laughing.

"I got wounded," Kafak said then. Remembered.

Gibbs stopped laughing.

"You did," he said. "Do you remember anything about it?"

"We were taking a farmhouse near Cisterna, during the Breakout," Kafak said. He frowned. "Something smacked me in the back." He stopped frowning and looked at Nurse Sullivan. "Was that you?" he said.

She laughed and the doctor laughed, too.

"I can't take credit for that one," Sullivan told Kafak. "But just wait until the next time."

"He is a lively one, isn't he?" Gibbs said.

"He's going to be just fine."

"You are," Gibbs told Kafak. "That's for sure."

"So how's it look?" Kafak asked. "For real, I mean."

"Well," Gibbs said, "you had a pretty big hole in your back. Shrapnel ripped you up pretty well. Most likely from a mortar shell. Could have been a couple of grenades as well. A pretty decent amount of shrapnel, though, so a pretty good explosion, I'd estimate. We had to remove the shrapnel, of course, and to do that, we had to cut away a good deal of your flesh at the site of the wound. A lot of that will grow back, but maybe not all of it. The muscles there were affected as well, but not so badly. All of that tissue will regenerate in time."

"And then I'll be ready to be sent back for combat duty, huh?" Kafak said. He looked at the nurse and smiled.

She smiled back. It beamed like a flare over a desolate landscape. Now he was all the way in love.

She looked at the doctor.

"I told him that when he was concerned he might have been negatively affected by the wound. It seemed the easiest and fastest way to alleviate his fears on that score."

"Really?" Gibbs said. He raised a brow. "Well, sending a guy back to combat hardly seems reassuring to me."

"It worked, though. Didn't it, soldier?"

"Yes, ma'am," Kafak said.

Gibbs laughed, said, "Well, good enough, then. You rest easy, soldier. Catch up on your sleep. I know you can use it."

"Sure can, Doc. Thanks a lot."

Gibbs smiled and patted Kafak, gently, on the shoulder.

"Certainly," he said.

He moved off, and Sullivan lingered behind just long enough to speak privately to Kafak.

"By the way, soldier," she said, leaning closer to his face so she could speak quietly, "I wouldn't want it to get around the ward, but it's not 'ma'am.' It's 'miss.'"

"OK," Kafak said, grinning like a damned fool.

She smiled back, then said, "Of course, it's First Lieutenant to you."

Kafak had been removed by the corpsmen to the aid station that had been set up for the Breakout. From there his wounds had been serious enough to have him evacuated to the 118th Station Hospital back in Naples.

Dr. Gibbs visited every day at first, then every couple of days as Kafak got better. Nurse Sullivan came by every day, sometimes more than once. Sometimes it was other nurses and she came only once. But she saw him every day. He checked to see if this was some kind of special treatment. He hoped it was. He saw soon enough it was just a matter of her dedication. She saw every one of the patients on her ward at least once each day. It was her ward, and she made sure to run it efficiently.

Radios played at the hospital during the afternoons and evenings. Not in the mornings or after ten at night, though. Those hours were for sleep. None of the guys seemed to have trouble sleeping through the music and news reports, though. Not here. Kafak surely didn't. He listened to the swing music that played. He especially liked the stuff that Benny Goodman and Glenn Miller and Louis Armstrong did. He heard on the radio that the Third Division had taken Cisterna the day after he'd been wounded. Two days to take that fucking town, he thought, once the Breakout started. And after all those months of stalemate. Mired in the mud and rain and fucking cold. And then—boom! Just like that. Well, it took a lot of men, a lot of casualties. Kafak himself could attest to that much. He could only shake his head over it all. He heard with the rest of the guys in the hospital when General Mark Clark marched into Rome on June 4, 1944. All the guys in the ward cheered. Kafak cheered right along with them. The Germans had declared Rome an open city, so Clark marching in wasn't as big a deal as it might have seemed. On the other hand, it was the first major Axis capital the Allies had taken. Everyone was arguing about who were the first guys into the city. Kafak thought that a stupid way to run a war.

Only it didn't surprise him any. One gung ho guy a few beds down from Kafak shouted, "On to Berlin!" Kafak recognized the guy. He'd been wounded in the first couple of hours of the Breakout. Hadn't been on Anzio much longer before that, either. Kafak offered no reaction to his shout. Some of the other guys cheered. A few others catcalled. Arguments started, though nobody got out of their beds. After about a minute of yelling back and forth, Kafak shouted.

He said, "Man on the end, let it go!"

That ended it. Everybody laughed.

Two days later, they heard about the invasion of northern France.

"This war will be over soon," Nurse Sullivan said to Kafak later. "Maybe you won't be going back into combat after all."

She smiled. Kafak shrugged.

"I feel pretty good," he said. "I don't figure you guys can keep me here much longer."

"Probably not," she said. "But a few more weeks, anyhow. Maybe that'll be enough to keep you out of combat. That's the talk in the officers' mess here, anyhow."

"From a lot of people who've never been in combat," Kafak said.

"And what does that mean?"

"Nothing," he said. "Nothing at all."

Kafak was still in the hospital on August 15 when the Third Division led the invasion of southern France. That news cheered him. He wondered if the war would truly be over before he was ready to go back. One part of him, maybe the largest part of him, if he were being honest with himself, hoped that it would be. He was sick of the mud and being shot at and the constant tension of being in a combat zone. Boredom and fear, in equal measures. Thinking nothing was ever going to happen and then everything happened. Knowing you could be picked off by a sniper at any second. Living through those barrages of explosions that shook the goddamned earth and rattled your fucking back teeth. Thinking they would never end. Praying just to get through it alive. To get through it without breaking, shattering your soul into a thousand little pieces you could never put back together again. No. He'd had enough of that to last him the rest of his life. On the other hand, there was another part of him that wanted to go back, that wanted to see his friends, wanted to support them, help them. Take what they were taking. Be by their sides when the shit went down. It was only right, he believed. That sort of thinking had been instilled in them all from almost the very first day of training, and it had all hit Kafak very deeply. He took it seriously. He genuinely believed in it. He didn't want to let his buddies down. He wouldn't. Not ever.

One time Nurse Sullivan found him wide awake about one in the morning.

"Can't sleep, soldier?" she said.

"Just thinking," he told her.

"Well, that's never good." She smiled. "Most soldiers use their time in the hospital to catch up on their sleep."

"I know," Kafak said. "I know it. In the foxholes, you're usually with just one other guy so you switch off, you know? Two hours on watch, two hours' sleep. But with all the shit going on and worrying about being shot at every fucking second, it's pretty hard to sleep at all, most times." Kafak paused, considering what he had just said. Then he realized something, and his face went red, and he looked to Nurse Sullivan and spoke quickly. "I'm sorry," he said.

"Sorry for what?" she asked.

"For swearing. It's just, it's gotten to be such a habit, you know."

"You don't have to apologize to me, Private. I've heard it all before. Believe me."

"I guess I probably swore some when I first came to, huh? I was pretty groggy then, though. Don't remember too much about anything."

"You were fine."

"You're pretty swell, Lieutenant," Kafak told her. "I'm going to ask the brass to give you a promotion."

She laughed. "Good luck with that," she said.

"Sure," Kafak said. "Sure thing."

"You probably went a long time without sleep when you were at the front, eh?"

"Yes, ma'am," Kafak said. "We all did. You just sort of got used to it." He paused, looking at her. Feeling suddenly stupid. "You know all this, though," he said to her. "I figure you've heard this stuff a million times from the guys here."

"Every soldier tells it a little different, even though it's always the same for all of them. I find it interesting. Every time."

"Sure. I guess so."

"Why is it you can't sleep now, soldier?"

"I think I've caught up on all the lost stuff."

"Then you ought to get ahead for when you go back into combat. You'll be sorry you didn't sleep more then, won't you?"

Kafak laughed.

"Probably," he said.

"Is that what's got you thinking?" she asked then. "Going back into combat?"

"Naw," Kafak said. "That don't bother me. I mean, not in the way you're thinking. Don't get me wrong, I'm not aching to get back, but I don't want to spend the war here while all my buddies are fighting, either. I need to go back and help, sure."

"So what is keeping you awake then?"

"Just thinking. That's all."

She paused, staring into his eyes. He could tell she wanted him to talk. Kafak didn't want to talk, though. Not about that. He'd been thinking about Marshak. About how Marshak had caught it. And about how Marshak had been there the whole time on Anzio until that day. It didn't seem right. That Marshak should catch one after all that time. It got so, after a while, when you didn't get your ass killed, you actually started thinking you wouldn't. That somehow you had figured it out. You knew how to survive this shit. You weren't going to get shot. It was always going to be the guy next to you, or somebody else, anyway. And then something like Marshak happened. And you understood that you didn't have anything, nothing at all, figured out because there was nothing to figure out, it was all just a matter of chance, bad luck, a random throw of the dice. Kafak wondered why Marshak, climbing out of that trench almost directly next to him, to Kafak, why that 20 had hit Marshak. And why not him? Why not Kafak? How did something like that happen? Who made those decisions? Why did Kafak have that luck, and not Marshak? Kafak had done nothing to deserve that luck. And Marshak had done nothing to deserve getting his head shot apart. Still, that's what had happened.

You couldn't figure it out, was the thing.

You only could accept it. Forget it. Move on.

Kafak tried to do that. He figured it didn't do anybody any good to spend too much time thinking about things like that. Not now, anyway. Maybe later. Sometime later. Only he couldn't see when.

He missed Marshak, and knew he would miss him for the rest of his life. But he wouldn't think about that either. He wouldn't allow himself to think about that.

"Well," Nurse Sullivan said after waiting Kafak out and finally realizing he wasn't going to say anything more, "if you ever want to talk about anything, Bobby, anything at all, you just give me a holler. OK?"

Kafak smiled at her.

"You're just swell," he told her. "I'll remember that."

A few days later, Sullivan asked him, "Why are you in this war, Bobby?"

Kafak knew she asked because of their earlier conversation. He grinned at her and said, "Don't ask me questions like that, Lieutenant, when I'm trying to sleep here."

She laughed, but she asked him again.

"Why are you in this war, Bob?"

"I got drafted," he said. He shrugged. "Why else?"

"You didn't try to get out of it? When you got drafted, I mean? I've seen your records, you know. I noticed a few things that might have gotten you out. Or at least stuck you to a desk somewhere."

Kafak frowned at her. He felt almost angry. But this was Nurse Sullivan. He couldn't really be angry at her.

He told her, "A guy doesn't do that."

"Plenty of guys did."

"That's for cowards. I ain't no coward."

"No, I can tell that."

He frowned again and shook his head, hard.

"Don't get me wrong," he told her. "I'm no hero. I keep my ass down. I turn down promotions on account of they get you killed. I'm not here to win any medals or win this fucking war single-handed. Pardon my French, ma'am."

"OK."

"But I ain't gonna shirk, neither. If some other guys wanna do that, let 'em. But I'm here to do my part, and I'm gonna do it. When they order me to, anyhow." He finished that with a smile.

Sullivan smiled back.

"You've got a few medals, though," she said. "So you must be more of a hero than you say."

"Aw, that's baloney," he told her. "Around Anzio, they give you medals if you survive. You outlive the other guys and you get medals and stripes. That ain't right. They shouldn't ought to do that, you know? It's all just dumb luck. That ain't nothing else."

"I think you're just being modest."

"Not me, ma'am. Got nothing to be modest about." Kafak paused, then he said, "There is one medal I'm proud of, though. Well, not really a medal. It's just a badge. The rifleman's badge."

Kafak nodded. "Yeah," he said. "Yeah. That one makes me pretty proud, all right."

Once, at three in the morning, when they had nothing left to really talk about, the guy in the next bed whispered across to Kafak.

"Can I ask you a question, pal?" he said.

Kafak looked over to him. They'd spoken about baseball and music and movie actresses and the progress of the war in general. And where they had served and a little of what they had seen. The guy had earlier told Kafak that he had been wounded at Cassino after only four days on the front line, and that straight out of the States. He said he was two months away from his nineteenth birthday. He looked like a kid, though. Then Kafak remembered that he was only nineteen himself. He felt sure he didn't look it, though. Not anymore. He often forgot entirely about it.

"Sure," Kafak said. "What's that, Billy?"

"How many guys you kill, Bob?"

Kafak was silent for a long moment. Long enough that Billy repeated the question.

Kafak said, "I don't know," finally, because Billy was insisting on an answer. "Maybe none," he said.

"Come on, Bobby," Billy said. "You were on Anzio for more than two months. You went on patrols, you fought in major battles, you were there, buddy, in the shit. You had to have killed a few Krauts. More than a few. So how many d'you think you killed?"

"I don't know."

"I wished I'd've killed a few Krauts before I got hit. They got me, but I don't think I got any of them. I wasn't around long enough. Never actually even seen a German. Just the bullets, you know?" Billy laughed. Then he stopped laughing. Then he said, "So, come on, Bobby, how many you kill?"

"I ain't killed nobody," Kafak said. The answer came firm and final and shut Billy up. After nearly a minute of silence between them, Kafak said, "But I know for a fact, I saved two guys' lives."

Kafak received his discharge. He was all healed up. There was a dent in his back where not all the flesh grew back. But he felt strong enough, the muscle having regenerated well. They told him he'd always have the pit in his back.

"You can prove you were in the shit," Billy told him.

"Don't need to prove something I already know," Kafak said.

He packed up. He carried his barracks bag and went looking to say good-bye. He found Nurse Sullivan first, and he told her so long, that he would miss her.

She said, "Just make sure we don't see you back here again, soldier."

Kafak grinned.

"Don't you like me?" he said.

"I like you fine. That's why I never want to see you again."

He wanted to hug her, but he didn't figure that was right. She was a lieutenant, after all.

Dr. Gibbs told him, "I spent a lot of hard work on you, Private. So make sure you don't waste it all by getting yourself killed."

"I'll do my best for you, Doc," Kafak said.

He went once more to the Bagnoli Repo Depo and got himself fixed up with new equipment, new uniforms. He was all set to go back. He told the officer there, "I won't go back unless you put me with the Fifteenth Regiment, Love Company. Sir."

Kafak was determined. One way or another, he was going back to his pals. And only there. He'd go to the brig otherwise, if he had to.

"You got buddies there, Private?" the officer asked.

"Yes, sir."

"Those boys are in the shit up there, you know. About to run up into the Siegfried Line."

"That's just it," Kafak said. "Those jokers probably need my help by now."

Kafak smiled, and the captain laughed and shook his head. "Careful what you ask for, Private, cuz you're liable to get it. The Fifteenth it is."

He stamped the papers and handed them over to Kafak.

Kafak felt good, pleased. Damned near happy.

Then he figured himself an idiot for feeling happy about something like this, and he stopped doing it. He still felt pleased, though.

Kafak was packed on board an LCI for the trip from Naples to Marseilles, France. It started out all right, but they ran into a storm, and the craft started tossing wildly in the sea. Everyone aboard got sicker than hell. Everything the soldiers could fill up with their vomit was filled up, then heaved over the side, then filled up all over again. The storm finally ended, then the sea ended, and then they were on land. They weren't in Marseilles long. The army moved them up by truck and rail to join the troops at the front. On the train, Kafak found a guy he'd been on Anzio with. Lester Carter from Alabama. Kafak liked him. He liked to hear Carter's stories about the farm he grew up on and hunting in the woods down south. Carter always used to tell him, "You oughtta come on down and see us after this shit, Dash."

And Kafak would always say, "Sure. Why not?" And nothing more.

Now Carter asked, "Where you comin' from, Dash?"

"Been in Naples, recuperating, Bama."

"Oh my shit. Me too."

Carter sounded surprised that they had been in Naples, both wounded, both recuperating, at the same time and hadn't run into one another until now, now that they were back heading for more fighting. Kafak didn't think it so odd. After all, there had been thousands of casualties during the Breakout, both the Anzio and Cassino sides. No surprise you couldn't find anyone in those crowds. The two traded information about their wounds, joking about them. They made the rest of the trip together. A third guy from Anzio hooked up with them as well, a guy named Bill Hastings. Kafak didn't know him as well, but he seemed all right and they got along pretty well the rest of the trip. Kafak knew he used to be a sergeant, though, and now he was a private, so Kafak wondered how he'd fucked up.

"Where you been, Coo?" Carter asked Hastings.

They called Hastings "Coo" as in "bill and coo," because he was a known womanizer, any chance he got.

"I been at the hospital," Hastings said.

"Us too," Carter said.

"When you get hit?" Kafak asked him.

"While I was in Naples," Hastings said. He smiled, sort of sheepish, Kafak thought. "I caught the VD from a whore there, even before I shipped to Anzio the first time."

No wonder he wasn't a sergeant anymore, Kafak thought.

"You fuckin' asshole," Carter said, laughing.

Hastings laughed, too.

"Fuckin-A right," he said, agreeing. "After we took Rome, I couldn't stand it no more, and they shipped me back to get fixed up. They took good care of me there, though. I'm good to go now."

"So they sent you back?" Kafak said.

"Sure, after they busted me. Probably woulda put me in the hoosegow except they'd rather have the fucking Krauts kill me off than have to feed me for doing nothing for a couple of years."

"Sure," Kafak said. "The Krauts take care of a lot of the army's problems, don't they, the fuckers."

"Fuckin' Krauts," Carter said, shaking his head.

"Fucking army," Hastings said.

They kept together as much as they could after that.

They passed by Montélimar, France, where the German army, retreating from southern France, had been caught nearly bumper-to-bumper on Route 7, the one main highway that led north from the Riviera. That had happened only a few days earlier, near the end of August. There were still bodies being removed. They hadn't even gotten to the equipment yet, the trucks and carriers and tanks and the rest that had been obliterated by the Third along with the Air Corps. There were supplies blown everywhere. Kafak saw more than a few dead horses, lying in the sun, bloating and stinking. The stench of burned human flesh still hung in the air, a choking miasma that overpowered even the cordite smell. Kafak gagged.

"That's the worst smell in the entire fucking world," he told Carter. "I don't think I'll ever get it out of my head, if I live to be a hundred."

"All them poor horses," Carter said. "Poor farmers coulda used them animals."

That came from living on a farm, Kafak thought. He hadn't really thought about the horses himself. Then he did, and he felt bad for them. At least the people killing each other had thought about it, had come here with varying degrees of willingness. The horses, they just got dragged into it. It wasn't their fault. They had nothing to do with it. Only they were just as dead. That didn't seem right to Kafak. Then he forgot about the horses; there was nothing he could do about the goddamn horses.

Most of the French towns they passed through greeted them with cheers and waves. The French were thrilled to have the Allied troops there, liberating them from the German yoke they had been under for four long years. When they were marching through some of the places, a few of the girls would run up and kiss the GIs. Usually on the cheek. Hastings would always try to French them. "Well, we're in fucking France, ain't we?" he'd say. One really pretty girl had approached Kafak in one village, and he had kissed her pretty good. She reminded him a little of Nurse Sullivan, and that was why he really let himself go to town with the girl. She seemed to like it. An older man from the village had had to pull her away from Kafak. He was laughing about it, though. The girl made Kafak think more about Nurse Sullivan. He wished now he had hugged her. If he ever saw her again, he swore to himself he would hug her for sure that time. Except he didn't much expect there would be that next time. What were the chances, after all? In the middle of a fucking war? It was a nice thing to think about, though. One village they passed through didn't cheer for them. The officer leading them back to the front told them that a lot of people had been killed there by a bombing that shouldn't have happened. An American bombing. The people held it against all Americans now. The villagers slammed their doors, barred their windows. Those that did remain on the streets as the American troops marched by either showered them with sullen looks or spit on the cobblestones. Kafak figured he understood it well enough. He'd be pretty upset just like these folks if someone had bombed his friends and neighbors. Still, it rankled a little, too. Because he knew they would never have been allowed to look at the Germans that way, act that way toward the Krauts. The Germans would have killed them for shit like that. We just let it go. They ought to realize at least that much is different, Kafak figured. The new guys marching and riding in the trucks with them had a lot of questions. About combat. About the Germans. About what to do and what not to do. Some of the veterans had plenty to say. Lots of advice. Kafak thought some of it was even good. He didn't offer much himself. He wondered how you advised a guy to be lucky. Because that was the thing of it, he'd concluded. Since he didn't know how to do that, he pretty much kept his mouth shut. One guy who wouldn't let up, though, he did tell him, "Keep your ass down and you'll be a goddamned veteran before you fucking know it."

That was the extent of what he had to offer.

They finally reached the Third near Lyon. They made silk there. They were famous for it, apparently. It was like that, though. Half the time you never knew where the fuck you were. You just followed the guy in front of you. Kafak didn't know the names of half these villages and towns, and he pretty much forgot the names of half the rest. Only occasionally did a name or a place stick in his mind. Like Montélimar. Because of all those dead Germans. And that overpowering odor of burned human flesh. That one he would always remember, he knew.

He and Carter reported to L Company together. Captain Cole was there to take their papers. He grinned when he saw them.

"You guys finally decided to stop goldbricking in Naples and join back up with the fighting men, huh?" he said.

"I tried to stay, but the nurses kicked me out," Kafak said.

Cole laughed, and Carter said, "I couldn't wait to get on outta there, Cap. The food was so good I was gettin' fat."

"And he didn't want to get too fat on account of he knew he couldn't run fast enough when the Germans started shooting at him again."

"That comin' from you, *Dash*," Carter said.

"That's why I didn't get fat," Kafak said.

"Well," Cole told them, "I guess I'm glad to see you two clowns." Then he said, "How you boys feeling, though? For real? You OK?"

"Good as new, Cap," Kafak said.

"Ready for anythin'," Carter said.

"Good, good," Cole told them. "So far this fight in France has been pretty much hurrying to keep up with the German army. They've been retreating so fast, we can barely follow them. Once in a while, though, they turn and fight, and we have to be ready for that. That's what I'm going to need you guys for. I'm desperate for good experienced soldiers like yourselves. We've got a lot of green boys with us now. They learn fast—"

"—Or they get killed fast," Kafak said.

"Right," Cole said, nodding. "Right. Anyhow, I can use all the experienced men I can get. I'll need you guys to be scouts for me. Feel things out so we know when the Krauts plan on making a stand. That sound all right?"

"Sure thing," Carter said. "Be just like huntin' in the woods back home."

"Why not?" Kafak said.

And that was how he became a scout.

14

The next night, Cole sent Kafak out on a night scout. To find Germans. See if they were just retreating or had left anyone behind for a rearguard action or if they had stopped and turned and were preparing for all-out battle. They hadn't reached the Siegfried Line yet, but they would be coming to it within weeks, maybe even days, depending on the German resistance. Kafak patrolled for three hours. He didn't see any Germans at first. He found some discarded equipment. Ration tins, broken weapons, one truck with a busted engine. All left behind. The evidence of a fast-retreating army. On his way back in, Kafak ran across a squad of Krauts. They were sneaking around the woods, not far from the American lines. Kafak steered clear of them, returned, and reported to Cole.

"Shit," Cole told him when Kafak reported about the German squad lurking nearby. "We can't have that. We've been getting a lot of infiltrators. They're trying to slow us up so the main body of German troops has more time to retreat."

"These guys didn't look like they could do too much damage, Cap. They didn't have any heavy weapons. No mortar. Not even a machine gun."

"An assault squad. All burp guns and hand grenades, yeah?"

"Pretty much. Yeah."

Cole frowned, looked around at the men, told a sergeant to wake them up. Cole turned back to Kafak.

"Figure you can find those Krauts again if you had to?"

"Could. Don't want to."

"Well, you're going to have to," Cole said. "Take Bama and Coo and a couple of the new guys. They could use the experience."

Kafak swallowed anything he might have said. Then he looked at the men still dropping the sleep from their eyes.

"Any volunteers?" he asked. These guys might have been new, Kafak thought, but they'd already learned the rule about never volunteering for anything. A rule Kafak didn't share, of course, and that had served him well some times and not so well others. He looked back at Cole. "No volunteers, Cap. You're gonna have to order somebody to go."

"Hell," Cole said, "you order them."

"I'm just a private."

"Not anymore. You're sergeant now. Acting until I can get the paperwork through to make it official."

"Aw, hell with that, Cap. I don't wanna be no sergeant."

"Not your choice, Kafak."

Kafak looked around, scowling. He waved toward Hastings then.

"Why don't you make Coo the sergeant, Cap? He's been one before. He's pretty fucking good at it."

"Thanks, Dash," Hastings said, smiling.

"Oh my shit, boy," Carter told Hastings. "He's only sayin' that to get out of it hisself."

"Well damn. That true, Dash?" Hastings asked.

"I'd say anything to get out of a promotion," Kafak said.

"Well, nothing you say is going to work, Kafak. I can't make Hastings sergeant if I wanted to because he's been busted for disciplinary reasons. There's no way. You're acting sergeant. Pick a couple of the greens and get moving. Wipe out that squad of Jerries. Got it?"

Kafak sighed.

"Yes, sir," he said.

Cole started off, then turned back.

"Oh, and one other thing," he told Kafak.

"Sir?"

"Congratulations."

"Aww, hell."

"And sorry, Dash."

Cole grinned, and Kafak cursed under his breath. He hated being a sergeant, hated having to give orders. Now he not only had to look out for his own ass but for four other guys' asses as well. It was too much responsibility, he thought. He didn't want it. He would get rid of it. He vowed he would. He kept in mind what Cole had said about Hastings being busted so that now the captain couldn't promote him back to sergeant.

"That's what I'm gonna do," Kafak said to Carter as they got their gear together.

"What's that, Dash?"

"I'm gonna get busted so I can't be no fucking sergeant no more."

"I'd be sergeant," Carter said. "I don't get it why you don't wanna be, Dash."

Kafak looked at Carter and shook his head.

"You dumb country boy," he told Carter. "You'll get your fucking ass shot off yet."

Carter shrugged.

"Did anyway, and I was only a private. Same for you, I remember correctly."

"You don't—" Kafak began, then shut up because he realized there was no arguing with Carter's logic.

They moved off through the night, carrying only their weapons. They left behind everything that might make noise. Just the way they'd learned it on Anzio. A good moon hung high above them, so they could see well enough. Of course, that meant the Germans could, too. Kafak led the group back to where he'd last seen the Germans. They weren't there any longer. He wondered which way they had gone. He asked Carter and Hastings what they thought.

Hastings said, "I think we ought to go back and tell Cole we lost 'em. Fuck it."

"Naw," Kafak said, thinking on that. "He wanted us to find them pretty bad."

"So when you go back and say you couldn't, maybe he'll bust you."

"I would if I thought that'd work. But he won't bust me. He'll just send me back out again."

"Yeah, you're probably right."

"I see some tracks headin' thataway," Carter told Kafak.

"'Thataway,' huh?" Hastings said. He grinned in the dark.

"Shut the fuck up, Coo," Carter said. "I seen 'em, City Boy, you fuckin' didn't."

Hastings only laughed, and Kafak said, "Let's go, then."

They followed some tracks and some roughed-up undergrowth that showed signs it had been trampled through. Soon enough they heard voices, low murmurs. German. Kafak signaled for everyone to get down and hold their positions. He moved forward to get a better look at the Krauts. They were sitting in a circle, back to back, resting and waiting for the American advance. They would look to ambush some guys; maybe pick off some stragglers. Anything to disrupt the advance. Kafak figured it that way, anyhow. He crept back to his comrades and whispered the situation. He sent Carter and Hastings around to the other side of the little clearing in which the Germans had hunkered down. He kept the new guys closer to himself but sent them off to either flank. He'd told them all not to fire until he did.

When he'd given everyone enough time to get into place, Kafak hollered to the Germans.

"You're surrounded! Surrender!"

They looked startled. Kafak lay close enough in the encircling brush to see their faces clearly. They darted glances at one another. He could see their eyes asking each other what they should do. Two of them started putting down their guns, and then a third guy opened up. He fired toward Kafak's position, and Kafak bit at the ground in front of him. The bullets whipped by, slicing leaves and limbs from trees a few feet above him. That started off Hastings and Carter. They fired into the clearing. The Germans started dancing. Kafak raised his head and fired a couple of bursts from his tommy gun. That got the new guys firing as well. Pretty soon the forest was filled with racket. Gunshots ripping through the night. It lasted about forty, forty-five seconds. Then it was done. Three of the Germans were dead; the other two were wounded. The Americans took them prisoner. One of the Krauts could walk all right, so Kafak had Carter keep him covered. The other guy was shot up pretty bad, so Kafak ordered the two new guys to help him. The German threw an arm across each of their shoulders, and they dragged him along between them. That was how they came back to their own camp.

Cole was happy he had prisoners for G-2 to interrogate. He congratulated Kafak on the successful mission.

"I knew I made the right choice," he said, grinning at Kafak.

"I still don't wanna be no sergeant," Kafak said. "Bama wants to. Make him fucking sergeant."

"Not a democracy here, Dash," Cole said.

Then he laughed and took the prisoners away.

There were a lot more buildings around, here in France, than there had been in Italy, at Anzio, where the shelling from both the Allies and Germans had laid waste to just about everything that stood between them. Kafak bunked down in an old barn. It smelled of sour hay and horse manure, but it was out of the weather. It was the very first days of September and already cooling, especially at night. No rain, though, and that was a blessing to Kafak. Some of the newer guys complained about the stink of the old shit in the barn. It had to be old because all the animals that had been in the barn were gone. Confiscated by the Germans. Carter said he liked the odor.

"That smell sure do remind me of home," Carter said.

"What?" Kafak said. "The horse shit?"

"That manure smell, yessir."

"What the hell?" Kafak said. "Maybe I won't come visit you, after all."

"You come see me," Carter told him, "you'll get used to it. You'll see."

"I don't figure I want to get used to it," Kafak said.

"Aw, this ain't so bad," Carter told him.

"Better than Anzio," Kafak said.

"Sure is," Carter said. "But what the fuck ain't?"

"Fuckin-A right," Kafak said.

The next couple of days there were more scouts. Kafak came up with nothing. He didn't shirk; he tried his best. Still, he found nothing. And he was glad of that, especially when he had men with him. Men for whom he was responsible. He hated that idea. He didn't want anyone killed because of him. The Allied troops moved forward. The Fifteenth was held in reserve for a lot of the time during that march, and that was good duty. Kafak liked it. You could relax a little more knowing there was nobody close enough to shoot at you. Still, you always had to be careful. Krauts might slip through. Try to pick you off. Just like the guys he had found that first night out. And then, during the patrols, the tension always ran real high. Still, it was not as bad as Anzio had been. But what the fuck was? to paraphrase Carter, Kafak thought.

Then they came to Besançon. They marched all day and marched through the night as well. They had marched for twenty-four hours so that they could block the roads south of the city. The Germans had decided to hole up there. One of the places they would make a stand. The Germans figured it for a good defensive position. There were a series of forts there that had been built back in the seventeenth century to protect the town. The biggest was one called the Citadelle. The Americans were ordered to take it.

Constant fire from small arms as well as machine guns, 20 mm flak wagons, and tanks beat at the Americans as they dug in and moved to take as much high ground as they could. Allied tank guns did little to disturb the walls of the various forts. Kafak watched as they brought up the 105 mm and 155 mm guns. Just pointing those big weapons at some of the smaller forts disheartened the enemy there. But the Germans in the Citadelle kept fighting. At the Citadelle, the guns fired at the three-foot-thick walls and exploded harmlessly. They did no real damage at all. Kafak shook his head and whistled.

"They're practically bouncing off the motherfucker," Hastings said.

Carter said, "Oh my shit. And we supposeta take that fucker?"

"That's the orders," Kafak said.

"And you know," Hastings said, "if the artillery can't do it, it always ends up in the hands of the fucking infantry."

"Which only goes to show," Kafak said, "we joined the wrong fucking part of this goddamned army."

"Oh my shit, yes," Carter said.

All three regiments of the Third Division, the Seventh, the Fifteenth, and the Thirtieth, were used in the attack against the Citadelle at Besançon. The assault began on September 4. Kafak thought it might be an interesting thing to attack the fortress, just like some medieval knight or something. Stupid, but interesting. In the event, he never did. Cole came to the men and told them, "We've been ordered to relieve elements of the Seventh Regiment at the Avanne Bridge. It's an important bridge because it's the only crossing left to us over the Doubs. We've been ordered to hold it at all costs."

Kafak exchanged glances with Carter and Hastings. They all knew what "at all costs" meant. None of them liked the idea. They'd do it, though. Because that's what you did.

Before seven they were moving toward the bridge. They held it for that first day of the assault and suffered little action. Random shelling kept them on the alert. No time to relax.

Anything could happen. They watched the fight progress, saw the US troops make gains. The next day they rejoined the rest of the Fifteenth and fought northward, closing in on the city. Kafak was under constant fire as he moved forward with Carter and Hastings nearby. Intense firefights broke out. Mortar fire helped the advance. Kafak didn't see any Germans, but he knew they were there from all the shit that they were firing at him. He kept his head and his ass down as much as he could. He'd been assigned to lead a squad in the assault, and he kept them moving forward as much as possible. He found he was running sideways, between his men, as much as he was going forward, and that was no good thing. It only gave the enemy more chances to hit him. He knew it, but he couldn't do anything about it. He cursed Cole as he ran. He cursed being a sergeant. He cursed the fucking Germans for shooting at him. The company eventually moved the enemy off the high ground and took it for themselves. Kafak ran past a lot of dead Germans as the squad advanced. He wondered if he had been the one that killed any of them. He didn't know, would never know. Not for certain. And that suited him just fine. They were ordered to hold it through the night. Although they took tank and mortar fire and some flak wagon barrages, the Germans didn't counterattack. Kafak wondered if they had the manpower left for it. The next day, troops from the Third overran the fortress and poured into the Citadelle. They took some two hundred prisoners in the aged fort. Some of those told the Americans that, while the guns didn't bust through the fort's walls, seeing those big guns aimed directly at them sure as hell fucked with them psychologically.

"Well, they were good for something, then," Hastings said.

"Yeah, just not much," Kafak said.

"We aren't done yet, boys," Cole told them all. "We've still got to take the city itself."

That attack began at 2000 hours. By 2130, L Company had come to the railway station, where they met stiff resistance.

Kafak got his men down behind a stack of trestles intended for track repair. The rest of the company had pretty much surrounded the buildings. They put heavy fire on the station house but couldn't dislodge the Germans. The firefight blasted through the night. Kafak tried to move up to a closer position behind some benches. He felt something kick him in the shin as he ran, and he fell midstride, rolling. He rolled all the way to one of the overturned benches and ducked behind it. He looked down. He'd been shot in the leg.

"Shit and goddamn," he said.

"You awright there, Dash?" Carter called out.

"Yeah, fucking hit in the fucking leg," Kafak said.

"Bad?"

Kafak looked at it. He cleaned it and dressed it.

"Nothing but a graze," he said.

The force of it had been something, though. Knocking him down like that. He was only glad it hadn't hit him full. And that it was just a burp gun bullet. Not a 20 mm. Or a machine gun. Kafak rose up to fire over the edge of the bench, but slugs smashed all around him and he hunkered back down.

"You under some heavy fire there, Dash," Carter said. "You want us come fetch you?"

"No. You guys stay there and keep your asses down. I'll figure something out."

"You'd best stay put a while."

"You bet your ass," Kafak said.

"Grand being a sergeant, ain't it, Sarge?" Hastings said.

"Fuck you too," Kafak said.

He could hear Hastings laughing and, despite himself, he laughed as well. He wondered what the fuck he was thinking. Then he thought he had to get out of this being a sergeant business. It was no good for his life expectancy. He really didn't much like it. He waited there, thinking about all these things, for a couple of hours. He didn't shoot anymore at the Germans. He wanted them to think he was dead. Or too wounded to fight, at any rate. So they would stop firing at him. At first it didn't work out very well. They kept pouring small arms fire his way. After about fifteen minutes, though, they stopped. Then they'd just throw a little gunfire at his position every so often, to let him know they remembered him. He waited them out. When they finally gave up firing toward him and hadn't shot at him at all for more than forty-five minutes, Kafak figured it was time to try to get back to his men. He didn't much like being hung out to dry all by himself here. He wondered again what had gone through his head that had made him try to approach more closely. Then he recalled. He had thought to flank the station. A one-man flanking action. That certainly wasn't going to do much good. "Shit," he said, but he muttered it very quietly. There was enough gunfire going on that nobody heard him but himself. "Fucking hero," he said. He sounded disgusted with himself. He thought he might be able to hit the station with a grenade from where he lay. His arm was good enough. He could do it. He felt fairly convinced. Still, he didn't throw any. It would have alerted the Germans he was still alive, and they would've pinned him down even longer. He didn't figure the grenades would've done much good anyhow. The place was fairly well buttoned up. He'd have to make a perfect throw through a small gap left in a window opening. The potential gain didn't measure up to the risk. At 0030 hours he made his go to get back to Carter and Hastings. He used the duckwalk for a bit, and it worked, but then some son of a bitch Kraut saw him and fired his way. The bullets flew over his head but forced him to bite the cobblestones. He crawled the rest of the way, skinning his knees pretty good on the harsh stones of the platform. He circled around the ties and collapsed in a heap against them, breathing heavily.

"Hell of a show you put on," Hastings said.

"You crawl near fast as you can run, Dash," Carter said.

They both laughed at his expense.

"Yeah, you fuckers," Kafak said. "I'm sending you bastards next time."

"Oh my shit, no. That sort of shit is for sergeants to do."

"The privilege of rank," Hastings said.

"That's right," Carter said. "A man can't follow where another don't lead."

"I already led."

"And now you're back," Hastings said.

"Shit," Kafak said, shaking his head. "I ain't cut out for this sergeant shit."

"Tell you a secret," Hastings said. He grinned. "Neither was I."

"What you need to do," Carter said to Kafak, "is find you a nice little Frenchie gal and catch the VD from her."

"Sure," Hastings said. "That'll fix you."

"Hell with that," Kafak told them. "The Germans'll go away eventually. The clap don't ever."

"Aw fuck," Hastings said. "Why you got to go and remind me of something like that?"

"Serves you right, you bastard," Kafak told him. "I wouldn't be sergeant now if it weren't for you fucking around."

Carter laughed. That time, Hastings didn't.

The firefight continued through the night. Sometimes it grew more heated. Other times it seemed to die down altogether so that somebody from the company thought to try what Kafak had done, and then the Germans erupted in a new barrage of blasting fire.

"Oh my shit," Carter said, "we gonna spend the rest of the war here, looks like."

"Naw," Kafak said, "come light, Captain'll get a tank up here. Blow that railway station to shit and back."

"He oughtta send somebody now, while it's dark enough for them to get away."

"He already did. I saw the guy go," Kafak said.

"Well, that's good," Carter said.

"You got places to go, or what, Bama?" Hastings said.

"Sure," Carter told him. "I heard about this nice little French whorehouse they got in Besançon. All we got to do is get the Germans outta there."

"Really?" Hastings said. Kafak thought he had to know that Carter was ribbing him, digging it in about Hastings's VD, but Hastings either didn't realize it or was so overcome by hope that there really was a whorehouse that he didn't care about the teasing. Either way, he wanted to know what Carter knew. He said, "Where is this place? What'd you hear?"

"Jesus, Coo," Kafak said. "How many doses of the clap you gotta get before you give it up?"

"Can't never get enough, Dash. Cuz they always clap when old Coo gets through with them."

"You mean, they always have the clap when old Coo gets through with them."

"Hell, that's their lookout."

"You a sick, sick fella, Coo," Carter said.

"Hey, I've got to get me a French gal," Hastings said. "I've had American girls back home, of course, and I had me a couple of girls in North Africa, and then a few more in Italy. Now, I got to get me a French girl."

"You a real world traveler, all right," Carter said.

"Then I have to get me a German girl, once we get into Germany."

"Yeah, you and Eva Braun," Kafak said.

"Who's she?"

"That's Hitler's girlfriend, dumbass," Carter said.

"Well shit," Hastings said. "I wouldn't have nothing to do with her. You'd likely catch something worse than the clap from fucking where Hitler's been."

"Why hell, Coo, I never knew you had a line you wouldn't cross."

"Tell you the truth, Bama, I didn't know either till you brought that shit up."

"Oh my shit, boy. You is really something, all right."

"You're so fucked up, Coo," Kafak said, and laughed. "Shoot your fucking gun instead of your dick for a change, why don't you?"

They all did.

It went like that for the rest of the night. With morning came K Company to assist them, and Love Company was able to fall back.

"We gonna get some rest now, Cap?" Carter said.

"No," Cole told them. "We've been assigned to clear out any pockets of resistance we can find left in the city."

"Like we did at the railway station?" Kafak said.

But only Carter and Hastings heard him. They all laughed. That hadn't gone so well. They could only hope any other "pockets of resistance" wouldn't hold them up for so long.

L Company moved through the streets of Besançon, looking for Germans.

"How we supposed to know where they at?" Carter said.

"We'll know when they start shooting at our asses," Hastings told him.

"Oh my shit, that ain't no decent way to go about the thing."

"No," Kafak said, "but it's the army way."

"Fuckin' army," Carter said.

"Fuckin-A right," Hastings said.

They moved along the streets. A shot would ring out and maybe somebody would fall and maybe nobody would, and they'd all duck into doorways and behind walls. Anything they could find for cover. Someone would locate the shooter. They'd bring up a tank if they could, and if they couldn't they would just pour fire on the location while some others would flank the sniper until the guy either surrendered or was shot up out of commission. Sometimes wounded; more oftentimes killed. Twice Kafak had to climb up to third stories of houses to see if a Kraut was actually dead or just playing dead. It was dangerous duty, tense. It could always be an ambush, after

all. Once Carter went with him, and once Hastings did. Each
time the one who went volunteered to back him up. Kafak
appreciated it. He didn't say anything to them about it because
you didn't do something like that, but he appreciated it and
he knew they knew he did. Both times, Kafak flung himself
through the door firing his tommy all the way. Both times he
stitched the German in the room. Each time he felt certain the
guy was already dead before he got there. Because if the German hadn't been, he would've fired at Kafak. That's how Kafak
thought about it, anyway. By the end of the day, the Germans
had either all been removed or had disappeared of themselves.
Besançon was finished.

It was still light out, and the people of Besançon poured into
the streets. Some of the girls wanted to kiss them. They didn't
argue about it. Hastings disappeared, and Kafak said to Carter,
"Well, I guess Hastings managed to find a French conquest."

"That old hound dog," Carter said.

Kafak smiled.

"Can you just imagine a Hastings Junior in every fucking
country in fucking Europe?"

"Oh my shit," Carter said. "That'd be a fuckin' disaster."

"Yeah," Kafak said. "For fucking Europe."

Carter shook his head.

"Well," he said. "Leastways, now I know what we fightin'
this fuckin' war for."

"Good a reason as any, I suppose," Kafak said.

15

The next day, the day after Besançon had fallen, German artillery shelled the town. The only building they hit was the whorehouse.

"It's like they don't want us to have any fun at all," Carter said.

"Just because they lost the fucking battle," Kafak said. "Poor fucking sports, is what they are."

"Hey, Dash," Carter said, "you don't suppose Hastings is in that ol' whorehouse, do you?"

"I don't know. I ain't seen him since yesterday."

"Think we oughtta go look?"

They did. They found Hastings standing outside of the bordello watching as troops helped clear out the rubble. A lot of the girls were standing around swearing in French at the Germans. Others of the whores were propositioning the GIs hanging around nearby. A couple came up to Kafak and Carter, and they were thinking about it when Cole came up behind them.

"You don't have the time, soldiers," he said. He sounded rather cross. "Get yourselves together and follow me. We're marching out of Besançon."

"Oh my shit," Carter said, "it's gettin' so a man can't even enjoy the spoils of victory anymore."

"I figure it's a good thing," Kafak said.

"How's that?"

"We don't need a bunch of Bama Juniors running around Europe any more than we need Coo Juniors."

"Fuck you," both Carter and Hastings said simultaneously. Kafak laughed.

Carter asked Hastings, "So was you in there when the bombs started droppin'?"

"Naw," Hastings said. "I never got a chance to go inside. I'd just found the place."

"So you haven't polluted France then?" Kafak said.

"I didn't say that," Hastings said. "I found me a French girl last night. We had a good old time."

"Fuckin' Coo. Always makes his way," Carter said. He sounded admiring. Kafak only shook his head. Then Carter said, "Where we goin' now that's so all-fired important, anyhow?"

"The next fucking town," Kafak said. "That's all that matters."

It was like that. They marched on from one town to the next, rolling right through the ones the Germans had abandoned and fighting for the ones where the Krauts made a stand. After Besançon, things got different. They were closing in on the border of Germany and Austria now. The Germans didn't seem to like that much. Resistance grew greater. They ran into more and more prepared defensive positions. Good ones, too. Roadblocks, pillboxes, machine gun nests. The vaunted Siegfried Line. Artillery fire picked up, too. The Germans still had plenty of life in them, seemed like. That was not good news to Kafak. Or any of the men of the Third, he figured. They'd have liked to be home for Christmas.

All the towns ran one into the other. Kafak couldn't keep track anymore. Every place was the same, whether they marched through it or fought through it. If they only passed through, it usually meant streets filled with crowds of French people cheering for them. Girls kissing them. Men shaking their hands, slapping their backs. Sometimes, if they were at the back of the column moving through a town, all the people had already spent their emotions on the earlier GIs that had passed through, and no one was left in the streets for them. It didn't make much difference, Kafak thought. The whole thing grew into one huge blur. He wished he'd written down the names of the places they passed through. He might want to remember them later. For now, he only wanted to get through them, one after another, until they reached Germany and ended this fucking war. In every town where they had to fight their way through, that was the same, too. They'd move in. Encounter resistance. Engage in firefights. Kafak would keep his ass down. He'd fire at the enemy and toss grenades and wait for the tanks to come up. The Germans would either retreat or surrender. Or they would die. He might have been shot himself at any time. But he wasn't. Hastings was. In a small town two weeks after Besançon, Hastings took a sniper's bullet. Right in the chest. He went down like a puppet without strings. Kafak darted over to him. He shook him.

"Coo!" he said. "Coo! You all right?" Hastings didn't answer. Kafak knew he wouldn't. He could see the eyes wide open. Nothing moving. He knew Hastings was dead. He only yelled at him hoping it was otherwise. Kafak slumped against Hastings's corpse. "Ah, fuck," he said. "Fuck, fuck, fuck. Goddamnit, fuck."

He felt something tug at his sleeve and then something else punch him in the back. He knew the sniper was firing at him, and he rolled away from the body and up against the wall Hastings had been running to for cover. The wall Hastings hadn't made. Kafak ducked behind it now. He checked his arm, but the bullet had only hit his uniform, not any part of his flesh. His back hurt a little, but that was just from the force of the slug. Because it had hit where his back was still tender. Not entirely healed, not covered over with scar tissue yet. Kafak had his backpack on, and that had stopped the bullet. He supposed when things quieted down he could pull off the pack and find the bullet and have himself a unique souvenir. That was the thought running through his head just then, and he knew it was stupid, knew he should have been thinking about getting at that sniper. Or getting away from him. Either way. Then he didn't have to. A tank rolled up and blew apart the clock tower the sniper had been nested in.

"Well," Carter said, running up to Kafak, "that sumbitch is dead."

"Sure figures to be," Kafak said.

"You OK, Dash?"

"Took one in the shovel," Kafak said. "Ain't nothing," he said.

Carter looked down at Hastings.

"Coo bought it, huh?" he said.

"Yeah," Kafak said, not looking at the body.

"Oh my shit, but that's a bitch of a thing."

"Yeah," Kafak said. Then he said, "Well. At least the German women are safe."

They spent the night in that village after clearing it. The Germans didn't even bother shelling it once they'd left. Kafak found a nice basement with floor-level windows. You could see if anything was coming, and you had more than one way out. Yet you were beneath the level of explosions if the Germans changed their minds about the shelling. It was a comfortable little nest for the night. They had hot food. They had cooks traveling with them now. Well, not far behind them, anyway. At night, they often had hot food brought up, and it was much better than things had been in Italy. Even the food was better. The army seemed to have figured out how to make the shit they fed the troops taste a little better. Some guys still complained, of course. Even Kafak did once in a while. He did that night. He took one bite of the chow and threw down his mess kit in disgust.

"What's up, Dash?" Carter asked.

"I can't eat this fucking shit," Kafak said. "It tastes like the fuckers cut up a motherfucking dog and put it in a stew. And not a healthy fucking dog either."

"Tastes all right to me," Carter said.

"That's because you're from the South where you're used to goddamned dog."

"Oh my shit, Dash. That ain't right."

Kafak turned and walked away. He stood in an alley that led out of the town and into some woods. He kept a close watch but didn't like the spot. A sniper could too easily sneak up on him. He found a doorway in which he could crouch protected. He had a smoke, cupping the end in his palm. He went back into the basement. Carter was there, eating. He stopped eating when Kafak arrived. Kafak sat down against the wall opposite the one where Carter sat. He lit up another cigarette. He held the pack out to Carter.

"Smoke, Bama?" he said.

"No," Carter said. "No thanks, Dash."

"OK."

Kafak smoked, and Carter started eating again. They went on that way for some minutes, in silence. When Carter finished he stood up and washed off his mess kit at a sink in the basement. They were lucky because the water still ran and it looked clean. Clean enough, anyhow. They wouldn't drink it. Not without the disinfectant pills. But it looked clean enough for cleaning, washing up. When he'd finished, he picked up Kafak's kit and washed that, too. He walked over and handed it to Kafak.

"I could use that smoke now," he said.

Kafak said, "Sure," and handed the pack to him.

"Thanks," Carter said. He crouched down against the wall next to Kafak.

"That dog," Kafak said after a minute or so, "it didn't taste that bad, I guess."

"Oh my shit," Carter said, "it was way better than any I ever had to home, I can tell you that much."

Kafak laughed. Carter laughed. Carter stood up and looked out the window.

"Somebody comin'," he told Kafak.

"Ours or theirs?" Kafak said without getting up or moving, except to smoke his cigarette.

"Ours. Oh, it's Muncher and some of the boys."

The guy they called Muncher came down the stairs into the basement followed by about four other guys. "OK we bunk here with you guys?" Muncher asked. Muncher was chewing on something; he was always chewing on something. How he got his name.

"Make yourselves to home," Carter told them.

"Sure," Kafak said. "We're all one big happy family."

"Fuckin-A," Muncher said.

Everybody settled in, and Muncher started a conversation. He was always talking about one thing or another. He should have been nicknamed Gabby, Kafak thought. But somebody else had already earned that one. So he got Muncher. From his other habits. They talked about the war and when it might be over and what they might have to deal with tomorrow and what they might find once they got into Germany proper since they weren't that far off from it now. After a while, most of them went to sleep. Kafak didn't. He waited until he thought everyone was asleep, and then he pulled out his picture. The one of him and the Italian girl in Naples. He stared at it for a long time.

Carter said, "Who's that in the picture, Dash?"

"I thought you were asleep, Bama," Kafak said.

"I was, only now I ain't."

Kafak grunted. He put away the picture and sighed as he nestled down into his bag.

"That your girl back home?"

Kafak didn't answer for a time, and then he did. "Naw," he said. "Just some girl I met in Naples."

"What was she like?" Carter asked.

Again it took Kafak a long time to answer and then he did and he said, "Do you know, it's been so fucking long that I can't even hardly remember anymore."

16

They moved so quickly through so many places that it took something special for Kafak to remark a place any longer.

One village stuck because he and his squad were traveling through a cemetery to look for Krauts, and then he found one. A dead one. The guy's boots were missing, and his corpse had been abandoned there. Flies were congregating all over it. The corpse already stank.

"That boy needs a bath," Carter said.

"Guess the FFI's been here," Kafak told Carter.

"How's that?"

"They always take the fucking boots. Haven't you noticed?"

"Oh my shit, yeah," Carter said. "Now you mention it."

Another place that made an impression on Kafak was a small farming village they had entered and found abandoned by the Germans. The French came out to greet them in the streets. All of that was the normal course. But at one house, they heard a woman screaming. Sounded like she was being tortured. Cole sent Kafak and a couple of guys to investigate with his squad. Kafak returned to the captain, smiling.

"What's it all about, Dash?" Cole asked.

Kafak tossed a thumb over his shoulder.

"Woman in there just gave birth to a baby boy. Fine-looking little guy."

Cole grinned back at the squad.

"Well, there's a hell of a thing."

"The priest was in there baptizin' the tyke," Carter said, "and that old boy could speak a lick of English. Better'n me, tell you true."

"That ain't saying much," Andover said.

A bunch of them laughed, and Carter said, "Well, he couldn't curse near half as well as me you fuckin' motherfucker, so there's always that."

"Whoo, boy!" Andover said, and laughed.

"Get on with it, Carter," Cole said.

"Anyhow, that priest fella, he thanked us for comin' since when the Krauts saw us headin' this way, they done hightailed it outta here. So the kid's parents were happier than hell that their son got borned in a free village instead of one conquered by the fuckin' Germans. Can you imagine that?"

"I can," Cole said. "I can completely understand that."

Kafak hadn't said anything else. He just kept grinning. Word spread through the troops about what had happened, and suddenly Kafak heard the French national anthem, "La Marseillaise," being played by the division band, who'd been tagging along the last few days. Kafak saw how a lot of the French people milling about the streets started crying. Tears were in most of their eyes. A couple of pretty girls came up to him and kissed him, telling him thanks. Thanks for something. He couldn't figure out what. He only recognized the words for "thank you very much." He didn't know too much of the other French they were speaking. But it was good enough. He felt fine. And then they marched on.

Two days later they came upon some French farmers in a field. The Frenchmen were elderly fellows, and they shouted with joy and raised their arms to the sky when they saw the Americans. Kafak and his squad were ahead of the main body of troops, scouting. They hugged the old Frenchmen and offered them cigarettes and then prepared to move on, but the farmers stopped them. In broken English, one of the Frenchmen told them they shouldn't go forward.

"Why's that?" Kafak asked.

"There are *les Allemands là!* There. Over there." The farmer waved in the direction he meant.

"How many?" Kafak asked, looking where the farmer had indicated. He didn't see anything. That only meant they were farther away than he could see just then. He looked back to the old Frenchman. "About how many, sir?" he asked again.

The farmer shrugged with his mouth in that way the French had. Then he looked to his friends and they held a quick discussion. Kafak couldn't follow the rapid French. Afterward, the farmers faced back to Kafak, and the one said, "*Quatre, cinq,* maybe four? Yes, four or five." He held up fingers in case he'd translated the numbers wrong. He hadn't.

"Oh my shit," Carter said. "There's eighta us, Dash. We can take them motherfuckers. Maybe get some prisoners. Captain likes his prisoners. Where they at? Ask 'im that."

Kafak glanced at Carter, looked down the road again, then put his attention back on the old man.

"Four or five," Kafak said. "Guys?" He frowned and then waved at his own men.

The Frenchman made a face showing he didn't understand. Then light dawned. His face brightened, and he smiled and shook his head. He paused, thinking of the word, Kafak could tell, and then he said, "Hundreds. Four or five hundreds."

"Well, hell," Carter said.

"And this many tanks," the farmer added flashing fingers for thirteen.

"Shit, Dash," Andover said. "We'd best get back and report to the captain."

"Yeah," Kafak said. Then he said to the farmer, "These Germans, *les soldats Allemands,* how do they travel? They on foot with the tanks?"

"Uhmmm, the trucks? Trucks, yes. The trucks come. They pick up the soldiers. Take them away." The farmer nodded. "They wait for the trucks to come now."

"Well," Waszinsky said, "let's hope those fucking trucks get here soon, then."

Kafak laughed. The others laughed. He led them back to the company to report to Cole. The German trucks didn't get there quickly enough, and they had to fight. A pitched battle, more than a firefight, in a field and woods. Kafak took his squad around the flank with about thirty other guys. A machine gun nest pinned them down. Kafak, Carter, Andover, and Jenkins crawled forward while the rest of the guys covered them, drew the machine gun's fire. When they were close enough, they hurled grenades. Kafak felt something bite at his thigh, and he dropped back down into the underbrush, cursing. The grenades took out the nest, and they moved forward. Kafak checked his leg. It bled heavily. He didn't figure it for much, though, since he could walk OK. They got behind the German lines. They had maybe twenty guys left. They put down a withering fire from the rear of the Kraut position. The Germans began surrendering in droves. Then a Panzer arrived. The Germans took a second wind.

"That ain't fair," Carter said. "Them boys done surrendered already."

"Report it to the Geneva Convention," Andover told him.

"It just ain't right, all I'm saying."

The tank gave them trouble. Forced a short retreat. A lieutenant in charge of the group told Kafak, "We're going to retreat again in a second or so. I want you to lay low. Stay right where you're at. Once that fucking Panzer passes you by, you slip this underneath it." He passed over a satchel charge. "You know how to use it?"

"Yes, sir," Kafak said.

"Good. Here's a couple extra grenades, case that charge doesn't blow it all the way."

"Sure," Kafak said. "That oughtta help."

"Just do it," the lieutenant said.

"Sure," Kafak said. "Why the fuck not?"

The lieutenant led the second retreat through the trees. In Italy, they'd been taught to dig a small slit trench and lay in it until the tank passed over you. Then you would pop up and fire at the infantry following the vehicle. That wasn't the plan here. Here, the lieutenant wanted them to take out the tank itself. Fucking lieutenant, Kafak thought. Carter and Waszinsky stayed behind with him. They all lay flat in fallen leaves of the woods. The leaves smelled pretty good, Kafak thought, lying there. Like mulch. Not decayed yet. Crisp and colorful still beneath him. They crackled with every move. Kafak called out the play to Carter and Waszinsky. Then he lay quiet, still; played dead. They all did. Kafak figured that soon enough they might not be playing at it anymore. He held as still as he could as a group of six or seven Germans walked through where he had been ordered to remain. The satchel charge was beneath him, covered by his body. Just my luck it will blow now, he thought to himself. He cursed the lieutenant again for sticking him with this assignment. He figured if he ever saw the guy again, he'd knock his teeth out. Let him give orders with a mouthful of gums from now on. That thought pleased Kafak, and he wondered if he could actually do it. He wondered if he'd ever see that lieutenant again so that he'd have that decision to even make. And then the Krauts were past him, and he heard the tank rolling forward. He figured there would be more guys walking alongside of it, or behind it. Protecting the tank from an action just such as this. Besides, a lot of guys liked to keep close to a tank. Made them feel more secure themselves. Kafak never did it anymore, not after that time near Cisterna. He waited until the tank was parallel to him. Then he shouted. "Now!" he said to Carter and Waszinsky. The two men rose up to their knees and laid down a withering fire at the infantry on either side of the tank. Even while they fired, Kafak rolled to the side of the tank and shoved the satchel charge in between its treads. The German soldiers were either dead, wounded, or too busy to bother with him. Kafak

rolled away from the tank just as quickly and shouted again at
Carter and Waszinsky. All three curled into the fetal position
and covered their heads with their arms. Another quick tick and
Kafak heard a tremendous explosion. He thought the charge
might have somehow got lucky and caught the tank's fuel. Or
a shell. He looked up. The tank had turned into a fireball. A
couple of guys jumped out of the lid. Flames ate them. They
shrieked. He thought he heard the German word for *mother*.
Maybe some cursing. He couldn't be sure. "Fuck," he said. He
fired his tommy gun. Carter fired as well. The slugs silenced
the two guys who were burning. Kafak figured they'd done
those boys a favor. Put them out of that misery. The stench
of their fried corpses made him retch. He was vomiting when
three Kraut infantrymen came running back through his position. They ignored him, running like hell. His own guys led by
the lieutenant raced after them. Kafak thought how he could
belt that lieutenant right now, only the lieutenant was already
gone, ran past. Besides, Kafak was in no fit state to fight with
anyone right then. He finished puking and looked up. Carter
stood beside him.

"You OK, Dash?" he asked.

Kafak's ears still thundered from the explosion, but he could
make out Carter's words as if through water. He nodded. "Ain't
nothing," he said. "Just that smell."

Carter looked at the burned Germans. "Yeah," he said. "I
know how much you love that odor." He tugged on Kafak's
arm. "Come on, boy. We gotta get outta here and join up with
the other fellas."

"Sure," Kafak said.

They caught up, but the battle was over. The lieutenant had
disappeared. A corpsman treated Kafak's wound. Just a gash
along the side of his thigh that bled a lot worse than it was.
That's what the corpsman said, anyhow.

"Not so bad as it probably looked," he told Kafak.

"Sure," Kafak said, "but it ain't your fucking leg, is it?"

He laughed and Kafak smiled, and Cole walked up. The medic finished and hurried off to the next case, and Cole said, "You OK, Dash?"

"I'm right as rain, sir."

"Good, good. You did a hell of a job today."

"Yeah," Kafak said. "I guess we all did."

"Every day, every fight," Cole said, "we get closer to the end."

"Yes, sir."

"Some lieutenant," Cole said then, "guy named Kravits, I think, something like that, anyhow, he's putting you in for a medal."

"Medal?"

"Yeah. For taking out that tank. Said you remained behind and took out a tank when everyone else retreated."

"Hell," Kafak said, "I only did that on account of he ordered me to. Besides, Carter and Waszinsky were with me. Give them the fucking medal."

"He named you, specifically."

"Shit, Cap. Tell you the truth, I'd much prefer socking him in the jaw than getting any goddamned medal. That would make me feel a hell of a lot better."

"Well," Cole said, grinning, "I guess you'll have to settle for the medal."

Kafak frowned. He remembered the guys on fire. Two of them.

He asked Cole, "How many guys in a Panzer, anyway, Cap?"

Cole shrugged.

"I don't know. Like ours, I suppose. Say, five, maybe. Why?"

"Because," Kafak said. "I don't want no fucking medal."

The next night, Kafak walked with Cole to attend a briefing. When it was over, Cole remained behind to socialize with a few of the other junior officers. Kafak walked away. He headed back to rejoin his men. On the way he came to a crossroads where troops were moving. He saw guys from his company as well as all the other companies heading west. They were coming down a long road to where the road T'd east and west, and a soldier there was waving them all west. Away from the enemy.

"What the fuck is this?" Kafak said to himself. He approached the GI who was directing traffic. He wanted to find out where this guy had gotten his orders, what was going on. According to the briefing he'd just attended, the entire army was pushing eastward, toward Austria and Germany, so Kafak couldn't figure out where this soldier got his directions. Going west made no sense at all. Kafak strode right up to the guy and said, "Who the fuck told you to send these guys that way?"

The soldier looked at Kafak. Glanced at his Thompson. The gun was slung, but Kafak held the handle and trigger in his hand ready to swing it up in a second. He always carried it that way, walked that way, when he was anywhere near the front. It had become a habit. Immediately, the soldier threw down his rifle and jerked his arms straight up into the air.

"*Kamerad! Kamerad!*" he said. He dropped onto his knees and hollered. "No shoot! No shoot!" he said.

"What the fuck," Kafak said. "You're a German."

"Surrender!" the guy said. "Surrender."

Kafak swung up his gun to point it at the guy. He still held it in just the one hand. He was laughing. The movement west had stopped as the nearest guys had halted to see what was going on. A major came forward in a jeep, his driver raising dust as he braked.

"What's the holdup here? What's all this about, soldier?" he asked.

"You guys are going the wrong fucking way, sir," Kafak said. He was still laughing.

"What are you talking about?" the major said. He didn't sound in any mood to join in the joke. Kafak didn't think the major liked him laughing about it either.

"This guy's a Kraut," Kafak said. "He must've gotten left behind during the last battle. He took a GI uniform. He was directing you all west when you should be going east."

The major looked at the captured trooper. The German demonstrated the picture of fear and submission. He was still begging not to be shot, and claiming surrender.

The major shook his head. His face was going red. Kafak couldn't stop laughing, though it wasn't loud.

"What a regular mess this is," the major said.

"Sure," Kafak said. "It's the fucking army, ain't it?"

The major scowled.

"I don't think your sense of humor is well placed, Sergeant," he said.

"I don't think your sense of direction is," Kafak said. "Sir."

The major went ballistic, but despite how hard he tried, Kafak couldn't keep himself from chuckling over the situation. Cole came rushing up. Kafak figured he must have heard the major's raised voice reaming someone. Then he found out it was Kafak getting reamed. And clearly not giving a shit about it. Cole tried to intervene, but the major wasn't having it. He told Cole, "I want this man broken, Captain. Take his stripes away."

"You can have 'em," Kafak said.

"Shut the fuck up, Kafak," Cole said. He snapped at Kafak, then turned back to the major. "Sergeant Kafak has been through some very harrowing experiences in battle recently, sir. He's not himself."

"I don't care if he fought with Hitler himself. He's a private now. You understand that, Captain?"

"Yes, sir," Cole said.

"And I intend to see about having him court-martialed and sent to prison as well."

"Sir, really, I—"

"That will be all, Captain," the major said, and ordered his driver to take off.

Cole turned to Kafak. He was burning with rage. Kafak was still grinning.

"What the fuck is wrong with you?"

"That guy was an asshole," Kafak said.

"He's a major, Kafak."

"OK," Kafak said. "A major asshole."

"Goddamnit! You want to go to prison, Kafak?"

"What?" Kafak said. "It's gonna be worse than here?"

Cole shook his head and bit off his next words. He was too angry to speak, Kafak figured. Cole told him to get back to his squad; then the captain swung away from him and marched off.

"That fella's pissed," one of the soldiers standing on the road said.

"Sure he is," Kafak said. "But that's OK. Cuz I ain't no sergeant no more."

17

Kafak returned to where his men were bivouacked in the barn of a small cottage. They had a nice little fire going and were warming themselves near it. Kafak sat down nearby and took off his field jacket and removed the stripes.

Carter smiled at him.

"Your papers come in?" he asked. "They givin' you the real thing, Dash?"

"Naw," Kafak said. "I been busted."

"What?"

"Yep. I'm just a lowly old private like you bastards now."

"Hey," Waszinsky said, "I'm a private first class, I'll have you know."

"Fuck off," somebody else said.

"What happened, Dash?" Carter said.

Kafak told them the story. They were all laughing when Cole arrived. They all shut up quickly then and moved away from the fire. Kafak stood to attention, saluted. Cole left him at attention as he spoke.

He said, "Well, I had to go over that major's head, but the general saw things my way. When he heard that a major who'd never seen a lick of combat and had just got over here from the States wanted to send a combat vet to prison, he had a conniption. I think he's ready to bust that major, tell you the truth."

"That sounds like it might cause you some trouble, sir," Kafak said.

"To hell with it," Cole said. "That son of a bitch has no right acting like that. Not here a week and he's acting that way."

"Yes, sir."

"You're still a private, though," Cole said. "I didn't ask the general to fight about that part of it."

"Thank you, sir," Kafak said. "I appreciate that."

"Wipe that grin off your face, Private," Cole said. "This war lasts long enough, you'll be a sergeant again, I'm sure, like it or not."

"Yes, sir," Kafak said. "I'm afraid you're right, sir."

Cole left then, and soon after a new sergeant came in. None of the guys knew him. He said he'd been with the Seventh but they had transferred him over because the Fifteenth didn't have enough NCOs around to cover the spot. He'd only just been promoted himself, so he tried to get along with the squad. That seemed all right to Kafak. He felt the situation was improved all the way around. He slept well that night.

The next day they ran into a German rearguard action. The firefight was short but intense. Machine guns, small arms, mortar fire. The company was momentarily pinned down, but then half a dozen tanks came up and broke the German resistance. The Krauts retreated. They lobbed a few more mortar shells as they were leaving. One of them landed near Andover. Took off his legs, one mid-thigh, the other just below the knee. He was shrieking from the pain. Kafak ran over to him shouting for a medic.

"Oh, mama! Oh, mama!" Andover said.

He tried to sit up and look down at his legs, but Kafak pressed him back to the ground.

"Don't move," Kafak told him.

He jabbed Andover with his syrette of morphine. Carter ran up. Andover was still screaming for his mother.

"Fuck," Carter said. "Oh my shit, fuck."

"Give him your morphine," Kafak told Carter.

Carter did.

Andover was still crying and screaming for his mother. Then he said, "Where are my legs? What the fuck, Dash? Where are my fucking legs?"

"You're gonna be all right, Stu," Kafak told Andover. "Just hang on. You're gonna be OK."

A few more mortar shells exploded, but nothing too close by. Then the Germans were silent, retreating. The American tanks rolled after them. Most of the company with them. Kafak, Carter, and a couple other guys stood around with Andover. They'd put tourniquets on his legs. Shot him with streptomycin. Some of the others added their morphine to what Kafak and Carter had already given Andover. They didn't figure it much mattered since none of them figured Andover was going to live anyway, but Andover settled a little. He was no longer screaming. He was crying and murmuring now. "Mama, help me," he said. Over and over again. "Mama, help me find my legs." Kafak held his hand. Two medics arrived and took over. Kafak stood up and began walking away. The others all walked alongside of him, forward, to join the company.

"Oh my shit," Carter said.

"Motherfuck," Kafak said. His chest hurt. It made him angry. "Motherfuck."

"Son of a bitching Krauts," Waszinsky said.

"Andover," Kafak said. "Son of a bitch."

They joined up with the rest of Love Company. The fight was over. The German rearguard was all either dead, wounded, captured, or gone. That night, over chow, the lieutenant who had ordered Kafak to destroy the tank came by. Kafak stood up. Before he could slug the guy, the lieutenant told them all, "Captain Cole has been captured."

"What?" Kafak said.

The other men rose up and crowded forward, asking the same question. The lieutenant patted the air to quiet them. Then he explained.

"Captain Cole was scouting for a place where we could cross the river. His jeep hit a mine. His driver was killed, but he was tossed out. Wounded. The Germans found him there and took him prisoner. A forward observer saw the whole thing."

"Why didn't he do something?" Carter asked.

"He was alone. He said he'd started down toward the captain but then about a dozen Krauts arrived. They got to Cole first."

"Fuck," Kafak said.

"The guy shoulda done something," Billings said.

"Yeah," Waszinsky said.

"He couldn't," the lieutenant said. "I'm telling you."

"Fucking piece of shit," Billings said.

"Leave off that," Kafak told Billings. "Them FO's are damned brave guys. He says he couldn't do nothing, then there wasn't nothing to be done." Kafak looked at the lieutenant. "Anybody getting up a search party for the captain?"

The lieutenant said nothing; he only shrugged.

"I'll go," Kafak said.

"Enemy lines are close by, Dash," Carter said.

"Cole's a good officer." Kafak glanced at the lieutenant. "Ain't a lot of them around. It's worth trying to get him back."

"He could be dead already, you know," the lieutenant said. "We don't know."

"We oughtta try," Kafak said.

"I can't order anyone to go on a mission like this," the lieutenant said. And Kafak thought how he could, though, order Kafak to stay behind to blow up a fucking tank. "But I won't stop anyone from going either."

Kafak turned to the others.

"Any other volunteers?" he asked.

"Oh my shit," Carter said. "You serious, Dash?"

"Yeah," Kafak said. "I'm serious."

Carter paused, frowned hard, then sighed.

"Well, hell," he said. "If you're goin', I reckon I am, too."

"Thanks, Bama."

Four others stepped forward. One of them, Anzini, said, "Cole's a good guy, like you said, Dash. He deserves whatever chance we can give him."

"Let's go then." They got their gear together and started off. Kafak stopped in front of the lieutenant. "One more thing," he said.

"What's that, Private?"

And Carter said, "Let's go, Dash. We ain't got the time for any of that shit."

Kafak took a deep breath, then he shook himself.

He said, "Nothing, Lieutenant. Nothing at all."

"If you're not back before dawn," the lieutenant said, "I'll figure you have all been killed or captured. No one will be sent after you."

"You're a regular sweetheart," one of the men said but nobody knew who for sure.

The group moved off into the dark. They had only their weapons and ammunition. Nothing that could make noise. Kafak carried a knife and .45 on his belt. His tommy in his hands. Plenty of ammunition and half a dozen grenades.

Carter said, "Any idea where we goin', Dash?"

"Other side of the river," Kafak said. That drew a couple of gasps from the others.

Carter said, "Oh my shit, Dash, that's German territory right now. They got heavy men over there."

"If they got prisoners," Kafak said, "where else you figure them to be?"

Murmurs shot around the other guys. Kafak ignored them. They could turn back if they wanted to, he figured. He figured he ought to turn back himself. But he didn't. He wouldn't.

Carter said, "OK, OK, then, Dash. That still leaves the question of how we gonna get cross that river. We ain't got a boat or nothin'."

"There's a town, just this side of the river. Not too big. Saw it from a distance on my last scout. I figure somebody there got to have a boat."

"So that's where we goin'?"

"Good a place as any, I suppose."

Everyone fell quiet for a time, considering what they were getting themselves into.

Then Anzini said, "You really gonna belt that looey, Dash?"

"I was about an inch away from it," Kafak said.

Carter laughed, said, "Oh my shit, boy, I could tell you was."

"You'll be in some big trouble, Dash," Jacobson said.

"Fuck," Kafak said. "What they gonna do to me? Send me to the fucking front?"

They all laughed at that until Kafak told them to quiet down as they approached the town. It was a small town and near completely dark. No lights to give either side a target to bomb. A single lamp barely burned in the town square. The moon and the stars supplied the only illumination they really needed. Kafak led them down one of the town's main streets. They stuck close to the buildings. They hadn't gone too far in when they heard voices. German voices. They all froze.

"Shit," Jacobson said.

He whispered. They all whispered. They were all scared shitless. Kafak was, anyway, so he figured the others were, too.

"What the Germans doin' here?" Carter said.

"They're supposed to be the other side of the river," Anzini said.

"Shut up," Pintarello said.

They listened some more. The voices were drawing closer, moving toward them. All of them flattened against the wall of the building they stood next to. Kafak was first in the column, so he drew his knife and slung his Thompson. He waited. Two men popped out of the nearby alley, still talking in hushed tones but not actually whispering. They were portly, middle-aged. They wore civilian clothes. They startled when they saw the Americans. They stopped in their tracks, their eyes gone wide in their pudgy faces.

Kafak put away his knife.

"Fuck," he said, "we must be in Alsace-Lorraine."

"What's that got to do with anything?" Anzini said.

"It's French territory, but they speak German here," Kafak said.

He walked toward the two men and the others covered him, still suspecting some sort of trap from the German-speaking townspeople. Kafak spoke with them.

"You know English?" he asked.

"A leetle," one of them said. The other hung back, observing. Still looking frightened. The burgher said, "I am a *française*. Citizen of France. Yes?"

"This is Alsace-Lorraine we're in?" Kafak asked.

The burgher nodded, smiled merrily.

"Welcome," he said. "When you came, the Germans left. So *danke* and *merci beaucoup*."

"Sure," Kafak said. "Are there any Germans left here? In this town?"

The man shook his head.

"They are all gone. They left days ago. Sometimes, though, they send patrols. Like you." He waved toward the American soldiers. He smiled. "But they are mostly gone."

"Have you seen any patrols tonight?" Kafak asked.

"Tonight?" The man frowned, thinking. Then he said something to his friend. In German. He turned back to Kafak and translated for him. "I haven't seen any Germans today, but he says he saw a few earlier, down near the river. In a drainage ditch there. About a mile south of the town."

"OK," Kafak said. "OK. Thanks."

He returned to the others and told them what he'd learned.

"So we goin' there first?" Carter asked. "Before we cross the river, I mean?"

"I figure it's a better bet, don't you?"

"Oh my shit yes," Carter said. "I don't wanna cross no river tonight."

"Well, let's go see, then."

They moved off toward the south end of town. They didn't see or run into any other citizens. Everyone was locked up behind closed doors and shutters. That was a good thing, Kafak figured. He didn't need another fright like that one. Though now he understood the situation, he didn't suppose he would be so startled again by hearing German voices where he didn't expect them to be.

At the edge of town they continued south. They moved carefully through woods and some dying undergrowth. They kept as quiet as they knew how to be. All the patrols and scouts helped them. They'd learned a few things. But then, so had the Germans. You never knew what might happen. Or when it might happen. Kafak tried never to think beyond just what he was doing. Focus on that. Leave tomorrow to focus on tomorrow. Focus on the here and now. Keep your senses alert and be ready to eat the ground. That was his philosophy.

They could make out the end of the ditch as they approached. It let out into the river, and a boat was moored there. A small rowboat, was all it was, but good enough to get a small party across the river. They didn't see anyone or hear anything. Kafak motioned them down onto the ground because that boat seemed out of place, tied there where they saw it. They crawled the last fifty yards or so to the ditch. At the point they reached it, the ditch was empty.

"What now?" Anzini said. Kafak was about to stand up when he heard something and dropped back down flat on the ground. "What?" Anzini said.

He put his hand on Anzini's arm for silence. All of them tensed; Kafak could feel it run down the line. Then he heard it again. The smoosh of a boot through mud. Someone was coming. Kafak didn't figure it to be townfolk. Not out here. Not at this hour. He motioned to all of them to be ready. He saw them then. Five Germans. Three of them carried burp guns, and the other two had their rifles slung and were carrying someone between them. It could have been a wounded comrade of their own; it was too dark to tell for sure. But Kafak would've bet his pay that the man they carted along was Captain Cole. He glanced down the line at all the others. They all nodded. Kafak put down his tommy and pulled out his knife again. The others followed the action.

When the Germans came abreast of them, crouching below them in the bottom of the muddy ditch, the Americans attacked. Kafak was on the end of the line, so he went after the lead German. Kafak leaped onto the man's back, trying to stab his body at the same time. The Kraut ducked when he caught a glimpse of something suddenly flying at him. Kafak nearly slid right over him but managed to grab onto the man's helmet. It was fastened on by a strap and the strap held and Kafak's tugging on the rim of the helmet brought the German tumbling down atop him. Kafak squirmed underneath the enemy soldier who was jerking around on top of him, trying to escape Kafak's grip. Kafak tried to clasp his legs around the German's legs to keep him from slipping away. While the two men grappled this way in the mud, Kafak struck downward with his knife. The blade bit into flesh. Kafak felt it. He didn't know where he'd stabbed the German, but he knew he'd hit flesh from the way it sank in. Kafak pulled it out and plunged it down again. And again. Three more times. Then more times after that. He lost count of how many times he pounded the knife down into the German's body, and he couldn't stop stabbing even when the man on top of him ceased moving. Kafak didn't even notice the man had stopped slipping about until well after the German was dead. "Shit," Kafak said under his breath, spitting out mud. He shoved the body off him as quick as he could and rolled away, coming up onto his knees and looking at the rest of the fight. Anzini was on his back, on the ground, looked to be in trouble. Kafak leaped on the back of the German attacking him, yanked back on the guy's helmet, and moved to slice the Kraut's neck wide open, but Anzini's knife was already shooting upward, sticking deep into the enemy's throat. "Die, you cocksucking motherfucker!" Anzini said as he plunged the knife into the German. It was an ugly cry, the growl of an animal. Fierce and amoral and without forgiveness or care except for survival. That was how it seemed to Kafak, anyway. The enemy soldier uttered a short, small cry, then a gurgle, and then he collapsed. It was a bitter-sounding thing in Kafak's ears. Kafak stood up. Anzini stood up. He was sprayed with the dead German's blood. Kafak looked away from Anzini and glanced around and saw all the Germans were dead. Jacobson was dead, his own knife sticking up from his chest.

"Shit," Kafak said.

"We got Captain Cole," Carter said.

Carter knelt beside the man the Germans had been carrying along, and Kafak rushed over to his side, genuflected in the mud next to the captain.

"Cap," Kafak said. "Cap, you hear me?"

A pause, then, "Kafak? Kafak, that you?"

"It's me, Cap. And Carter, and Anzini, and—"

"What the fuck you doing here?"

"We came to bring you back, Cap."

"Who allowed that? You guys shouldn't be here."

"Well, you got that much right, Cap," Kafak said. "So we need to get the fuck outta here right now. Shut up so we can leave, why don't you?"

Kafak grabbed the captain and drew him over his shoulder. He carried Cole over one shoulder and his Thompson in his other hand and started along the drainage ditch, back toward the American lines. Carter was right beside him, keeping him covered. Anzini grabbed Jacobson's body in the same fireman's carry with which Kafak was carting Cole. The others followed, watching their backs. They returned to their lines without any other problems, and Kafak turned Cole over to the medics. Kafak returned to the cottage in which he was bivouacked and he collapsed, covered in wet mud, and it didn't bother him at all. He fell straight into an exhausted sleep.

The next morning, after breakfast, Kafak went to the field hospital to look in on the captain and found him being loaded onto a truck.

"I'm being evacced to Naples," Cole told Kafak. "They say I'm too banged up to fight for now. But I'll be back."

"Take your time. Maybe we can knock this thing off before you get back here."

"Don't you dare do it. I want to see Berlin."

"All right, Cap. We'll save some fight for you."

"You do that. And by the way, Kafak."

"What's that, Cap?"

"Thank you, Bob. Tell the other men, too. Will you?"

"No need, Cap. You'da done it for us."

"Still. Pass it along, will you, please?"

Kafak nodded.

"Sure thing, Cap," he said.

Kafak patted the captain on his chest, softly, and then moved away as the stretcher was fastened into the bed of the truck. He stepped off and found a corpsman.

The medic asked him, "You one of the guys who brought Captain Cole back?"

"What about it?"

"Lieutenant Kravits wants to get all you guys a medal for doing it."

"That fucker is medal-happy. Jesus Christ. You'd think he'd never been in a motherfucking war before."

"Some officers are like that. Show their appreciation, you know?"

Right, Kafak thought. Order you to stay behind enemy lines and take on a fucking tank and then, if you live through it, show you how much they appreciate it. What kind of shit was that, he wondered.

He said, "He gonna be all right?"

"Who? Captain Cole?"

"Yeah."

"Sure, he'll be fine. Had some broken ribs, a busted leg. He ought to be up and about in no time. They'll likely send him back here, if we're still fighting in six weeks."

If we're still fighting in six weeks.

For some reason, those words struck Kafak. He'd never thought about things like that before, not until the medical corpsman had put it into words in that way. Could all of this really be over in six weeks' time? Was that even possible? Kafak didn't think so. On the other hand, the officers kept telling them the Allies were making tremendous progress on the northern European front. They would likely hook up, the two armies, one coming south, their own heading north, any time now. Soon. Everyone was certain it would be soon. Kafak didn't feel so certain about that. He knew the Germans were retreating, but then they'd turn on the Americans and fight like hell, and there'd be more casualties, more guys killed. They'd fight a quick rearguard action during the daylight and then, when darkness covered them, they retreated to the next place from which they wanted to ambush the Americans. Kafak didn't think the fight had gone out of the German army just yet.

Six weeks?

No, Kafak didn't figure on that. He figured it would go a lot longer than six more weeks. He'd be surprised if it ended in six more *months*.

He put the thoughts out of his head along with the corpsman's words. He understood what had so suddenly struck him about those words, what had gnawed at him so abruptly and oddly. The words had given him hope. Kafak hadn't felt hope in a while and that was why it felt so strange to him. He didn't like that it felt strange to him, but he understood why it did. He didn't want to feel that hope. Hope, he figured, was the sort of thing that could get a guy killed. Just live through the day you were in. Just focus on that and get through that. Reach tomorrow. And once you did that, focus on that day until you reached the next one. Every day, you did that, and every day you survived was one day closer to the end. But to hope for the end at any given point, that wasn't going to help him. That wasn't about to help anyone.

Kafak stopped hoping.

He returned to his squad and they soon moved out once again. The cold grew colder and the rain started up. September weather came and got worse. Still not as bad as Anzio, where it seemed the rain never stopped and the mud never ended. You could never get out of the rain and the cold on Anzio. Not until the spring had come. And that got ruined by the Breakout. Here, it was different. At night, you often got to bed down in a building, under a roof. Out of the rain. Sometimes, even out of the cold. That was good. Better than Anzio, that was for sure.

Kafak was pretty filthy after the fight in the drainage ditch, so the rain felt all right on him as he marched. He threw his face up to the sky, let the raindrops fall on his face, cleansing him. He didn't think about what had happened in that ditch. He concentrated on bringing Cole back safely. He focused on marching and keeping an eye and ear out for the enemy. No time to think about yesterday if you wanted to live through today. He focused on today. There'd be time to remember yesterday, all the yesterdays, later, afterward, when it was all over. And if he didn't live through it, that was all right too, he figured, because then he would never have to remember it. Not any of it.

Kafak stopped thinking.

He marched.

18

More firefights. More rearguard actions by the Germans. They lost Anzini. Then Billings and Postlethwaite and Hodecki. Waszinsky bought it from a sniper in some town the name of which Kafak couldn't even remember. He and Carter kept going. Lieutenant Kravits was killed by a mine one day.

"Well," Kafak said, "there goes our medals."

"That's a shame," Carter said. "Cuz the girls, they like them medals."

"Fuck it," Kafak said.

They came to a farmhouse. A new captain was in charge of the company now, and he'd only been with them about a week, since Cole had been evacuated. He'd been in the war a little longer than that, though. At least, that's what he had told them. The company hunkered down on the crest of a hill, looking down on the farmhouse, and the captain decided they should rush the building before the Germans could form up their defense. He ordered the men to charge. The entire company ran forward screaming and firing and attacking that farmhouse. Only the farmhouse was empty. Not a German in sight. And, thank God, Kafak thought, not the French owners of the house either. They'd have been dead by now with all the firepower the men of L Company had poured onto that building. Some of the men searched the house with the captain while the rest surrounded the outside and kept watch. Kafak saw movement by a woodpile that stood a good thirty yards from the front of the house. A woodpile that was located behind them now, surrounded by high brush. He elbowed Carter.

"Lookit that," he said.

Carter looked.

"Well, oh my shit, will you lookee there?"

They saw two German officers slipping out of the woodpile, through the brush, trying to sneak away into the nearby woods. Both of them held pistols and looked harried. Kafak laughed.

"Should we capture them ol' boys?" Carter asked.

"Fuck it," Kafak said. "What good are they to us?"

"Make us look good to the new captain."

"Fuck that. Fuck him. Those bastards are alone behind enemy lines. They can't hurt nobody. Let the motherfuckers go."

But some of the other guys had seen them, too, and they weren't in as forgiving a mood as Kafak. They started firing at the Germans. Instead of surrendering, the Germans only ran faster. A couple of the riflemen picked them off then. The two Germans went down.

"Two less, I guess," Carter said.

"Sure," Kafak said. "What's the difference?"

Some men went to see if the German officers were dead or alive. Turned out they were both dead. The captain came back out of the house and reamed them all for killing the German officers. "They would have made good prisoners," he told them all. "They probably could've provided some really good intel." Nobody said anything back. You didn't argue with an officer. Not like that, anyway. The captain shook his head, looking sour, said, "Well, nothing more to do here, anyhow, let's go, men." They marched on, up the hill that rose gradually behind the house. They reached the top of the hill and looked down onto a long valley stretching out before them. A road ran through it, from left to right as they viewed it.

"Hey, watch over there," Carter said, pointing.

A bunch of the guys were pointing, indicating a lone German soldier coming down that road. The guy was on a bicycle and pedaling for all he was worth. A couple of guys took potshots at him, but he was out of range. The Kraut was hunkered down and pumping hard on that bike, moving fast. Trying to escape the approaching Allied forces. Some of the guys made jokes about it and then the regimental commander arrived and he had a tank with him, a kind of bodyguard, Kafak figured. The captain greeted him and pointed out the German. The colonel told his tanker to see if he could hit the soldier. The gunner took a few shots, but he couldn't hit the guy. That German was just too small a target that far off and moving way too damned fast. The guys were whooping it up at the near misses, though, and the colonel told his tank gunner, "I'm going to have to send you back for some target practice, son." The gunner's face was red, and everybody was giving it to him, including Kafak. He and Carter were laughing with most of the others. Only the newer guys weren't laughing. They looked embarrassed, exchanging glances.

"This ain't right," a guy named Clarkson said to Kafak.

He'd only just joined them a few days earlier. The farmhouse had been the only combat he'd seen so far, and Kafak didn't figure that counted since no one was shooting back at them. That made it nothing more than an exercise in assaulting an empty farmhouse.

Kafak shrugged.

"I guess I oughtta feel bad about it, too," he said.

"You don't, though, do you?" the newbie said.

Kafak paused, frowned, then said, "I felt a little bad, at first. Then I think about Sleepy Ass and Anzini and Andover and Coo and I don't feel so fucking bad about that motherfucking Kraut anymore. No."

"Still," the new guy said. "You ought to."

Kafak looked at him.

"See what you think in another few months," Kafak told him.

"If you last that long," Carter said.

"Don't fucking jinx me," the new guy said and moved off.

Kafak and Carter looked back to the pedaling German, but they weren't laughing any longer. Kafak fell silent until the guy was nearly out of sight, and then he spit and he said, "You know something, Bama?"

"What's that, Dash?"

"That right there," and he pointed down toward the road with his chin, "that's why we're gonna win this war."

Carter frowned at him.

"Why?" he asked. "Because some tank gunner can't hit a single solitary Kraut on a goddamned bike?"

"No," Kafak said. "Because some tank gunner can waste half a dozen shells firing at a single solitary Kraut on a goddamned bike."

"I don't get it, Dash."

"It's how come everybody should know, should always have known, that we were going to win this fucking war. Because we can waste all that time and all that ammo on one guy who's no harm to anyone, just wearing the wrong uniform. What other country in this thing can compete with resources like that? You know?"

"I suppose you're right, sure," Carter said. "But resources or not, we still gotta fight to win this thing."

"Sure," Kafak said. "Sure, we do."

Things began changing then because they were nearing the Vosges Mountains. The mountains offered natural defensive positions and were as far as the German army wanted to go. No more hit-and-run, no more rearguard actions, no more fight until dark and slip away. Now it was going to be all-out battles for every scrap of ground. Artillery fire picked up. They hadn't seen a tank in over a week, and now they found fucking Panzers every time they turned around. The mountains were tough going, covered with trees and brush, and the rain didn't help anything either. The rain came down steady and created a mist throughout the entire woods. Visibility couldn't have been more than fifty feet. They had a new lieutenant as well as their new captain, a guy named Holbrooke, and Holbrooke came to them one day and told them, "We're loading up on some trucks, boys. They're moving us up to relieve the Thirty-Sixth. They're already in the foothills of the Vosges, and we're gonna give them a rest while we kick some Nazi butt. Let's go." They piled into trucks, with only the new guys fired up by the new lieutenant's speech. Then, when the trucks started off, carting the regiment toward the front line and the heavy sounds of fighting, the new guys' faces began reflecting not excitement or energy but fear. Kafak didn't figure there was anything wrong with that. They ought to be afraid, was what he thought. Hell, he was afraid. He'd been through a few battles and plenty of firefights and countless number of patrols and scouts, and every time, every single time, he still felt afraid. And he didn't believe anyone who said they weren't. If you weren't afraid, you must be crazy. And he would always take the former alternative to the latter. Kafak didn't want to be anywhere near a guy who wasn't afraid. That guy would get you killed. Kafak would take a frightened soldier any time. So long as they guy could fight through that fear and do the job he was supposed to do. That's all Kafak asked of anybody in the company. In the entire division.

Kafak was already sitting at the back on one of the trucks, waiting while the others loaded, Carter across from him, when the captain came up. He was carrying a BAR, and he held it up, showing everyone in the truck. "Any volunteers?" he asked.

They knew what he meant. Volunteers to take the BAR. No one spoke up. One of the new guys started to but then took an elbow from the guy next to him and shut up. Quick. Nobody wanted to volunteer for BAR duty in a squad. The going rate for a BAR gunner in combat was all of about thirty seconds. And that was no exaggeration and all the veterans in that truck knew it. Since it was the heaviest firepower a squad carried, the Germans had learned pretty quickly to target the guy carrying the light machine gun. That was why they supposedly always gave the BAR to the smallest guy in the outfit, the hardest target. Kafak had seen no evidence of that kind of selective assignment for the gun. Guys just somehow ended up with it. Anyway, Kafak thought, it didn't really matter how small you were, a bullet could always find you. Or a shell. Or a mine. Something.

The captain waited it out for a couple of seconds, and when no one spoke up, he handed the gun up to Kafak.

"Here," he said. "You take it, Kafak. You were a BAR gunner before, right?"

Kafak had been. Once when a new guy, Judson, had transferred into the company from the States, he came trained out on and carrying a BAR. One of the new ones that didn't foul so easily when you cleaned it and didn't jam and break down so much as the ones they'd had earlier in the war. Judson lasted a day with the squad, and then he got killed. Riddled by machine pistol fire in a small firefight outside a tiny French village. Kafak had been assigned the BAR then and had used it for about four days before a new guy shipped in and Kafak passed it over. The new guy seemed happy to have the BAR. Now, he was dead, too, only just yesterday, in a shelling. So now Kafak had it again.

Carter said, "That ain't right, Captain. Dash done his time on the BAR."

"You want it?" the captain said, snapping at Carter.

"Oh my shit, no," Carter said.

"Then shut up. Here, Kafak."

Kafak slung his Thompson. By rights he should have handed it over, but he wasn't about to do that. The more firepower he carried, the better he felt. Kafak was a big believer in firepower.

He took the BAR from the captain without looking at the officer. The captain walked away.

Carter said, "I'm sorry, Dash." He shook his head. "I just couldn't take it."

"Ain't nothin'," Kafak said.

"Fuck me," Carter said.

"Forget about it," Kafak said. "Here." He offered Carter a smoke. Carter took it and smiled. He lit them both up. They smoked while they waited for the rest of the trucks to load. It wasn't long after that the engines growled and the bed lurched and they were moving toward the front.

When they disembarked the trucks later, Kafak and Carter waited at the assembly point to march to the line and relieve the Thirty-Sixth. They sat sharing a smoke. Kafak was thinking, not talking. He was thinking about all the talk he'd heard, the stuff from the officers, the rumors, conversations overheard and directly participated in. All of them indicated that the Germans had stopped running and were making a stand here, in the Vosges. Saint-Amé, Remiremont, Cleurie. The Allies were closing in on the German border and the Krauts didn't want them any closer. The talk, the strategy, the perfect defensive positions offered by the rough terrain and weather, all of it meant one thing. A battle. A tough one. Maybe tougher than anything Kafak had faced since the Breakout on Anzio. The fortress at Besançon had been tough, but nothing like Cisterna. And nothing like this, Kafak suspected. He felt an odd sensation run through his mind, then ripple through his guts. A premonition. That's what it was, Kafak thought. A premonition. He knew such things were never good; he'd seen other guys get them. They never boded well. You ended up turning it into a self-fulfilling prophecy. Kafak didn't want to do that. He worked to put it all out of his mind, just take what came.

That's what a guy did, he thought. You just took what came next when it came and you got through it and you didn't look back and you didn't think ahead.

And that was how you survived hell.

Carter said, "You awfully quiet today, pal. You OK?"

"Sure," Kafak said. "Why not?"

Carter glanced at him, looked away, puffed on his cigarette. "We headin' into the shit now, ain't we?"

"Ain't nothin'," Kafak said. He worked his own cigarette. Slowly. Painstakingly. Enjoying every bit of it.

Carter said, "You scared, Dash?"

"Shitless," Kafak said.

"Oh my shit," Carter said. "Me, too."

He chuckled and Kafak laughed and then Kafak stopped and he waited for Carter to stop and then he said, "Say, Bama."

"What's that, Dash?"

"You remember Andover? What happened to Andover?"

"Oh my shit, yes," Carter said. "That was only a week or two ago."

"Seems like years."

"Yeah. It does that, all right."

"Listen," Kafak said then, "I want you to do me a favor, Bama."

"How's that, Dash?"

"Don't let what happened to Andover happen to me. All right?"

Carter looked at him. He frowned. Smoke curled around his squint.

"What you talkin' about, Dash? How you mean?"

"I don't wanna be no cripple, Bama," Kafak said then. He took a deep breath. "I can't be no fucking cripple, you know?"

"You ain't gonna end up no cripple. Don't think on somethin' like that."

"I don't mind dying so much. At least, I don't think I do."

"Shut up now, Dash. You'll jinx yourself somethin' terrible."

"It's just being a cripple. Being like Andover. I don't think I could handle that, that's all. I couldn't stand it, Bama."

"Goddamnit, Dash. You're messing me up here, real bad. Stop it, now. You hear me, boy?"

"You gotta do me that favor, Bama."

"I don't get what you want, Dash. How'm I supposed to stop you gettin' blowed up by a shellin' or somethin'?"

"No. Not that. You gotta kill me. I mean, if what happened to Andover, something like that, if something like that happens to me, you gotta kill me."

"Dash, what the fuck? You fuckin' bastard. I ain't gonna kill you."

"You got to. I can't be no fucking cripple, Bama."

"Dash, oh my shit. Oh my shit, Dash."

"Promise me, Bama."

"I can't do that."

Kafak clutched Carter's forearm. He squeezed it hard, not even realizing he was doing it. He stared into Carter's eyes. He spoke in an urgent growl, low and angry.

He said, "You gotta do it, Bama. You gotta promise me. Promise me, goddamnit."

"Oh my shit, Dash, you know what you askin' me?"

"I know exactly what I'm asking you, pal."

Carter paused a long time. He turned away. He dropped his smoke and ground it out under his boot. He took a deep breath. Without looking back at Kafak, Carter spoke.

"OK, then," he said. "If that's how you want it, Dash."

"That's how I want it. Say you promise."

"I promise," Carter said.

"All right," Kafak said. "All right." He let go of Carter. He turned away. He nodded. "All right," he said again, this time more to himself than to Carter. He smiled, just a little. He took a deep breath of his own and nodded again.

A feeling of relief washed through him like a cleansing rain. A sharp, intense, suffusing feeling. Kafak lit another cigarette, offered one to Carter. Carter wouldn't take it, but Kafak smoked his.

Kafak felt better after that, with Carter's promise tucked away in his mind. He could face it now. He could march forward and do what he had to do and not worry about how it would end up. He felt better.

He was ready.

19

The Third Battalion started off providing support fire for the Second, covering its flank. There was a lot worse duty, Kafak thought, and then the second day of the battle, they got some of it. Holbrooke told them to move forward, toward the town of Cleurie. The entire battalion, including L Company, moved along a ridge to their northeast. In the morning they faced no opposition. They moved through thick trees. The rain fell down steady and cold. It rose up in a mist from the ground.

"I can't see a goddamned thing," Carter said.

"The visibility here is for shit," Vinzani said.

"Keep your ears open, then," Kafak said.

He whispered, Carter grunted, and everyone shut up.

They moved along and didn't stop to eat any lunch. In the afternoon, a machine gun opened up on them. Kafak hit the cold, wet ground, looked around. The gun fired again, off to his right. The Germans were unloading on some of the guys from King Company. That meant L Company was in the clear.

"Come on," Carter said. "We can flank those bastards."

He stood up into a crouch, and Vinzani and a couple of the others followed him. They moved to circle around the machine gun nest, and then four Krauts armed with machine pistols fell in behind them. They fired quickly. It was loud but not so accurate. The Americans hit the dirt. Kafak thought a couple of the guys might have been hit. He took the BAR and labeled the four Germans with it. They jerked around and collapsed onto the ground. Kafak moved up toward them, carefully, waiting and looking and listening for another squad to attack like this first one had. No other Germans erupted out of the mist this time, though. By the time he had reached the four men, Vinzani had finished spraying them with his Thompson. They were all dead and the Americans could move forward.

The machine gunners had heard the commotion, though, and turned their weapon to fire toward Kafak and the others. Kafak didn't figure the Germans could see them, just heard the firing and so they shot in their direction. All the Americans dropped flat and waited out the bursts. A staff sergeant rolled over to them.

"Hey, Murph," Vinzani said. "How you doin'?"

"I'm feeling great," Murphy said. "You fellas ready to take out those Jerries?"

"After you, Sarge," Carter said.

Murphy smiled.

"Come on, then," he said.

He led the way, crawling quickly forward under the constant barrage of the machine gun. Kafak somehow ended up right beside him with Carter on his other side. When they had reached to about twenty yards of where the gun sounded to be coming from, Murphy stopped and looked over to Kafak and Carter.

"What's up, Sarge?" Carter said.

"You boys got any grenades?"

"Got a couple, yeah," Kafak said.

Carter said, "Me, too."

"Toss one, on my count. Right?"

"Sure thing, Sarge."

Kafak plucked the grenade out of his jacket. Carter took one from a pouch. They readied theirs, watching Murphy do the same. Murphy counted in a low voice.

"One, two, three!"

He hurled his grenade, and Kafak and Carter threw theirs. The three small bombs exploded in unison and Murphy was up before all the clumps of dirt had fallen back to the ground, charging the nest and screaming like a madman. Kafak said, "Oh shit," and jerked up right behind him. Both men fired their weapons without cease as they charged forward. Kafak saw Murphy jump into the nest. There were three Germans there, they were all dead, and Kafak couldn't tell if they had been killed by the grenades or by their small arms fire. It didn't matter either way, he supposed; they were dead enough.

"Nice job, soldier," Murphy told Kafak as Carter arrived.

"What happened to you?" Kafak asked Carter.

Carter scowled.

"Slipped on some fuckin' leaves and fell flat on my fuckin' face. I'm here now, though."

"Day late, dollar short."

"That's my motto, all right. Help me live through this fuckin' war, I hope."

They both laughed, and Murphy joined them.

"What's your names?" he asked them.

"They call me Bama," was all Carter said, nodding toward the sergeant.

"Kafak."

"I'm Murphy," the sergeant said. "Audie Murphy."

Kafak didn't finish any of the introductions because he saw two ghostly forms lurching out of the mist behind Murphy and he shoved the sergeant down and landed on top of him. He heard Carter firing his M1. Kafak rolled off to get back to his feet and join Carter's attack, but Murphy leaped up in front of him, spinning and firing. He took out the two Krauts who were charging through the mist. Carter had ducked them, but it was Murphy who finished them off.

Carter looked at Murphy. Kafak was watching the two Germans, making sure they didn't get back up.

"Oh my shit," Carter said, "that was a hell of a thing."

"You saved my life, Kafak," Murphy said.

"I doubt that, Sarge. I figure if I hadn't tackled you, you just woulda killed those Krauts a lot sooner, is all."

Murphy laughed and slapped Kafak on the shoulder. The other guys had come up now, and Vinzani said, "Good work, guys."

Carter shook his head.

"Oh my shit," he said, "these fuckin' woods are messin' with my head."

"Still not as bad as Anzio," Murphy said, grinning.

"Nothing bad as Anzio," Kafak said.

Murphy grinned at them all, said, "Well, I'll see you boys in Cleurie!" and then darted off into the mist to rejoin his company. Leastways that's where Kafak figured he was going. Still, he thought Murphy was something of a maniac, and there was no telling where a guy like that would end up.

Holbrooke found them then and gathered them up with the rest of the company. He moved them all forward once more. Again Kafak crept through the trees with Carter close by, searching through the heavy mist. The sun couldn't break through the canopy of dead or dying leaves and the trees' thick branches to burn off the ground fog, so they just had to deal with it. About forty minutes after the machine gun nest, another German platoon materialized right in front of Kafak and Carter and the others. Not fifteen feet away. Both sides opened up simultaneously. Kafak found cover behind a tree trunk. He blasted the Germans with the BAR. Immediately, a heavy round of fire blistered back at him. He ducked behind the tree trunk. Carter emptied his M1, Vinzani his Thompson. Other guys joined in as well. The Germans stopped firing. The Americans moved forward. Kafak saw that the other side of the tree trunk behind which he'd been hiding had been chewed up all to hell.

"They were tryin' to chop down that ol' tree," Carter said.

He grinned at Kafak.

Kafak shook his head, pulling a face.

"Goddamn BAR," he said.

Carter laughed and Vinzani said, "Need any more ammo?"

"Naw," Kafak said, "I still got some on me. Thanks."

All the other guys in a squad were tasked with protecting the BAR gunner since they knew he would be the man who drew the most fire. A rifle platoon was set up around the BAR man. They also carried extra ammunition for the weapon because no single man could carry enough by himself. It weighed too much.

"Let's go, men!" Holbrooke said.

They followed again. Kafak thought Holbrooke was all right, even if he was new. He kept his head and did his job. That was all a guy could ask. A Kraut popped up right in front of the lieutenant not ten minutes later, up from the ground, thick fog swirling around him like the broken surface of a pond. He came up with a knife, and if Holbrooke hadn't moved fast, he would have been gutted from belly button to sternum. He swung his carbine's stock around though and knocked the German's thrust off direction. The blade sliced through the lieutenant's sleeve, maybe got some of the arm. Holbrooke fell backward, flat on his ass, on the ground, trying to bring his rifle to bear on the German who was moving forward, trying to bring the knife down into the lieutenant's chest. Kafak fired the BAR. He'd been standing right behind Holbrooke and just off to his side. He had a sudden clear field of vision at the German now, and he pulled his trigger and stitched the enemy soldier almost in half. The guy lay groaning on the ground, and Kafak helped Holbrooke back to his feet.

"Thanks, Kafak," Holbrooke said.

"Nice move," Kafak told him. "Dropping down like that."

Holbrooke grinned.

"I didn't mean to," he said. "I just slipped."

"Well then," Kafak said. "Lucky thing."

Holbrooke nodded.

"Let's go," he said.

They moved along and fifteen minutes later ran into about twenty Germans with an MG42 and lots of potato mashers. They fought an intense firefight, and Holbrooke sent Kafak and three others off to the right to flank the Kraut position. The guys kept Kafak in the middle of them until they had reached their spot, and then they all threw grenades while Kafak unloaded a twenty-round clip into the Germans. At the same time, Holbrooke and the others charged from the front. It took about ten minutes, but it seemed like a few days, the fire had been so heavy. The Germans were all either dead or wounded then. There'd been no prisoners. Anyone they might have taken alive had scurried off in the fog. The wounded left behind were too far gone to do anything for them. Holbrooke left them there and moved the company on.

They encountered two more groups of Germans that afternoon and handled them in the same manner, each time flanking the position through the fog and trees and then collapsing on them. They never caught any prisoners. Not that day. By late afternoon, the entire battalion had gained the position they had sought, the high ground south of the town of Cleurie. At dusk, a heavy artillery barrage started dropping on King Company, not far off from where Kafak and L Company were hunkered down. They kept their heads down and hoped the shells didn't move their way. They didn't. They just suddenly ended. The moment they did, a company of Germans, screaming their love for Hitler, erupted out of the darkening mist, firing machine pistols at the men of K Company. The surprise of the attack pushed back the Americans, and they retreated right through where Kafak and his buddies were located. The men of L Company provided covering fire, and then K Company regrouped and formed up and fought back, and the German advance was halted. The fight went on for three hours. Small arms fire a constant presence, zipping over their heads, plucking up dirt in front of their faces, nipping at their packs and uniforms. Killing them. Wounding them. Kafak didn't think much about it. Not while he was in the middle of it. He just kept his ass down and fired the BAR where he thought the Germans were. Mortar fire started dropping on the attacking Germans. It went on for what seemed an hour. The sound was deafening but welcome. It broke the Germans and they started falling back, and K Company's troops charged after them, regaining all the ground that had been lost in the original push. The entire action had been a waste in terms of strategic position, but it had killed or wounded a good number of men, both German and American.

After the battle, after the wounded had been cared for, Kafak lay down in his foxhole and kept watch while Carter and Vinzani ate cold rations. Then it was Kafak's and Wolocheck's turn, and Kafak ate some stew and took a piss while lying on his shoulder and aiming at the side of the muddy hole. Then he went back on watch while Carter and Vinzani tried to sleep. Kafak didn't know if they did or not, but two hours later, when it was his turn, he knew he didn't sleep. They kept hearing sounds during the entire night. Scufflings in the dark. German voices calling to one another. They could never be sure where the voices were coming from in the darkness and through the echoing tree trunks. Every so often, the unmistakable sound of burp guns would explode in the night and American weapons would answer. These firefights were always quick and intense. Then the Germans would either move on if they succeeded in killing their targets or melt away into the thick woods if they couldn't sustain their assault. Or they would be killed themselves. Kafak and the men in his foxhole all waited for the assault that would come to them. None did that night, but no one got any real sleep at all.

The next day was a replay of the day before. Vinzani was wounded. The medics carrying him out of the fight on a stretcher required an escort because the Germans had infiltrated all through the American lines. And they had no qualms about firing on wounded or medical personnel. The Germans were everywhere; there really were no set lines as L Company moved on. Kafak sometimes wondered if they were just moving to move, like a shark had to move, and killing Germans as they came across them, or if there existed some purpose, some final goal to all this movement and fighting. By the end of the day he knew that there had been a goal and the company had achieved it.

Holbrooke told them, "We're on Hill 785 here, men. And we've been ordered to hold it at all costs."

"At all costs," Carter said, whispering to Kafak.

Kafak only shook his head.

That night they fought off attempted German incursions upon the hill on four separate occasions. Most of them consisted of bullets flying out of the dark and the rain and the fog as if nobody shot them at all; and the Americans fired back in the direction from which the sound of small arms came, but they couldn't see anything or anyone they were shooting at. A guy three over from Kafak bought it. A slug ripped right into his face, just below the eye, and came out the back of his head, ricocheting around inside his helmet. "Oh my shit," Carter said. "I don't even know who to fuckin' shoot at, Dash." "Just keep shooting out that way," Kafak told him. "Maybe we'll hit something like they did." One of the incursions threatened to break through, though. Thirty Krauts had charged forward in the night, screaming wildly and firing their burp guns, trying to overrun the American position. At about forty yards away they were nothing but ghostly forms in the dark and fog, and Kafak leveled BAR fire at them. In the darkness he couldn't tell how effective it was, but he could hear the Germans screaming and charging still. Guns were popping and firing in a constant roll of sound, trying to drown out the Kraut shrieking with death and destruction. Half a dozen enemy troops actually made it into the American line. One German leaped into Kafak's foxhole and Kafak ducked and the man landed on the far side of Kafak and Kafak spun to fire at him but the BAR was too cumbersome to bring around quickly enough and the German fired his burp gun point blank at Kafak only the gun jammed and Kafak saw the German's eyes go wide and suddenly frightened when he realized the situation he was in and then he stared at Kafak and Kafak brought the gun to bear, finally, and he ordered the Kraut to surrender, put up his hands, and the German's face went abruptly black and he shouted his love for Hitler as he dropped his gun and drew his knife and Kafak yelled at him, said, "No!" but the man was lunging forward and Kafak shot him and the force of the .30-caliber bullets knocked the German backward and off his feet and Kafak cursed and then moved over to see if the man was still alive but he wasn't and Kafak kicked him once, just to make sure, or maybe for some other reason, and then Kafak turned away, still swearing and cursing the "fucking stupid fuck Nazi" and then he got back to his position on the line but the fight was over by then.

They spent a little time policing the field, and Carter and Wolocheck picked up the dead German and rolled him down the hill, out of sight.

"Good thing that fucker's gun jammed, ain't it?" Carter said.

"You think it was the mud or something?" Wolocheck said.

"Something," Kafak said.

"What else?" Carter said.

"Maybe he was outta ammo," Wolocheck said. "That coulda been it, too, you know."

"All I know," Carter said, "wasn't your time, Dash. Cuz if it had been, that gun woulda worked."

"Hell of a thing," was all Kafak said.

"It was," Carter said. "It was a hell of a thing. Unbelievable, when you think about it."

Only Kafak didn't think about it. Didn't want to. Because there was no reason to. Because all the thinking in the world wouldn't have helped figure out a thing like that. There was just no figuring something like that.

You just turned your back on it and you moved on.

"Fuck," Kafak said, later, quietly, and only to himself. "Fuck."

20

"We're taking Cleurie Quarry," Holbrooke told them.

The men looked at one another. Already they'd heard horror stories about the quarry. They had been able to see it from their various positions during the preceding days, if not in detail, at least in its broad outlines. And it looked like a piece of hell waiting for them to arrive. Kafak thought to himself that it reminded him of what he'd read about Devil's Den during the Battle of Gettysburg in the Civil War.

"What's so fucking important about Cleurie Quarry that we gotta take it, Loot?" Wolocheck asked.

The lieutenant started to explain, but the captain arrived then and cut him off.

"Never mind that," he told the lieutenant. He looked at the men. "The reason that Quarry is important is this," he said. "The Germans got it. The brass want it. Case closed. Got it, soldier?"

"Yes, sir," Wolocheck said.

He snapped off a salute.

"Good. Now get your gear together. We're moving out."

They all saluted because the captain waited for it. After he was gone, they looked at Holbrooke and he scowled.

"You heard the captain," he said. "Let's move it, guys."

"Fuckin' jerk," Carter said to Kafak.

"Least the loot's OK," Kafak said.

It had been more than a week of near constant fighting or, at least, the constant threat of fighting. The Germans had attacked and counterattacked in force. They had infiltrated through the night and fog and trees, getting in between the American companies, behind the Allied lines, wreaking havoc. You never knew when an enemy soldier was going to pop up out of the mist practically right on top of you. A constant tension ground at Kafak and, too, the taxing and debilitating need to be always alert, ready. It took a toll. Sleep came only with exhaustion and was never settled. Kafak existed on shots of pure adrenaline and then crashed down into an almost fatal stupor from being overtired and overtaxed. He kept going, though, because he knew every other guy in the entire division felt the same way, was going through the same things. If they could do it, Kafak reasoned, then he could, too. And he did.

The fight for the quarry had been going on for a couple of days when Carter told Kafak, "You realize this is our third day trying to clean out this fucker?"

"You keep track of shit like that?" Kafak said.

"Sure, a course, I do. We started fighting this battle more'n a week ago. We been at these rocks for three days now. The captain is calling this the mop-up operation. Mop-up, hell. Them Krauts ain't any more outta there than the day we begun."

"Fuckin' captain."

"Got that right," Carter said. "Oh my shit, Dash, I wonder are we never gonna pry these fuckers lose from them rocks?"

"We will," Kafak said.

"You got a lotta faith, pal."

"Remember the tank and the bicycle Kraut?" Kafak said.

"Sure," Carter said, "I remember that."

"That's how I know we're gonna get the Germans outta there."

"Yeah," Carter said. He nodded. "Sooner or later, I suppose. Sooner or later."

"That's the spirit," Kafak said.

"Just so long as we still around to see it."

"Don't fucking jinx us, Bama. Shit."

"Sorry, Dash."

"Let's go!" Holbrooke said, marching through the collapsed troops. "Everybody up. We've got orders. Let's go."

"Where we going this time, Loot?" Wolocheck asked.

"We're going to move around the top of the quarry, flank these bastards. Hopefully we can give the guys down in the rocks some relief."

Kafak stood up with the rest of the men from the company. There were only about half of them left, half of the men they started with that week or so earlier that Carter had talked about. It was 0530, and they moved out, threading their way through the trees on the ridge that overlooked the quarry. Every so often, Kafak could look down and see the men in the rocks, fighting nearly face-to-face with the Krauts holding the quarry. L Company ran across a machine gun nest. Holbrooke used his usual flanking maneuver, and it worked. The nest was wiped out within fifteen minutes. A little while later, they came upon a second nest, but the Germans there saw how outnumbered they were, and they packed up and beat the wet ground in a fast retreat. The next nestfull of Krauts did the same. They fired for a couple of minutes, got the Americans' heads down, then took off. Kafak kept moving, with Carter and Wolocheck nearby. A couple other guys, too. Manning and Cooper had joined their little group. Kafak slipped around a high mound of wet grass and dirt in the midst of some thickly grouped trees and found Holbrooke holed up there with about four other guys. Kafak hit the ground, then Carter and the rest followed suit. Holbrooke pointed ahead. Another German strongpoint, an MG42 with about six guys. They had a mortar there as well, but none of them were manning it as it came fairly useless in combat this close. The Krauts didn't know where their own guys had slipped within the ranks of the Allied troops. Sending off mortar rounds might have killed their own as easily as it would the enemy. So they kept the mortar there in reserve and prepared themselves to use their small arms and grenades in support of the machine gun crew. Holbrooke looked at all of the men with him and then pointed to Kafak. "You're with me, Kafak. Keep that BAR in plain sight, give them something to think about."

"Sure," was all Kafak said.

"I want to take these men alive," Holbrooke said.

"Oh my shit, Loot, we could wipe 'em out from here," Carter said. "Just pointin' it out, is all."

"I want them alive. Prisoners. For the intelligence."

"That ain't too intelligent," somebody said from the back.

A couple of the other guys laughed, quietly. Holbrooke even smiled.

"Maybe not," he said, agreeing and defusing any objections to his command. "But it's worth a shot. Be good to know just how much more the Jerries got that we're going to have to fight. Don't you think?"

"Let's just get it over with," Kafak said.

"Right. Let's go. On my move."

All the guys got into crouches as quietly as they could so they could charge on Holbrooke's word. Then he gave it and everyone was up and running and screaming like banshees, but nobody was firing. One of the Germans fired a quick burst of his machine pistol but then dropped it. All the rest dropped their weapons as well and shot their hands up high in the air. The short burst though had done some work. Wolocheck lay on the ground. Kafak bent next to him, and Carter stood over Kafak's shoulder.

"He dead?" Carter said.

"Yeah, the fucker," Kafak said.

"Oh my shit, Dash," Carter said. "That fuckin' Kraut couldn'ta shot more than three fuckin' rounds."

"Only takes the one."

"Oh my shit, yes," Carter said.

They moved on, Holbrooke shouting at them. He'd already sent the six prisoners to the rear under two guards.

"Wish he would send me back," Cooper said.

"Hell, me, too," Manning said.

"We all wish that," Carter said.

"They can't send Dash back," Manning said. "He's got the BAR."

"Fuckin' BAR," Carter said.

"Ain't nothin'," Kafak said.

"I'd rather be taking prisoners back to HQ than moving forward into God knows what," Cooper said.

"Ain't no back," Kafak said. "Not in these woods."

"Oh my shit, if that ain't right, I don't know what is," Carter said.

That quieted them all and they followed Holbrooke through the fog. Kafak figured the lieutenant would be happy. They'd already taken out one machine gun nest, forced two more to retreat, and captured six men of a fourth. And it wasn't quite 0730 yet. Kafak thought, At this rate, this battle has to end today.

Then they came upon a platoon of Germans. Suddenly. One moment, the Americans were simply walking along, alert and ready, but just moving forward, and the next, just that fast, there were twenty or so Germans in front of them. A bone-cutter opened up. Several Krauts fired their machine pistols. The Americans hit the ground or scurried for cover. Kafak was far off on the left flank of the platoon, covering with the BAR. He found a spot, quick, behind a tree. He stood and fired the BAR at the machine gunners. Everyone was firing, on both sides. The sound was intense, rapid, nonstop. A German popped out from behind a dead, fallen log and fired his burp gun at Kafak. The BAR seemed to explode in his hands and he felt a sharp, incredible pain and something smacked him in the face and he went down, onto his back, on the ground. "Fuck," he said. "Fuckfuckfuck!" The burp gun continued firing, but now the Kraut was shooting where Kafak had been, not where he was, so all the slugs flew harmlessly over him. Kafak shouted to Holbrooke.

"Loot! Give me some cover fire so I can get the fuck outta here!"

"You got it, Kafak," Holbrooke said. He shouted to the men. Then to Kafak: "Get ready to move." A moment's pause and then the lieutenant shouted again to the men. "Now!"

The platoon nearest Kafak's exposed position let loose a withering fire. It suppressed the Germans attack long enough for Kafak to run, stumbling, with his hand covering his one eye, from where he'd been on the flank back to the main body of troops. He ran, he fell to a knee, he crawled, he pushed himself back up, and stumbled some more. He fell back against the trunk of a thick tree and slid down it onto the ground. Carter rushed over to him. Out of his one still-seeing eye, Kafak saw the look of horror on Carter's face.

"What?" Kafak said. "What the fuck, Bama?"

"Your face, Dash," Carter said. "It's covered with blood."

"It's my eye," Kafak said. "I can't see out of my fucking eye."

"Medic!" Carter said.

Holbrooke was kneeling by Kafak's side now as well. The other guys were still blasting. Tossing grenades. The fire from the Germans was starting to fall off. Then it stopped altogether and they shouted their surrender. The corpsman arrived and tried to pull Kafak's hand away from his eye. Kafak fought against it.

"You gotta let me see your face, soldier," the medic said. "Let loose now."

Kafak took a deep breath and said, "Fuck, oh fuck," and moved his hand away from his face.

"Your fuckin' arm and hand's all shot up, too, Dash," Carter said.

"No more fucking updates, Bama, you don't mind," Kafak said. "Ah," he said, then turned the near shout into a groan as the medic probed his eye. He wiped away blood, but more kept pouring out from inside Kafak's face.

"I can't stop this bleeding," the medic said. "I'm going to wrap it up." He looked to Holbrooke. "We gotta get this guy back to a first aid station, sir."

"Right," Holbrooke said. "Carter, you and Cooper help Kafak back."

"Yes, sir," Carter and Cooper said simultaneously.

"You need morphine, soldier?" the medic asked.

"I maybe don't need it," Kafak said, "but I won't fight over it."

"We'll wait until we get back to the station, then. If you can make it, that would be better for all of us."

Carter ducked under one of Kafak's arms and helped him move. Kafak couldn't see straight, so walking was more of a stumble. More than half of his head was bandaged over by now. He wondered how bad it was. The corpsman had also wrapped up his hand, very tightly. Kafak wondered would he lose it. He placed a couple more bandages around Kafak's arm.

They started walking back, toward the aid station, the four of them.

Carter spoke quietly to Kafak.

"Looks like you might lose that eye, Dash," he said.

"Fuck," Kafak said. "What the fuck."

"You know that promise you made me make?"

"What?"

"The promise you made me make. 'Bout you becomin' a cripple and whatnot. You remember."

"Yeah," Kafak said. He grunted. Groaned. "Sure," he said.

"Well," Carter said. "You want I should kill you now?"

"What the fuck?" Kafak said. He sounded outraged. "I can see with one fucking eye, Bama. What the fuck?"

Carter laughed.

"Just makin' sure, Dash, is all," he said.

"Fuck you, you fuckin' maniac," Kafak told him.

Carter laughed all the way back to the first aid station, and, against his better judgment, from somewhere deep within his pain, Kafak sometimes joined him.

21

At the station, Carter, Cooper, and the medic left Kafak with the doctors. Kafak grabbed the first guy that came at him, a corpsman, who was unwrapping the field bandage. "I can't see," Kafak told the guy. "I can't see."

"You got about a foot of bandage covering your eye, soldier. Of course, you can't see."

"Before," Kafak said. "Before they put it on, I couldn't see."

"Let me get it off so the doc can take a look at things, OK? Just calm down."

"I am fucking calm," Kafak said.

The doctor arrived and told the orderly, "Give him some morphine so we can work on him."

Kafak felt the prick of the needle, and then he felt nothing more.

He came to in a field hospital. A corpsman was shaking him awake, and he opened his eyes and looked up with one of them, groggy, at a doctor. The doctor said, "We've cleaned a lot of bullet fragments out of your hand, son, but I'm afraid we can't save that finger. We're going to have to take it off."

"My . . . finger?" Kafak said.

"Yes, soldier. Just wanted you to know."

Kafak fell back into a hazy, morphine sleep.

He had a dream.

He was in Naples. Near the fountain where he had met the girl. She was there again, seated on the edge of the fountain, and the fountain was filled with flowing water, spraying water, and that didn't seem right to Kafak, even in his dream, because he remembered there had been only a little water in the bottom of the fountain because the fountain had been cracked by a shell and the water had mostly drained out of it and the mechanism of the fountain, the one that made the water fly and spray, that had been broken, so the water just lay in the bottom of the broken fountain all green and slimy. But in his dream it wasn't like that. In his dream, the fountain looked the way it had looked, the way it must have looked, in its greatest glory. And the girl sat there, smiling at the water flying all round her. Kafak walked into the little plaza and saw her there. He pointed her out to the guys.

"There she is," he said. "That's her."

"That the girl?" Carter asked.

"That's her," Kafak said.

He frowned, though. Because that wasn't right either. Carter hadn't been there, in Naples. He hadn't met Carter until later, on Anzio. Carter might have been in Naples, but not with Kafak.

Kafak looked at the other guys with him. Marshak was there and Sergeant Collins was there and Captain Cole and Andover, too. No, Kafak thought, none of that could be right. None of them had been there with him, not in Naples. And Marshak and Collins and Andover couldn't be there at all, could they? No, it wasn't right. But Kafak turned away from this, turned away from them, and he looked again at the girl and he saw how pure and beautiful she was and she was smiling at him and he smiled back feeling suffused with wonder and joy and a warmth that sort of itched within his breast, but he couldn't scratch it, it just filled him up and made him want to go and sit beside her. He started to do that and then Jankowicz pulled him back, yanking on his arm. That was right, after all. Jankowicz had been there, in Naples, when Kafak had met the girl. Jankowicz was a big, goofy guy, one of those guys who could break you in two with his bare hands only he was so gentle he wouldn't hurt a fly. He'd been in the artillery so he never had to see what damage his work did. He could live with that, Kafak figured. Because he was just a big, gentle softy, truth be told. Jankowicz had taken the picture. He'd had a camera, and he'd been taking pictures of everything and everyone they came across as they walked through Naples that day, and now he took a picture of Kafak and the girl. A couple of them had pictures taken of themselves with the girl. Kafak hadn't been the only one. Hadn't even been the first one. But he had been one of the ones. And, later, Jankowicz had made certain that all of the guys who'd had their pictures taken with the girl got their picture. That was how Kafak had the picture in the first place. They'd all taken pictures with her and she had laughed and teased them in beautiful Italian none of them understood but that she was teasing them and laughing, that they all could tell, they all understood that much, and it had been a beautiful afternoon with the sun shining down, and now here it was, all over again, only now with the fountain flowering and the girl laughing and speaking broken English with her pretty Italian accent so now Kafak could understand her teasing and it was sweet and beautiful and then he took a picture with her but before he could ask her her name, another guy with them, a guy named Nosh from Brooklyn, he'd elbowed his way in, saying, "My turn," and he'd moved up alongside the girl and grabbed her around the waist and pulled her to himself and she didn't like it, Kafak could see that, she had stopped laughing, then she stopped smiling, and then she had tried to push away from Nosh only Nosh wouldn't let her and he tried to pull her closer, stuck his face toward hers, tried to kiss her and Jankowicz had said, "Aw, Bobby, don't do that," and Nosh had told him, "Shut the fuck up, me and this dolly are gonna have some fun," and then Kafak had said, "Let her go," and Nosh looked at Kafak and said, "What the fuck did you say?"

"I told you to let her go, you fucking son of a bitch," Kafak said. Nosh thought about letting her go and coming to fight with Kafak, Kafak could see that on Nosh's face, but Nosh didn't, he only grinned at Kafak and then he turned back to the girl, tried to force a kiss on her again and now Kafak grabbed Nosh by the helmet and yanked back on the front rim of the helmet and that drew Nosh's head back because the helmet was strapped under Nosh's chin and then Kafak stuck a knife into Nosh's throat and the blood spurted out, landed all over the girl's dress and hands, ruining her clothes, and the girl screamed, looking down at herself, more upset by the lost dress than by Nosh being stabbed and then Nosh fell to the cobblestones of the plaza, blood shooting out of him like he had ten men's worth, and he was writhing on the stones and bleeding and yelling at Kafak, "Look what you did! Just look what you did!" and then Carter pulled Kafak aside and told him, "Oh my shit, Dash, you can't be doing stuff like that no more." But Kafak wouldn't listen. He looked down at Nosh and kicked him and Nosh howled in pain from the kick in his ribs and then Kafak said, "You fucking Nazi. Die, you cocksucker."

And then Kafak woke up.

"Where am I?" he asked.

He heard a steady thrumming drone, felt everything around him vibrating, and he thought he must be in some kind of hell, a kind of chamber of hell, set aside especially for men who killed their own. Then he recalled that was only a dream, that had only been a dream, and none of it had happened that way at all. There had been the little plaza, and the broken fountain, and the beautiful girl. Jankowicz had taken pictures of three or four of them with the girl and had given their pictures to each of them later. All of that much was true. And Nosh had been there as well, Kafak remembered, but Nosh hadn't wanted a picture with the girl. "I only want to fuck her," he had said.

And Kafak told him, "Don't ruin it, Nosh."

"What the fuck does that mean?" Nosh said.

"Forget it," Kafak told him, but mostly because he wasn't sure himself what he had meant.

And the girl had left then, before anything else could or did happen. She had skipped away, laughing and smiling. Kafak remembered that clearly. The skipping. He hadn't seen anyone skip in years. Since he'd been a kid. So that stuck out in his mind particularly about that sunny, beautiful afternoon in Naples.

"You're on an airplane," a medic told Kafak. "You're being flown to Marseilles for a hospital ship."

"Huh," said Kafak. He still felt half under from the morphine. "I've never been on an airplane before."

"Well, here's one more thing you can tell the folks back home you did in the war, soldier."

"Sure," Kafak said. "Why not?"

"So how you feeling, anyhow?"

"I feel," Kafak said, "like I'm in hell."

They gave him more morphine then, and he fell back asleep. He had another dream.

Andover was there again. He was standing up, standing over Nosh who was curled in the fetal position on some cobblestoned street. Andover was beating hell out of Nosh with a piece of a leg. He was smashing Nosh with the booted foot of the leg while he, Andover, held on to the knee of the leg with both hands. He was just pounding on Nosh with that piece of leg. "Oh my shit," Carter said. "What's all this, then?" He started forward to stop Andover from delivering this beating but Kafak grabbed Carter's arm and wouldn't let him go. "Don't," he told Carter. "Just don't." "But, Dash," Carter said, "he's like to kill that ol' boy." "Good," Kafak said. "That's good." "Oh my shit, buddy, how is that good?" "Because he deserves it. Nosh deserves to die." "Nobody deserves it, Dash," Carter said. And that made Kafak let go of Carter and he stared into Carter's eyes and he said, "Why didn't you kill me, Bama? You promised me you would kill me." And then Kafak suddenly couldn't see Carter at all. Couldn't see anything at all. He'd gone blind. He felt himself screaming in his dream and he couldn't make himself stop.

He woke later aboard the ship and all around him were other guys in bandages in beds and finally a guy who could walk came down the aisle between some of the beds and Kafak asked him, "Where am I?"

"You're on a hospital transport ship. We're just outside of Naples."

"Say," Kafak said. "Do me a favor, will you?"

"What's that?"

"Don't give me no more fucking morphine, will you?"

"You say so, soldier."

He didn't sleep much more after that and just gritted his teeth against the pain when it came. It came in waves, beginning kind of slow and then building and then peaking and he wanted to scream out loud at the pain then but he didn't, he only ground his teeth together all the harder and clutched hard to the side-rail of his cot with his good hand. Then the pain would begin to lessen and then it would wash away until only a little was left until it started all over again the next time. They landed, and while he was being carried off on a stretcher from the ship, an NCO stood on the dock with a clipboard and he was assigning each wounded man to a hospital in Naples, so when it came Kafak's turn, Kafak said, "Can I have the 118th?"

"Sure," the NCO said. "Anything to keep our boys happy."

So Kafak ended up in the 118th, and his first day there Nurse Sullivan helped get him situated and told him, "I can't tell you how happy I am to see you, Private."

"I knew you would miss me," Kafak said.

She pulled a face.

"That's got nothing to do with it," she said.

"What, then?"

"Because seeing you here means you're still alive."

"Sure," Kafak said. "But I'm in the hospital."

"I did notice that," she said. She laughed.

"How am I?"

"Let's let the doctor decide that, shall we?"

"No. I mean, what do I look like?"

"As handsome as ever."

Kafak reached up toward his eye. The bandage still covered it, wrapping across most of his head in a sharp slant.

"This ain't so handsome," he said.

She smiled at him.

"We've had it off already to put on a clean one. You look fine under there, soldier."

"There aren't any . . ."

"No scars. That's what you want to know?"

"Sure," Kafak said. "I mean, I guess a little one or something, that would be all right."

"Oh right, the girls would just love that, wouldn't they?"

"But nothing disgusting, you know?"

"You survived without being disgusting," Nurse Sullivan told him, smiling.

"You mean to say, no more disgusting than what I started out, right?"

"I mean, not disgusting at all, soldier."

"Good," Kafak said. "Good." Then he said, "Am I blind?"

"No, the doctor thinks you'll see again. Not perfectly, of course, but your eye will work well enough for you along with the good one."

Then Kafak remembered something else and he lifted his hand and he looked at the place where his finger had been, the middle finger of his left hand; about two-thirds of it was gone now. There were other wounds on his hand and arm as well, but they were all sewn up and healing already, not covered with bandages. He'd been days in traveling to this place, he realized. He moved his hand, clenching and unclenching it, gently, then more fervently. It felt fine. It worked fine. He smiled.

"What happened to my eye?"

"Well, there were some shards of wood in your eye. The doctor thought they looked like they might be from the stock of a gun."

"My BAR. The front stock got blown all to hell by that German burp gun. I thought it was a bullet that hit me in the eye. Or shrapnel."

"No. It was the wood. The doctor removed a lot of it, but there was a piece he just couldn't get to without doing more harm than good to your eye. You're going to have to learn to live with that piece. And be careful that it doesn't slide up and cut into your eye."

Kafak grunted.

"Anything else I should know?"

"You had a couple other wounds, bullet wounds, in your left arm. Those have all been removed, stitched up, and bandaged. They're all going to be fine."

Kafak nodded. He didn't say anything more. Nurse Sullivan gave him an odd look when he fell so quiet, but she let him be, telling him, "You rest now. I'll be back later."

If she did return, Kafak didn't know it because he either slept or feigned sleep the rest of that day and night. He didn't want to see anyone; didn't want to talk to anyone. Because something had occurred to him.

He figured he would be going back into combat.

It was October 1944. That much he knew, could figure out. Unless he'd been out a lot longer than he thought and maybe it was November, but he doubted that. He doubted that very much. The point was, the war was not over. They hadn't even reached Germany yet. They'd go on. The war would go on. And he'd very likely be back in it. A part of it again. He wasn't quite sure how he felt about that. He didn't want to let his buddies down. He knew that for sure. So if they sent him back, he'd go. For them. Because it's what a guy did. Only he knew he didn't really want to go back, either. If he never heard another gun fire or shell explode in his life, he'd be fine with that. If he never had to smell another burned body, he'd rejoice in that. If he never had to fear being turned into a ghastly, disgusting apparition again, he could live in peace.

But if he had to face all of those things again, then he'd do that because that's what you did. And he wasn't going to do anything less than anybody else would do.

The next day, Dr. Gibbs passed by on his rounds. He clearly remembered Kafak. He took one look at him, and he told Kafak, "That's all for you, son."

Nurse Sullivan stood nearby, and as the doctor walked off, she said, "How does it feel, soldier? To have it all over with?"

Kafak shrugged. Lieutenant Sullivan thought he wasn't going to say anything and Kafak could see that in her eyes, on her face, but then he did say something. He didn't want her to leave just then, so he said something to keep her there.

Kafak said, "I don't know."

"It's a lot to take in," she said. "I know."

Kafak shook his head.

"You don't know," he said. His voice came quiet. He looked at Nurse Sullivan then, a sheepish expression turning his face. He smiled halfway, said, "I mean, who knows anything, right?"

"It must have been hell out there."

Kafak said, "It's just . . . it's hard, you know, always being in the dark like we were. I mean, never knowing when the war's going to end, never knowing where you were going or going to be from one day to the next, never knowing what you were going to have to face, to deal with, one day to the next. Never knowing if you were ever going to go home at all. And every second at the front, you just never knew what was going to happen. Were you going to be shot at? Bombed? Shelled? Were you going to be wounded or killed? You just never know and so you're scared. All the time, you're scared. I don't care what anyone says, everyone, all of us, we were all scared. Until something happens and then your reflexes take over, you know? But the waiting. The waiting could be boring or tense, depending. But it always made you scared. And maybe the worst of it, the worst of it all, see—I wonder why I wasn't killed. I wonder why so many of my buddies were killed and I wasn't killed. I wonder did I do as much. I wonder why did I deserve to live and they didn't? Because I don't, see. I don't deserve it any more than any of them did. So why did I get something I don't deserve and they didn't? I just don't know, I mean."

"Well, I don't know the answer to that one, Bobby, but I can offer you this. You did survive. Whatever the reason might have been, you did. Now you've got to take that survival, take that life that's been given to you, that gift, and make sure you don't waste it. Make sure you use it well. Right?"

"Sure," Kafak said. "Why not?"

"Are you happy?" Nurse Sullivan asked him then.

Kafak frowned, thinking over this. Then, not really answering her, he said all he could think to say.

"I don't know if I'm happy," Kafak said. "I only know I wouldn't give up what happened, not any of it, not for a million dollars. I just wouldn't ever want to do it again."

And then Kafak smiled.

And then he wept.

EPILOGUE

My father would never go hunting. He had no ethical reserve about killing and eating animals; he never minded spending time with his boys. His reasons for refusing to take us out hunting ran deeper.

He never explained them to me, nor to anyone else, until one day we were sharing a drink. I was in my midtwenties by then, and somehow the subject came up, and I asked him once again, "Dad, why is it you never took us hunting when we were growing up?"

He smiled a crooked little smile and shook his head and spoke, not looking at me, or at anything else really. He said, "Because of the war."

"Tell me about the war, Dad," I asked him.

He laughed and told me, "I'll tell you how losing a pair of glasses saved my life. That happened in the war."

"Tell me."

Only then he changed the subject. And not subtly, either.

When I tried to bring things back around to his time as a soldier, and told him, "You were telling me about the war," all he said was, "It was the worst part and the best part of my life."

It wasn't until years later, when he was nearing his death from prostate cancer, that he finally decided to relate his experiences from the war. It was almost as if he needed to talk about them then, to let someone know what had happened to him, so that none of it would be lost when he passed away. He told me much about it, then, but he never told me all of it.

I don't think anyone who lived through it was ever able to tell all of it.

Still, here is the story—as much of it as he told to me—relayed so that it will not be lost.

Because what my father went through, what all the men who fought in that war went through, all of that pain and suffering, all of that sacrifice and horror, all the duty and honor, none of that should ever be lost to the world.

AUTHOR'S NOTE

The landings at Anzio-Nettuno (Operation Shingle), the action that begins Bob Kafak's real war, were designed to be an end run around the German Gustav Line, which had halted the Allied advance up the boot of Italy. This area was about thirty miles southwest of Rome and had been marshland prior to the Second World War. Benito Mussolini drained it to create a fashionable resort spot. The drainage ditches that cut through the terrain would play an important role in the fighting as it progressed.

On the Anzio beachhead, the surrounding Alban Hills became a fact of life that wreaked tremendous damage on the Allied troops. This range looked down upon the Allied lines and gave the Germans a view of everything done by the troops there. Night and smoke were the only methods the Allies could use to move with any degree of safety whatsoever. While Major General John P. Lucas built up his forces so as not to be driven off the beach by a German counterattack, the German command took the opportunity to move reinforcements into those hills. By the time Lucas felt ready to break out from the beach, the Germans were prepared and outnumbered the Allied force by some several thousand men.

Kafak's first action comes as a result of the attempt to relieve the US Rangers who had been sent to infiltrate and take the nearby town of Cisterna. Cisterna was a linchpin of the German defense, but Army Intelligence thought it undefended when the Rangers were sent in. The relief never got through, and the Ranger forces were decimated. Only seven men of the eight hundred plus who attacked returned to Allied lines—803 casualties killed, wounded, or captured.

The next major fighting in which Kafak is involved resulted from the Germans' fierce counterattack over February 16–20, 1944. The Germans wanted to destroy the beachhead and drive the Allies back into the sea. To Hitler and his General Staff in Berlin, this desire was fired by their knowledge that the Allies intended a cross-channel invasion soon. The German High Command wanted to use this opportunity to show the Allies that such a beachhead could not be held and, even if it was, would prove disastrous to their troops. Field Marshal Kesselring, in charge of the Italian theater of operations for the Germans, threw everything he could against the Allies during this counterattack in hopes of destroying this abscess behind the Gustav Line. After the four or five days of fighting, the Germans, though having nearly rolled up the Allied lines at one point, could not execute a full breakthrough. They created a salient, which the Allies took some time and cost to flatten out, but the Allies held on to their beachhead. After the high losses of men killed, wounded, and captured during this counteroffensive, both sides realized they had no alternative but to enter into a period of consolidation and the reconstituting of their forces. Once more each side began a buildup of troops and equipment and fortified their positions. This was the time of patrols and small-scale skirmishes. It would be months before truly heavy action took place at the Anzio-Nettuno beachhead again. And that would come with the Allies' Breakout in May.

The episodes dealing with trench foot are true and a little-known aspect of this campaign. Trench foot is an insidious and debilitating affliction. It occurs when the feet become cold and wet and go unused; blood fails to circulate properly, and the tissue of the feet begins to rot and die. Gangrene can set in.

The potential for a person to lose a foot or leg due to required amputation is very real; even death can result from cases gone untreated for too long.

In the Italian Campaign, trench foot (as well as frozen feet, which has much the same results but can occur far more quickly under fierce weather conditions) proved a real danger and affected many troops. This was due to the weather conditions exacerbated by the sort of war being fought there: a kind of trench warfare reminiscent of the First World War. Eventually, so many men were lost to the trench foot–and–frozen foot epidemic that the army enforced shoepac discipline. Officers and NCOs either enforced it with their troops or were removed from their leadership positions.

Kafak's illness is another example of a serious fact of this battle. On Anzio, the Allies lost about four times as many men to illness and accident as to enemy fire. This was not an unusual ratio for troops on the front line in harsh conditions such as those suffered by the men on the Anzio-Nettuno beachhead in February and March 1944.

When Kafak returns to Anzio, he begins preparing for the Breakout. On the first day of this Allied attack, the Breakout from the Anzio-Nettuno beachhead, estimates of killed and wounded for the Third Division range from just under a thousand to around fifteen hundred. The official history of the Third Division, while warning that casualty estimates in battle can be notoriously untrustworthy, states that the division suffered 995 killed and wounded on May 23, 1944. Whatever the exact amount, it stands as the greatest number of casualties suffered by any single division in one day during all of World War II, including the invasion of Normandy.

Kafak's next major bout in combat is as a foot soldier during Operation Dragoon. This was the designation for the invasion of southern France, the area of the Riviera, by American, British, and French troops. The idea of the invasion was that Allied troops would fight northward and link up with the troops from the invasion of northern France. Once linked up, the Allied forces would turn eastward, toward Berlin. General Eisenhower himself would say that nothing so aided the troops in northern France in their breakout from the beaches as the Allied troops advancing on the Germans from the south.

The major actions of the novel end with the battle of the Cleurie Quarry. According to *The History of the Third Infantry Division in World War II*, Cleurie Quarry is a battle that will always be remembered as a tribute to the men who fought there:

"The importance of the battle for the CLEURIE QUARRY cannot be overemphasized. For us, it was an obstacle controlling our main route of advance—the LE THOLLY-GERARDMER Road—which had to be cleared before we could continue on the overall mission of penetrating the VOSGES Mountains. From the quarry positions, the Germans could, and did, pour a murderous fire on this avenue of approach, limiting and even stopping all traffic and movement . . .

"There were several reasons which made the quarry position particularly impregnable. First, it was situated on the slopes of the large, thickly wooded hill mass northeast of ST AME. The only approaches to it were up the steep almost cliff-like sides of this mountain and the heavy woods offered excellent concealment to the defenses. On the north and south sides of the quarry were steep cliffs covered by machine guns and in order to gain entrance to the interior, our men would have to charge up the sides in the face of furious fire. Both the east and west ends were blocked by huge, stone wall roadblocks which the enemy constructed. The steep cliffs on either side made it impossible to by-pass these, and thus the only way left open was to go over the top of them which again was covered by terrific concentrations of small arms fire, and snipers in almost undetectable positions."

A few definitions that might assist the reader:

BAR: Browning Automatic Rifle, the most powerful non-stationary small arm carried by a US Army Rifle Company.

FFI: Forces Francaises de l'Interieur, the name given the French resistance fighters during the latter stages of World War II. The designation was made by Charles de Gaulle, self-proclaimed leader of the Free French. In the early stages of the war, the French resistance had no formal organization or name. Once France had been invaded by the Allies, however, de Gaulle no longer considered the country occupied, but a free nation fighting against the Axis armies. At that point, he designated the resistance fighters as a part of the French army, using the name Forces Francaises de l'Interieur, or French Forces of the Interior.

G-2: The designation for a combat unit's intelligence section.

LCI: Landing Craft, Infantry

LCT: Landing Craft, Tank

Rifleman's badge: What Kafak calls the rifleman's badge is actually known as the Combat Infantryman Badge. It was established during World War II by Army Chief of Staff George C. Marshall, who said that a relatively small handful of men in the armed forces, perhaps one out of ten, were actually the frontline infantrymen who went through a living hell, enduring every conceivable hardship, including maiming, disfigurement, and death, and massive deprivation of life's conveniences and ordinary comforts. He wanted a special designation for those men who had borne the brunt of combat, who had served in the worst and most dangerous conditions—the one out of every ten men who actually saw frontline combat during the war. Though all soldiers played essential roles in a military at war, these frontline grunts were the men who suffered the most casualties and the most deprivation.

Any reader who wishes to know more about this part of World War II might consult the following works:

Clark, Lloyd. *Anzio: Italy and the Battle for Rome—1944.* New York: Grove Press, 2006.

Department of the Army, Historical Division. *The Anzio Beach-head: 22 January–25 May 1944*. Nashville: Battery Press, 1986.

O'Rourke, R. J. *Anzio Annie: She Was No Lady*. Fort Washington, MD: O'Rourke Services, 1995.

Pratt, Lt. Col. Sherman (Ret.). *Autobahn to Berchtesgaden*. Baltimore: Gateway Press, 1992.

Rathbun, Glenn E., and Robert C. MacFarland, eds. *The History of the 15th Regiment in World War II*. Society of the Third Infantry Division, 1990.

Salter, Fred H. *Recon Scout: Story of World War II*. New York: Ballantine Books, 1994.

Shirley, John B. *I Remember: Stories of a Combat Infantryman in World War II*. Livermore, CA: Camino Press, 1993.

Taggart, Donald G., ed. *History of the Third Infantry Division in World War II*. Nashville: Battery Press, 1987.

ACKNOWLEDGMENTS

For you, Louise, always. Special thanks to Jordan and Anita Miller and Cynthia Sherry, whose vision made this happen, and thanks to all the great people at Chicago Review Press, especially my wonderful editor, Ellen Hornor, and Andrew Brozyna for his superb cover. Thanks to Clarence Fioke, Wendy Hill, Christopher Escareño-Clark, and Angelica Michelle Lopez, whose belief sustained me. Thanks to Marinda Kippert, whose love strengthened me. And thanks to my father, Robert J. Kippert Sr., my true hero, whose life inspired me. This book is for him and all those who fought that war, so that their stories, their sacrifices, and their lives will not be forgotten.